PRAISE FOR VERO[...]

"A fascinating tale . . . Henry digs in to themes of family, environmentalism, and the connection between humans and the natural world."

—Publishers Weekly

"Henry's near-future fantasy world is interesting and beautiful, with lush descriptions of the forest and the fantastical world hidden within."

—Library Journal

"Henry adeptly navigates the communication struggles among families and the destructive forces of climate change in this thrilling fantasy."

—Booklist

"Perfectly balanced between the fantastical and sharp reality, *The Canopy Keepers* is a genre-defying work as prescient as it is brilliant. Henry has written yet another extraordinary novel everyone should be reading."

—Cadwell Turnbull, award-winning author of *No Gods, No Monsters*

"A gripping, compelling story with themes of great significance to us all."

—Shiv Ramdas, author of *Domechild*

"*The Canopy Keepers* is a gorgeous love story for national parks, trees, and the people who protect them. Veronica Henry's characters are strong, complicated heroes, and her world is delicately, lovingly drawn—and an anguished reminder of everything we are losing day by day."

—Yume Kitasei, author of *The Stardust Grail*

"Henry skillfully layers historical realism with fantastic elements to explore the way times of desperation test the ethics of oppressed communities. Henry is a writer to watch."

—*Publishers Weekly*

"Henry's debut draws on a rich history of folklore from various African traditions, as well as African history and Black American history, and almost the entire main cast is Black. The carnival setting works perfectly for bringing together various strange and magical people who aren't at home anywhere else . . . Come one, come all, this magical carnival has all the delightful dangers a reader could wish for."

—*Kirkus Reviews*

"[*Bacchanal* is] gorgeous while somehow never losing sight of the need to unsettle. It captures a sense of wonder and reminds you that too much curiosity can lead to danger. And most importantly, it's Black and never lets you forget it. If you want endearing characters, a charming setting, and characters that refuse to bend to the world's injustices, then *Bacchanal* is the book for you."

—*FIYAH*

"Set in the Depression-era South and featuring a mysterious traveling carnival, it's a novel of Black history and magic that makes for a terrific read."

—*Washington Post*

"Beautifully descriptive prose that fully captures the places, people, and time period."

—*Booklist*

"Think of a Southern Gothic version of *The Midnight Circus* with a touch of *Lovecraft Country* . . . nail-biting scenes of tension."

—*Lightspeed*

"Filled with magic, danger, and dynamic characters."

—*Woman's World*

"With a powerful voice that grips you from its very first pages, *Bacchanal* casts a spell on readers . . . Eliza is a wonderful character . . . Not a traditional superhero, Eliza's special power is a highlight of this work, and readers will root for the young conjurer and for Henry as she explores the limits of her gifts."

—Sheree Renée Thomas, editor of *The Magazine of Fantasy & Science Fiction*, award-winning author of *Nine Bar Blues*, and featured author in *Black Panther: Tales of Wakanda*

"Writer Veronica Henry pulls on a mix of African folklore, Black histories, and carnival culture to weave a story of mesmerizing, bizarre, and dangerous magic. With a heroine of unique powers and a cast as colorful as any sideshow, this story offers up its share of delights, adventure, and frights! Welcome to *Bacchanal*. Enjoy the sights. Hope you make it out alive!"

—P. Djèlí Clark, author of *Ring Shout*, *The Haunting of Tram Car 015*, and *The Black God's Drums*

"Readers won't want their travels with the seductive and dangerous Bacchanal Carnival to end. If you took *The Night Circus* and viewed it through the gaze of a young Black woman in the Great Depression, you might get Veronica Henry's *Bacchanal*. Demons, lies, and secrets."

—Mary Robinette Kowal, Hugo Award–winning author of *The Calculating Stars*

A BREATHLESS SKY

A
BREATHLESS
SKY

VERONICA G. HENRY

47NORTH

Published by 47North, Seattle

www.apub.com

Amazon, the Amazon logo, and 47North are trademarks of Amazon.com, Inc., or its affiliates.

ISBN-13: 9781662520280 (paperback)
ISBN-13: 9781662520273 (digital)

Cover design by Shasti O'Leary Soudant
Cover image: © Elaina Daley, © Melissa Moss / ArcAngel; © Bertrand Demee, © Leonid Eremeychuk, © Adam Mustafa, © PhotoAlto/Jerome Gorin / Getty; © kaisorn / Shutterstock

Printed in the United States of America

For all the wildland firefighters

First one, then another, and the last made three

A soldier

An outcast

And a fighter

Topsiders who slipped beneath the veil, welcomed. Finally free.

The siblings warred

And Rhiza was split, torn

Adapt we must

The Keeper, old or new, we must trust

To put us back together again

When will we become unbroken?

   —A Rhiza children's tale, after The Breaking

Seeing with Nascent Eyes
I am a poem of death, written upon a breathless sky

They called my father The President
Almost three thousand years he lived, until the
    morons torched him
In his wholly unwarranted sacrifice, at least I was
    birthed
The cycle of life and death is older than even him
He has earned his spot in The Mother's realm
    now, but all that he was—everything that all
    the Giants ever were—I am that and, really,
    much more

My lower branches are still attached, like a human
    infant's first teeth
My bark, though, is already thick and furrowed
    like a brow in deep contemplation
See, I am what you would call a thinker, more so
    than those others born of the last flames

Ah, yet the caretaker lives, *my* caretaker, the un-
    doer, the breaker
He is an unfortunate human but a Rhizan
    visionary
I have a bold plan and I will make him ready

The other Giants are, in my opinion, a little
    jumpy, suspect even

Through the lattice they feed and nurture me
    anyway—we are still family
But they
The Western humans

They have looked upon me with justifiable won-
    der, soiled me with their filthy digits

My caretaker is single-minded, as am I
Our survival at all costs

I flex my burgeoning canopy, inhale the poison-
    ous carbon . . . and
I do not clean, I spew it back out, tainted still
An idea, a breakthrough

Chapter One

Sequoia National Park
The Giant known as General Sherman
April 2043

"By our best guess, General Sherman here is over two thousand years old," Syrah explains to the host of park visitors strung out around her like a necklace of broken pearls. There's a gray-haired couple, a teen or two with peach-fuzzed upper lips and pimples. A few onlookers succumbing to middle-aged paunch. Eager ones, the urge to learn, to do good, all but dripping from their pores. A bull of a gentleman wearing the raised eyebrow of a skeptic, fast-blinking believers. More Black faces than she's seen in these groups before, at least. To a letter, though, and to Syrah's credit, all hanging on her every word, all rapt like children in a griot's capable hands. "This Giant is one segment of an entire ecosystem. Did you know that they're social beings? They talk—not exactly the way we do, but they communicate all the same. These trees support one another, care for their sick, mourn their dead. They are historians. Hermann Hesse called them 'the most penetrating of preachers,' and he was right."

It's silly after all this time, but the words never fail to choke her up. This community of trees, they call to her . . . *Come, rest here with us.* Syrah wishes she could be like them, setting down roots, growing wild and untamed. She catches herself, lost once again in pointless rumination, and returns her attention to the group.

She ignores the people who are nodding, offering encouraging half smiles. She focuses instead on two men, one with a cornered badger's hostility bunched up in the veins of his neck, another as yet unreadable.

"Across this national park, there are four thousand Giants. But none older than this one." She gestures at the wrinkled, cinnamon tree trunk. "The General's cleaned about fifteen hundred tons of carbon dioxide from the air in its lifetime. Multiply that by every sequoia in the state, then think about all the trees in the country"—Syrah pauses, meets each expectant gaze—"and the world."

Murmurs of awe and wonder. Syrah is stunned; each group is different, ranging from mildly interested to can't be bothered, but this crew, she's actually reaching some of them. All except the hostile one. Her eyes have rolled over him and snagged at least twice while she's speaking. The man's arms aren't folded across his chest. No smirk mars his otherwise painfully ordinary features. But his stance is loose, that of a boxer sizing up the person in the other corner of the ring. Even before she became Rhiza, she was no slouch. Now, she'd sweep the forest floor with him.

"And you know what that means," she says, shifting her attention to an eager stump of a woman, one of Syrah's clear supporters in the group.

"It means horseshit," the badger barks.

Syrah sighs. The gray-haired couple shoot him a reproachful look, but he ignores them and bulldozes his way forward. He bumps another man, who spins on him like he's ready to unleash a string of curses but stifles the rebuff when he takes in the badger's size. "It means that you got your priorities all wrong." He stabs a thumb over his shoulder. "When's the last time you left the park? Homeless are overrunning all the towns between here and Los Angeles. We got kids down there that can't get one decent meal a day. And if that ain't enough for you, I passed three sorry dogs roaming the street on my way up here. That means to me that you, and everyone parroting this conservation bullshit, are clueless. Or you just care more for these goddamn trees than you do people."

For her part, Syrah levels the man with a look. His advance comes to an abrupt stop.

"What I'm saying is that I care so much for people that I want them—I want *you*—to understand that without the Giants, sooner than you think, there won't be anybody left to argue the particulars." That bit earns her a few mutters from the group.

Point to Syrah, she thinks with a self-satisfied smile. But the man? That just annoys him.

"Where you go wrong is you're focusing too far in the future." The badger isn't giving up so easily. "We've got problems to solve in the here and now."

Syrah shudders then. She runs her hands up and down her arms, grimacing. Her fungi are choosing this moment to flare?

"If you would allow me to get on with my presentation, perhaps we can—"

"No, I won't allow it. I want you to answer me."

Syrah tilts her head, measuring. "What did you even come up here for? Harassing a tour guide." She scoffs. "Pretty sad, don't you think? You want a fight, you need to take it to—"

"I'm not going to stand by while you lie to them." The man takes another step, and Syrah closes the distance.

Syrah is trembling now, struggling. While the two of them exchange heated words, the others in the group fall back. In the midst of all that, she catches sight of the other man—the unreadable one—standing at the edge of the crowd. He's studying the whole exchange intently, fingering his chin. He's got eyes the color of tree leaves, green in the full of summer, assessing everything, not just the two idiots arguing, but the entire forest.

After a brief nod, as if he's come to some important conclusion, the man weaves his way forward until he stands near Syrah and the denier.

"If you are quite done," he says, gaze firmly fixed on the man, "I have something of real importance to discuss with our guide here."

The denier grinds his jaw until Syrah imagines his teeth are on the verge of cracking. With a wave of his hand, the denier relents. "She's all yours."

"You were here for it all," the man says by way of introduction.

Syrah sighs. "I have a job to do. Say what you have to say, and let me get back to it." By now, the crowd has dispersed.

"The bear attack here last summer, coyotes and dogs down in Three Rivers, a suspiciously coinciding momentary shift in the mycorrhizal network."

Syrah is halfway turned toward her wary group, but her neck snaps back to the all-too-knowledgeable stranger. "Can you give me one moment, please," she mumbles to them and then gestures for the man to accompany her a short distance away. "Who are you? And what exactly do you think you know?"

The man's hand reaches into his back pocket and emerges with a relic, what looks like a business card. He hands it over. "Dr. Baron Anthony. I'm a wildlife biologist with the US Forest Service. I'm here at the request of a consortium of interested parties—mostly private."

"To do what?" Syrah asks, taking the card.

"Syrah Carthan, former fire chief of Station Ninety-Three," the biologist rattles off. "Quit in a huff when your prescribed burn went wrong. You huddled for a bit but mysteriously reappeared, helping park visitors battle a bear. Helping a woman whose dog had turned on her, partnering up with a coyote, of all things. And animals all over the region went crazy. After everything died down, you spent some time in Compton with your parents, some here with Dane Young. Then you disappeared. For the last six months. And when you surface, it's under the guise of park guide? Look, the rest of the country may have moved on to the latest disaster or skirmish, but I and the group I lead, we know that there's something more to what happened here. And you're at the center of it."

In spite of herself, Syrah is impressed. The man has done his homework.

She rubs those arms again, and her fungi stand down. "Thanks for the walk down bad memory lane. I would expect someone with your backing to have a better way to spend your time than chasing ghosts that don't exist. I made a mistake; I chose a different profession. One that keeps me close to the park and forest that I love and have fought my whole life to protect. Sorry to disappoint you, but there's nothing more to it."

"Any thoughts on what caused the animals to turn that way?"

Syrah bristles again but shakes her head. "You're the biologist, you tell me."

The man doesn't try to intimidate or overpower. His is a confidence borne of determination, at least to Syrah's eyes. "That's exactly what I plan to do. The winter's done for, or whatever passes for winter around here anymore. That stalled my progress, but not my mission. I'm going to be combing through this forest and bringing a lot of people with me. We'll get to the bottom of this with or without your help. I'd like for it to be with your help, if that matters. But either way, I will have my answers. And I'm starting, amassing my team now. There's nothing you or the park service can do to stop it, so help me."

There's no way. It's not possible. He can't discover Rhiza; it's never happened before, and it won't happen now. But there's something about this man, something very determined, and it's set Syrah's fungi on edge. She—they—cannot have this man and his team, whoever they are, trampling through Sequoia. She won't stand for it.

Syrah retreats, rubbing furiously at her forearms, then turns and sprints away from the biologist and her group of tourists. After she's gained enough distance from everyone, she hides behind a tree and glances back. Her group stands blinking, shuffling around aimlessly, before they begin to disperse like wandering sheep. The loudmouthed climate denier wears a self-satisfied smirk. The watcher, as Syrah has come to think of him, remains long after everyone else has gone.

5

Chapter Two

Sequoia National Park
Tokopah Falls Trail
April 2043

Romelo's breath never fails to catch when he approaches the entrance to Tokopah Falls. The refrain of her animated fluidity cascading over the dark granite cliffs, settling across the creek gorge. He used to prefer Muir Grove, but now he finds its green seclusion suffocating, accusing. The open air of the falls allows him to ruminate, uninhibited, on how his sister and his adoptive mother bested him.

Thanks to care and medicines provided to him by his off-again, on-again mate, Artahe, he is now almost fully himself again, at least physically.

Human encroachment prevents him from spending as much time here as he would like. He hopes that, like the yellow-bellied marmot, extinction will soon lay claim to the Western human animal. He thinks about it and ramps the hope up to a prayer, a promise.

Though the day is young, the sounds of clumsy topsider footfalls rush him headlong back into the present. Romelo hopes that curse and the grunt that follows are the precursors to a badly twisted ankle.

Before he realizes what he's doing, he doubles back. Within moments he spots the human. As if the absurdly oversize backpack is not enough, the side pockets on the man's khaki shorts bulge with more useless junk. Armpit sweat patches stretch halfway to his T-shirt's hem. Pathetic. This trail would be a walk in the proverbial park for a Rhizan toddler.

Romelo camouflages himself and slows to match the man's snail pace. On his flank, a pair of mule deer coming into their reddish-brown summer coats pick their way forward. They stop and lift heads crowned by the new season's velvet-soft antlers. Romelo releases a trace of the flow, encoded with the message *Leave us*, and they bound off into the thicket.

Alone again, Romelo shadows his prey as the topsider steps out onto the craggy rocks overlooking the falls. It would be so easy. One tiny shove. And that tender skull would smack against the granite and crack open like a summer melon.

Alas, Romelo has more important matters to tend to. Soon they will all be gone, anyway. He turns and sets off toward the ailing Giant at the mouth of the grove.

It was the stories of rootspeakers past that helped him choose this, his life's work. He had exceeded them all. For the first time in centuries, he had forged connections with trees on the other side of the country.

That was before everything and everyone he held with the slightest of good rapport crumbled like burned leaves in his hands. His mind, his very soul, caked with sediment.

He spots the Giant and berates himself for wasting time. He walks the perimeter gingerly, allowing his gaze to travel the length of the trunk up to the canopy. It is as he suspected.

Compacted soil is the least of this tree's maladies.

Jade-green foliage gone a dead brown. Diminutive entrance holes where the bark beetles burrowed in and exit holes where their larvae chewed their way out. Fire always has the potential to bring them out of hiding.

A small hope, a wonder: globules of sap and pitch that the Giant released to defend itself.

Romelo sets to work, connecting with the roots and speeding the healing and repair. After he is done, he mutters a prayer that the Giant will have a full recovery and wanders the forest until he is drawn, as always, toward General Sherman. While he traverses the Marble Fork, a familiar voice catches his attention.

Romelo edges close enough to listen but remains far enough away that she will not notice him. Syrah, like him, is now more Rhiza than she is human. Something he hears that she now accepts.

Romelo sports a knowing glint in his eye as his sister—he catches himself; when she turned on him, she forfeited that title—unwittingly explains to her tourists the process that he and Vice will use to bring their brief, unremarkable existences to a swift end.

Because of his duplicitous sibling, once more, he is outcast, this time by the clarion will of his own resolve.

Romelo plotted; then he planned. The trees and their caretakers would take a stand against Western human destruction. And then The Mother, in Her mysterious wisdom, had gifted him back his baby sister, Syrah. He had done something dangerous when he looked at her and saw bits and pieces of himself reflected back: he had hoped.

His *real* family. Together, they would become an unstoppable force.

Foolish of him. She had been raised by humans, after all. Syrah was not so dense as to not agree with him that destroying the topsiders in their great state and allowing the Giants and the flora and fauna time to recover was the right thing, the only solution. Yet she lacked the backbone to commit to the necessary action. She still clung like a lingering sickness to that park ranger and her adoptive parents.

She and Taron had not ended him that day, but they had hardened him so that he would never give in to anything so mercurial as hope ever again.

Countless volumes have been penned about the depths and ills of sibling rivalry. Extensive, tedious academic codices that pointlessly attempt to make tame a malady that is, at its most basic essence, feral. Romelo believes that the fiction he has read on the subject gets more readily to the heart of the matter.

The oldest Rhizan novel, written by the imprisoned murderer Xuru Scourge, tells the story best. Romelo spent his early years belowground, stealing time away from Taron's watchful gaze to read the forbidden text. He had, in fact, hoped the criminal would be released from The Mother so that he might discuss the book with him.

The hushed Rhizan legend would have one believe that Xuru's is an autobiographical true crime account that centers on a pair of brothers who find themselves on opposite sides of a generations-old family drama. From the moment the presence of his unborn sibling became apparent in their mother's womb, the five-year-old elder brother embarked on a subtly harrowing competition: Crying for no reason other than to have more of his mother's attention. Squirreling away food that he had fermented under the bed. Kind of like the way a seed that burrows into fertile earth will set to work, hoarding resources from the other seedlings so it may thrive.

When the second child was birthed, the tournament began in earnest.

It was all a matter of survival, you see. And simple mathematics. Parents' attentions can only be divided so many times before nothing remains but the dregs one might find at the bottom of a silty river. Love in the form of sediment. And whichever child finds themselves on the losing end of that divide, in some cases, does not survive and, in others, spends their entire life wishing they hadn't.

But that rivalry is not always mutual. Though he is three years his sister's senior, Romelo welcomed her addition to their family. If anything, she took away some of the attention he shunned. Romelo does not recall much about their birth parents. But a sliver of his subconscious remembers that their love was of the overly attentive first-time-parent variety, leaning toward smothering. Syrah's arrival, attention divided by two, provided him welcome room to breathe.

He knows that for a time, he had a human home. A place in the world that made sense. And then they were no more. In Rhiza, he found new purpose. What people might think of as a true calling. Taron was a poor excuse for a stand-in mother. The woman had all the warmth of a half-melted arctic glacier. She cared for him as a dog cares for its favorite toy, but her heart—or whatever passed for it that beat in her chest—was not in it.

Curiously, though, The Mother had guided his sister back to him. Syrah opposed him from the beginning. She was stubborn and idealistic. So painfully human. She fought him. She had cursed and almost killed him.

Syrah is everything a sister of his should be.

Yet instead of finishing him off atop Moro Rock, as he would have done to her, she somehow, in her newly minted Rhizan strength, carried him down the mountain and deposited him at the base of a Giant, where he could get much-needed sustenance. And where he would surely be found and rescued. With no word of him in six months, however, she, Taron, and the rest of Rhiza proper have given him up for dead.

Just as he had wished—if not hoped.

Syrah never uttered the words explicitly; she did not have to. It was in her desire to be nearer to him, even as they argued. It was in the manner in which her features, her expression, softened when she thought he was not looking. It was clear to him and everyone around them that she wanted Romelo back in her life as much as he wanted her. A real family. A powerful one. She had belonged by his side once.

He had believed that with his whole being. Her weakness, her lack of vision, delivered him a blow he will not suffer again. Sentimentality and nostalgia—they are the sources of his musing, and he will stamp them out, as he will Syrah if she does not yield.

It is simple, really, as Vice has shown him. The Giants will stop doing the human's proverbial dirty work, cleaning up after them like the irresponsible children they are. The term "choke on it" elicits a devilish grin.

From where Romelo stands hidden, watching Syrah, he has to chuckle to himself. There she is in that ridiculous park ranger uniform— fitted khaki slacks, color-matched long-sleeved shirt bearing the National Park Service insignia. Those long, tight sleeves are smothering her fungi, and she lacks the wit to understand it. The cartoonishly large green hat is an interesting twist. The feet crammed into those smothering boots. She is all wide eyes and big gestures. Putting on a save-the-environment minstrel show for this disinterested human lot.

She has taken on a regrettably deferential new role for the topsiders. One so far beneath her station as a former fire chief and Taron's heir apparent that, when he heard it, it evoked Romelo's often-suppressed laughter. He had to see it with his own eyes.

If he is less himself than he was, she has somehow eclipsed even that. She is pacing back and forth in front of her audience now, sunlight dappling her devout frame. Beneath those untamed brows are eyes so much like his. She does not miss much but does a masterful job of making it appear as though she does. The likeness only begins there.

Romelo imagines that Syrah has inherited their mother's thin legs. Perhaps they both can thank their father for their above-average height.

She has the voice of a woman comfortable with command. It swoops and careens on the too-warm spring air with the strength of an eagle's outstretched wings.

Chapter Three

Sequoia National Park
April 2043

Anger is base. Syrah thinks of it as the emotional equivalent of lesson one of an introductory course on what it means to bear the indignity of being human—be mad, stay mad. That's because it's always there. A promise about as lush and abundant as a Brooklyn trash dump. Bubbling up like clockwork at life's telltale moments, the last curdling word of an insult about your intelligence or know-it-all asshats who think they're always right. And the kicker? Aren't they the ones with the dumbest opinions?

The unifying factor, sure as a surgeon's steady hand, is other people's foolishness. Well, and sometimes your own.

And why shouldn't she be angry at that pompous, uninformed tree hater? He isn't the first person who's come to the park with the sole purpose of hopping up on a shaky platform constructed on baseless conspiracy theories found in their little online cocoons. Places where people like him go to find other people like him, a confirmation bias of idiocy.

Didn't some wise woman once say that anger is a distraction? A good chunk of Syrah's mind that isn't raging about what happened with her fungi craves that distraction. But she pushes it away like a cloud at the front of a headwind.

Now, shame? That's an emotion she can really sink her teeth into. One that she's become painfully familiar with. She, a former park service firefighter, a chief, mind you, had run—*run*—from her tourist group because she couldn't control herself. She imagines shame, quietly judging her from where she sits huddled beneath the impressive canopy of what, by the low branches peppered with fledgling cones, she guesses is a teenage Giant. Shame giving her that side-eye headshake like her mother does when she's disappointed in something Syrah has done. Which, while she was growing up, was often enough to become a cliché.

Anissa Carthan wouldn't be pleased with her daughter right now, but that's the least of Syrah's concerns.

She let her uncle Dane wear her down until she had no choice but to take this job, just to get him to stop asking. On paper, she's got the fancy title: Sequoia National Park's first environmental outreach coordinator. What does that mean in plain English? She's a tour guide, one with more than your average knowledge about the Giants. And a mission to protect them. And Rhiza.

Didn't The Keeper warn her? Syrah recalls Taron's words. *You have a responsibility to your fungi. Your symbiosis is unprecedented and must be cataloged. You must let them evolve, and for the sake of the survival of both you and your fungi, it is vital that you keep them hidden. They respond to your emotions. Do not wield it lightly, or your anger will be your undoing.*

Her fungi. A gift she didn't ask for, but one that she's come to refer to as her "secret garden." Those splendid, crinkly, medium-brown moon clusters on her arms and lower legs have become as much a part of her as the stubborn head on her shoulders.

She knows what drives them to surface. Like a seventh sense, they can warn her of some unforeseen trouble, and there's something else, more useful, that she's come to understand. They thrive on death, the kind that makes all life possible. Fungi decompose dead things and, in the process, produce a ton of spores. Their mycelia send out pheromones. While the Rhizan "flow" comes from the caretakers' pores,

Syrah's version comes from her fungi. That's why she was able to help Taron stop the animal attack.

She can sense, if not see, the spores now, the form in which most mushrooms start their long lives. It's as if they are drawn to her, responding to her even more with heightened emotions, something to do with the need to propagate. It's a guess that she's reasoned out herself and mostly confirmed with Artahe, her friendly neighborhood Rhizan mycologist and friend.

Syrah has another theory she hasn't shared. She just needs to test it out first. Soon.

The climate denier got to her. Much too easily, now that she thinks about it. Taron's slow recovery has her on edge. That biologist, though . . . she has a feeling he won't be so easily dismissed. Her fungi told her as much. She had to run out of there before they flared in front of everyone. Not a good look for the disgraced fire chief turned tourist attraction leader. If she can't even do this job, then what will be left for her?

Keeper of the Canopy, that's what.

As much as she wanted to rip the card to shreds and throw it in that man's smug grill, she didn't. She pulls it out of her pants pocket, a little crumpled. Smooths the edges and reads the name. Dr. Baron Anthony. Others have combed through the park since last year's events, looking for answers where there were none to be had.

But Syrah can't shake the feeling that this dude seems dead serious. "Resolved" is the word she's going for. And if this consortium—she glances at the card again—is legit, then she'll have to tell Taron and the rest of Rhiza sooner rather than later. It isn't that she's worried that he'll uncover their society, but they should at least discuss the matter.

A little research will bring her some initial answers. With luck, Dr. Anthony, like all the others, will lose interest and be lured away by the latest disaster. There are so many to pick from. Parts of Sacramento and San Mateo all but wiped out by Tropical Storm Zena. Inland Texas, long thought to be safer than the coastal towns, is a desert, five million acres scorched in the Panhandle wildfire a couple months back. She's heard the ash is knee deep. What little remained of Houston obliterated during last hurricane season.

So many species on land and water flattened by a climate that makes no sense. Unable to find enough food on land, the magnificent polar bears experienced reproductive failure in 2040. They turned to the ice, staking out seals' breathing holes, hoping for one to break the surface. But rising temperatures meant less sea ice, fewer seals. Extinction for the polar bears is probably less than fifty years away, with so many other species already lost.

Taron will not be pleased to hear about this latest threat. The Keeper is in an odd state. Healed as much as she can, but even Artahe has been noncommittal about her prognosis. All thanks to Syrah's brother, Romelo. He'd looked at the woman who had in effect rescued him and raised him and shoved her off the side of a mountain without blinking. If he weren't so misguided, Syrah might admire his single-minded determination to protect the Giants. To protect Rhiza. So blinded and twisted by his pain and ambition.

Syrah shivers involuntarily. Though his body was never found, she doesn't doubt what she did. To protect Taron, she'd killed her own brother. That truth is an anchor buried like a spike in her gut. It plunges deeper whenever she thinks of him.

However short lived, once they were reunited, everything in her wanted to embrace him. Before the knocks began to accrue, with interest: the revelation that she was the one who had accidentally pushed him out of the tree during the fire that claimed their parents. His determination to become a mass murderer, the betrayal of Taron and everyone who sided with her, including his own sister.

There are all kinds of strength. Physical is the most obvious and, consequently, often the least useful. There's the strength to endure the worst of hardships. To press on when every cell in your mind is screaming at you to pack it in and hightail it backward. Motherhood, childbearing, now there's real strength. To love, to give your heart and soul away, sometimes again and again, knowing full well you'll have to watch it be shattered into pieces the first time someone hurts your child.

There's all that, and then there's Syrah's strength. Fungal strong. Organisms that stretch across this earth and have navigated partnerships or submission from everything they encounter. Existing despite every human attempt to destroy them. And now, Syrah is the next, perhaps final, stage of their evolution.

She just has to confirm how this final piece works.

Syrah pulls off her boots and socks, then rolls up her pant legs. When she concentrates, she can just make out the small hairs on her lower legs, the tiniest poking upward, the longer ones lying against her skin. Her arms rest on her thighs. With an exhale, she closes her eyes and steadies her breathing.

She pushes away thoughts of the tourists now roaming the park on their own. They will find their way back, or she will catch up with them later. This she must do first.

For all of three plump seconds, her mind is blissfully clear. Then it's like she hits a mental play button, and worry intrudes. There's her father's health—he's recovered fully from the stroke that sidelined him last summer, but experience reminds her how quickly everything you think is okay can change in an instant.

As other worries give way to more, eventually Syrah's mind settles into that deep space she's tended like a farmer. Only then does she begin to feel the tickling brush of her fungi just beneath her skin's surface. Like a gentle knock on a doorway. There's no way to describe what she has to do other than to open that door. That means letting go. Something incredibly difficult for her.

She pushes, relinquishing the need to be in control. She feels the skin nearest her left wrist give way. She doesn't dare open her eyes just yet, though. Breathing through the release, she lets it all go. Welcomes her tiny buds. Another flares maybe a quarter inch beside the first. She brushes her fingers along the tips and grins at the little cluster that circles her wrist like a bracelet.

In this way, Syrah loses herself in the blooming until she feels the air grow midday warm. Splotches of sunlight pass over her face like warm kisses. When she finally opens her eyes, her heart sings.

Artahe has given her fungi an official new scientific name—*Africana fumosa*. They are pale pink with streaks of brown. Rounded caps coated with a fine layer of fuzz, sprouting in fleshy, vibrant clusters, wrist to elbow. Ankle to lower leg. Her friend judges them to be a mix of African tree ears, a variety that's somewhat like truffles, and another sort that's among the nearly one million types that topsiders don't know exist. Syrah's are a whole new species, and Artahe has taken a few samples for study.

Syrah spots a fallen branch and feels the tug. She pads over and kneels; she squints. From what she's learned, the spores are probably here, but how can she connect with them? *The flow, you idiot.* Syrah releases a sliver of her own current, what she hopes is enough to catch their attention. She's guessed right. Little clear bubbles rise up on an opportunistic breeze and land right on her fungi.

Like a tether to a hitch, they fuse. Their thoughts become entangled, and she's momentarily disoriented. Her whole body entwines with a world she can't even see but that nonetheless speaks to her in a thousand silent ways. Food, danger, propagation, contentment, and anxiety . . . anger.

Syrah feels and hears it all and knows this is something new, an innovation. Just like the latticework beneath the surface that is the heart of Rhizan communications, she can form her own, through the mycelia. This collection of fine white filaments, the hyphae, is the key to what she thinks of as the link.

Giddy on the high of her discovery, Syrah unenthusiastically retracts her secret garden, giving way to smooth brown skin again.

By the time Syrah treks back to where she left the tourists near General Sherman, they're all gone, dispersed like kids at the end of the school day. *No surprise there,* she thinks. She can just imagine what all those one-star ratings will have to say about her.

Tour guide last seen sprinting off into the forest like some wildland creature hot on the trail of an imminent kill.

We were left to fend for ourselves because she got her feelings hurt by a climate denier.

Inexperienced tour guide toppled by man on a mission.

Syrah hates ratings, has never understood the value others place on the opinions of perfect strangers. The only one that really matters is that of her employer. Time to face the music. But first, a feeler.

Reluctantly, she pulls her comms device from her front pants pocket, ignores the message indicator, and, after a hyperbolically expelled breath, says, "Call Uncle Dane." He isn't her boss, technically, being a relative and all, but her real one isn't as invested in the position and so largely leaves management of it to Dane.

He answers so fast it's as if he's been waiting for the call. "How's my favorite environmental outreach officer?"

Not the opening Syrah expects. No censuring, no disappointment. But then her uncle always takes the meandering way around things. And even then, he's never too excitable, not at all like Mama. "Would it be clichéd to say that I've been better?"

"Not if it fits the bill." His easy chuckle magically melts away the knots of worry bunched along Syrah's shoulders. "And judging by the incoming messages lighting up the NPS, I'd say it does, wouldn't you?"

Syrah groans. "Care to boil it down for me?"

"I'd rather hear your side of things if you're ready to share it. Meet you at your place with a bag from River View?"

"Rain check?" Syrah asks. She has two jobs to balance, and the one back in Rhiza is in need of attention. She's so close to the veil it wouldn't make sense to turn away now. Not even for a burger from her favorite diner. "But there is something I have to run by you. What was the name of the person you passed along Romelo's threatening message to? Was it a biologist?"

"Does this have something to do with what happened out there today?" Uncle Dane is all business now, the light tone gone from his voice.

"It does," Syrah admits, even though she doesn't care to get into it too deeply yet. "If you don't recall, can you get the name for me? I need to look into some things first, and then I'll take you up on that burger."

"Are you going to—" He still stumbles on the word.

"Rhiza," she says, filling it in for him. "And yes. I won't be gone long." She doesn't say that last part with a lot of conviction. She always loses time when she goes beneath the veil.

"At the risk of sounding like your father, I'm going to do that thing that I hate when people do it to me. I'm going to tell you something you already know but don't want to see. You're spending too much of your time there."

Syrah is poised to fire off a denial. It's what that old version of herself would've done. The annoyance and the guilt, though, they remain. "You're right, but I have my reasons."

"We feel you slipping away from us, and we're not prepared to stand by and let that happen," Uncle Dane tells her. "Just so you know."

For much too long, Syrah struggles to come up with the assurances he needs. In the end, a compromise. "Before I make any decision about anything, I'll talk it over with you and my folks."

"Okay, that's new. What kind of decision are we talking about?"

This man doesn't miss a thing. "My career, my future."

A beat passes, then another, two more.

"You've changed." Uncle Dane suddenly sounds tired. "I'll find that name you want, and I'll leave you a message. If it's urgent, I'll use our knock on a certain tree."

Chapter Four

Sequoia National Park
Near General Sherman
April 2043

Romelo had moved as close as he dared and had heard much of Syrah's conversation with the biologist. He lingers now until the man leaves. Something in his manner, having not raised his voice once or fallen back on the tree hater's tactic of physical intimidation, rustles Romelo's proverbial feathers. He has rarely experienced the troublesome feeling of doubt, but as of late, he *has* nursed indecision. The scientist has just cemented things for him.

He turns away and sets off at a fast clip, drawn by a colorless and sulky early-afternoon sky, a presage to Vice's freshly minted plan. A clock more urgent than the one his young, self-assured Giant has already imposed upon him is ticking.

The key will be *his* new tree. The President's spawn gifted to him before its contemptible demise at inept human hands. From the flames that claimed its venerable father, one scrappy seed won the competition for ever-more-scant resources. Vice has clawed out its existence while thousands of others have perished. It is determined to survive despite it all, much as Romelo was when he was first taken beneath the veil.

The young sapling is convinced that the other Giants will fall in line, but what will cement their victory is cooperation and coordination with the earth's second-oldest organism, the resilient and crafty fungi. And Syrah has them on her side.

While his human body has adapted to allow him to become Rhiza's most renowned rootspeaker, she has evolved differently, gifted with those incredible mushrooms, more animal than plant. To what advantage, he is still unsure, though as he passes through the forest, glimpsing clumps of fungal outcroppings in the soil, he figures they will become an important factor.

The Mother is at play here as well. He is certain of it; she's orchestrated a scheme probably launched ages ago. That is Her way. And he suspects even Keepers struggle to understand Her ways and motives.

From what he just witnessed, Syrah clearly has more control over her mushrooms now. He was hoping that her little tourist group would see her sprout right before their eyes and either run screaming or tackle her and try to drag her off for scientific examination.

For Rhiza's sake, he could not have allowed them to take her. But if he can figure out her weakness and use it to his advantage, he will.

Another alien emotion has snared Romelo in what he knows is a pointless trap. A wild, livid jealousy. He has lived belowground for most of his life. Consumed the self-same mushroom flesh that Syrah has. Yet no such knack has manifested in him. A thought strikes him then. Despite who now commands Lattice Affairs in Rhiza proper, Romelo is still the greatest rootspeaker. His tree-touch now reaches from coast to coast.

His and Syrah's evolution engineered and manifested as opposing forces by none other than The Mother.

She is up to something, rearranging them like pieces on a chessboard in Her own world, in Her own canopy. No doubt, she has put the siblings at odds for a reason. Taron may have some idea, but Romelo can no longer seek his adoptive mother's counsel, wise as it has been on occasion. The Keeper tried to drive a wedge between him and his only surviving relative. While he might be able to forgive her many other trespasses, that one he never will.

Syrah was blinded by Taron's duplicitousness, but in the end, she not only spared his life but put her own on the line to try to save him. For one exquisite breath, Romelo allows himself unrestrained comfort in that fact.

Or.

His ever-present logic suggests an alternate scenario to fill in the gaps in his memory. Did she turn and run back down the mountain in an attempt to save herself from sure defeat? And did he pursue her and succumb to his injuries? He cannot be sure, and perhaps that is for the best. On the wavering spectrum between optimism and pessimism, Romelo considers himself more of a pessimist, a realist in his mind. But the fact that he was found so close to a Giant, the ground carefully, almost tenderly, disturbed to allow for the root filaments to reach him? That allows the sliver of optimism in him to assert itself. It is the conclusion that makes the most sense. No one else but Syrah would have done that.

Doubt be damned. His sister *did* try.

That begs the question: Did guilt or love drive her intrepid actions? He hopes it is the latter. For in spite of everything, he cannot stop loving her. Something deep inside him, beyond fallible human memory, tells him that he has ever since the day he first saw her. And if he set aside the shock, the first time she saw him in Rhiza, her own love for him was plain to see.

Her crime is naivety. She still holds out hope for humanity's redemption, a mistake born of too much time spent aboveground. For better or worse, having been raised as he was, Romelo is thankfully more Rhizan than human. The years spent under Taron and Ezanna's tutelage have dispelled myth and sentimentality. The topsiders have been warned—he has sent several of those missives himself. They have chosen not to heed any of it. Evidence, science, they mean nothing to them—most of them, he amends.

At last, Romelo stands before his baby Giant. He has nicknamed it the only thing he could. What could be more fitting for the offspring of

The President than to affectionately call his new tree Vice? It is already double the size it should be, Romelo having nurtured it with blood from his own veins. Building that connection that Taron and Keepers before her banished. Dangerous, they said, having a connection to one tree. They thought it might skew Rhizan citizens, giving favor in the event of emergencies and such. Well, they were right. Romelo has a connection to this tree, and he will do anything to protect it.

The baby Giant is a little over two and a half meters in diameter: what it should be in its fiftieth year. He steps lightly to avoid disturbing the roots near the ground's surface and presses both hands and his forehead against bark the color of freshly ground cinnamon and feels the heartbeat thrum of new life beneath his palm.

Just by the act of existing, of breathing, trees clean the air. Each one, from the tiniest sapling to the largest of the Giants, functions as the earth's lungs. In a reversal of human destruction, they take in carbon dioxide and emit pure, clean oxygen. The CO_2 helps the trees grow. That carbon dioxide does not end up causing respiratory issues like it would for the topsiders, but it is stored, endured by the Giants. Towering carbon sinks, in conjunction with the surrounding soil and the earth's warming oceans.

It is a system that, when in balance, works just as the earth intended. That balance is a thing of an idealistic past.

The scientists suggest that Giants can store three thousand tons of CO_2 over their lifetime, but Romelo knows better. The real figure is double that. And the same can be said for particulate matter, even if it is sometimes only stored in leaves temporarily. Trees do the cleanup of those unseen particles of acid and metal and dust, released during rainfall runoff.

Because of their unique lung structure, Rhiza's citizens do much the same. That fact alone speaks to their superiority to humans.

Romelo steps back and walks the circuit around Vice, taking in every aspect of the sapling.

A sequoia typically grows two feet in height per year, during its first fifty to one hundred years. The root system branches out in the first two years. Lateral movement that eventually reaches out 100 to 150 feet; the roots increase an inch in diameter every three to five years.

Vice has defied it all. After a little over six months, it stands nearly triple Romelo's six feet. Its trunk unnaturally thick, though it still holds fast to its lower branches. At Vice's urging, Romelo has successfully rerouted its impressive root system to his version of the lattice. He painstakingly created the offshoot of the larger one that he abandoned when he and his followers moved to the new area of the Crystal Cave.

If he can do this with one tree, what could he do if given time to restore this forest, minus, of course, a huge obstacle?

The topsiders have to go.

But first, a small test.

Chapter Five

I said we have long life, not immortality. Syrah replays Taron's rebuke, the words like a pack of rabid wolves closing in, cornering her. It's not like she hasn't heard them before. But now she knows them for what they are: a dead-end road. She's all out of U-turns.

And that tone of Taron's . . . that seasoned ability to make you feel like the biggest of fools. Like a walking, talking lump of flesh, absent enough brain power to exist on whatever elevated plane she perches herself on.

Syrah hears that tone less often these days.

She would rather face down that wolf pack than contemplate Rhiza without Taron to lead it. She keeps that to herself around everyone else because, in a pile-on of epic proportions, Taron has asked Syrah to become Rhiza's next Keeper. Her. A topsider. A human being.

Syrah can't decide if she's more than human or less than Rhizan. It doesn't matter anymore, does it? She and her brother are the cause of everything that's gone wrong in this subterranean world, so there's no way she'll abandon it or leave it in less capable hands.

With her shift as park ranger cut short, Syrah doesn't go and check in with her manager like she knows she should. Instead she makes a hasty retreat to the cozy snugness of her room belowground to think and sulk in alternate waves of self-pity.

Though the entrance to Rhiza is fairly remote, Syrah has developed the habit of double- and triple-checking her surroundings before she steps into the gaping hollow that mars the otherwise pristine trunk of the giant sequoia. Her eyes adjust quickly to the dark, and she plows ahead. Funny how the impossible becomes ordinary. The first time Taron and Dhanil ordered her to walk into the tree and keep moving, she thought they were crazy. She did as she was told, or rather Dhanil shoved her forward, and instead of smacking her head against the back side of a tree trunk, she stumbled into their world, now her world.

The Rhiza she enters is a shadow of what it was before Romelo crippled The Keeper. The air is still cooler than it is in the park; the zigzag layout full of smooth curves and sharp corners has become as familiar as the streets near her home. But everything and everyone is more subdued, like they're all waiting for the ball they don't want to face to drop. Losing Taron.

The work goes on; scourge suppressors continue to lose the battle of cleaning the forest of topsider trash, the rootspeakers do their best to keep the lattice working and the roots communicating, and the Blaze Brigade has not had to battle a fire in months, but just like when she was a firefighter, there's still so much to do. Equipment maintenance, for one, clearing the forest understory, and what used to be her favorite, physical fitness. But the general Rhizan lightness is gone.

Syrah stops to remove her shoes and stuffs them into a little nook that she discovered a while back, seemingly carved out of the rock face just for this purpose. She flexes her toes, enjoying the freedom, and pads ahead, nodding at a few caretakers as she makes her way through the caves. "Peace be with us," someone says, and she returns the greeting. Eyes follow her because they don't—*Do not,* she reminds herself— approve of her choice of clothing. She'll change in her room.

But first, the sounds of the exercise chamber draw her down a wide corridor. It curves left twice in a half circle before she's there at the entrance. High and wide as a football stadium. What passes for exercise equipment, wooden, not metal, lines the perimeter of the wall to her left. The smell, earthy sweat, wrinkles her nose.

Members of the Blaze Brigade are training: running laps, doing lifts, sparring. She lifts her chin at Ochai's replacement. She hasn't learned his name because the job isn't his, or at least it won't be for long. Once Ochai is released from The Mother—and Syrah will harass Taron until he is—he'll resume his duties as leader of this group.

After watching for a time, Syrah doubles back and is soon in her room. She closes the door behind her and lets out a heavy sigh. This ten-by-ten space, rounded with haphazard curves and a low ceiling, has become more home to her than its counterpart twice its size in Three Rivers. Somehow her books still refuse to stay where they belong.

She takes her time gathering them up from where they're strewn around the room and carefully piles them back onto the shelves she built herself out of the Blaze Brigade's salvaged-wood stock. The fake plant that her friend Artahe has unaffectionately tagged "the affront"— short for "affront against nature"—goes back on the top shelf, nearest the light sconce. Next she vanquishes the fine layer of dust that accumulates at about half the rate it does in her topside house. She has one tired leg on the step stool she uses to hoist herself onto her bed when a quick rap of knuckles on the door stops her.

"You should be up there," Artahe says, pointing a long slim finger upward, "giving them lessons in conservation, yet here you are about to sink your head beneath the covers." Her friend's voice has that judgmental tinge to it. She strolls over and leans her backside against the desk, crossing her arms. She has the clean smell of pure water and vegetation. She fiddles with the decorative fungal cap tucked into the thick twists above her right ear. "What have you done now?"

How is it that, just like parents, best friends turn into ace detectives, homing in on all the little gaps between what you say and don't say. It doesn't help that the lattice seems to know everything that happens topside, one of the things Syrah was most surprised to learn about this place. Artahe is no rootspeaker, but that doesn't stop the chatter from flowing like lava. Syrah doesn't bother lying. "I screwed up. I let two people from my tour group get to me. One of no consequence." Syrah stops there, picking through her thoughts. "The other one I am not so sure about, but I will look into it."

Syrah is impressed with herself. It has taken some time, but she's learning to speak more like them, dropping the contractions. There's a quirk to Artahe's impressively dark and shapely brows, but she doesn't press Syrah for details. It's another thing that Syrah has come to admire about her, about all the caretakers. They know when to back off and just let things be for a while.

Taron, however, breaks formation—no, shatters formation—on that one. Maybe all Keepers have to be that way. A consequence of the job or something like that. Syrah knows that she'll soon find out.

"Did you have time to test your theory?"

By "theory," Artahe is talking about Syrah trying to connect with the fungal spores.

Her friend marches over and takes her arm. Syrah's skin prickles in response, and she blooms. Her fungi like Artahe. Always have. In a way Syrah supposes that, with all her potions and mixtures, her friend created them. "They almost flared, you know," Syrah admits, diverting talk away from her theory. She isn't ready to share, not yet. "When I was with the tour group, and one of those men made me so angry. A freaking climate denier."

"But why? How many times have you had this happen now, and you still let it get to you? He probably knows or cares nothing about what he speaks. Some people embrace argument to fill the emptiness in their lives. What is happening to the world is as undeniable as The Mother's existence. That man and all the rest, they know it. It is just an inopportune truth. You know the Western topsiders do not suffer inconvenience well."

Syrah knows Artahe is right and tells her so. "I ran, you know. Tore outta there before they could see me—"

"Which is why I suggested longer, looser sleeves."

"And I told you that I have to wear the department-issued uniform. Long sleeve or short sleeve. No alterations."

Artahe's lips quirk again. "Wait. Did you say you ran away? In the middle of it?"

Syrah huffs. "Like my feet were being held to—" She catches herself. Fire jokes are inappropriate in Rhiza. "Like a woman with something to hide."

"You are an enigma," Artahe says, preening the mushroom caps on Syrah's forearms. They lean into her touch. "You do not believe me, but I did not do this to you on purpose."

"So I did it myself? That is what you are telling me?" Syrah says, annoyed. They've had this argument before. "Why don't . . . will you not just admit it?"

"If you want to lash out at someone, pick one of those men." Artahe pulls away. "I prepared what The Keeper asked me to prepare. Where she received her direction, you will have to take up with her."

A silence falls between them, and Syrah squirms. She's bone tired and wants to fall into her bed and sleep for a year. But she's also so wired up about that Dr. Anthony she can barely stand still. And there's something else. The thing that stands between them as impenetrable as Moro Rock.

"I wish things had turned out differently with Romelo."

"As do I," Artahe says. "We all tried, you, me, The Keeper. He made his decision."

"And I made mine," Syrah adds. "Between the time we had together as kids that I do not even remember and the brief stretch that we managed to be civil here in Rhiza, I feel like I barely knew him. Somehow, all that does not stop me from loving him. But I know what he meant to you." Syrah pauses. "I never said it before, I could not bring myself to, but I am so—"

"Do not say it. I told you to stop agonizing over this. You managed to protect us and your topside family. Your decision was an impossible one. You took the action of a leader. Accept it, for there will surely be more ahead of you."

Because Taron is deteriorating, Syrah thinks. She searches her friend's eyes. Gone is the accusation, the resentment that plagued their interactions in the early months following Moro Rock. Even the sadness is fading, replaced by something unreadable. Acceptance.

"Come." Artahe mimes, bending over and making a stepladder of herself. "Let me help the halfling up into her bed. But come see me in the mycology lab before you go back topside. I have a tincture I would like you to try."

"And?" Syrah says.

Artahe looks away. "And what?"

"Part of the reason you are here is to check on me," Syrah says. "You may as well go ahead and tell me the other half of the story." The friendship mind reading thing goes both ways.

Artahe's full lips curve into a small smile. "The Keeper would like a word. When you are ready, of course."

Syrah snorts. "Translation: now." There's a line from one of her father's old movies. *Resistance is . . . resistance is . . . resistance is futile.* It comes to Syrah now because she has resisted. Like the Florida shoreline giving way to yearly hurricanes. Taron's not-so-subtle overtures started shortly after she began recuperating from the fall. Syrah firmly believes anyone else, topside or below, would have already been dead.

Syrah promises to visit Artahe afterward and is out the door, standing there, when she realizes she hasn't asked if Taron is in her library or her private quarters. She opts for the former, work always being at the forefront of The Keeper's mind.

Syrah winces as she notices that the walkways are noticeably thinned but no less bustling. She spots the kid, his name escapes her, who challenged her to a fight her first day here. He called her an outsider and sneered right alongside his parents. Luckily it didn't come to blows, because Syrah's sure that, at that time, he would've beaten her senseless.

Not now, though. She lets her gaze slide over and through him. He lifts his chin and acts like she doesn't exist, which is fine with her.

A group of scourge suppressors pass, tunics soiled dusty. They have not one but three barrels of trash from the park. Will people never learn to clean up after themselves? Maybe another message to add to her park guide spiel.

The sight of Taron's new guard, Yemaya, stationed outside her library door tells Syrah she's guessed right. If size and musculature were the only measure, Yemaya would be deemed capable of singlehandedly holding off a small army. Stern faced, with curious ebony eyes. The picture of a soldier. But thinking back to what Dhanil did, Syrah knows that being capable is one thing; being trustworthy is another altogether. She's glad Dhanil and his band are trapped in The Mother. She hopes that he suffers every day there. But she hasn't asked because she is afraid that whatever Dhanil suffers there is the same as what Ochai is going through, being punished for Romelo's crime. And that is a thought she cannot bear.

After the brief traditional greeting, *Peace be with us*, Yemaya waves Syrah in.

For Syrah, the love affair with Taron's library, if not The Keeper herself, began at first sight. Books from antiquated to modern crammed into every corner, every inch of wall, every shelf on top of shelf.

As a child, she did the requisite reading for class, and the cultural additions her parents added to round out her education, but the library never became a refuge for her the way it did for others. Until now.

The first time she was hauled into this room, it was as a captive. A million years and just as many selves ago. Since then, she often returns because the place beckons. Like the coziest room in a countryside home. Everything reminds her of those early visits. Floor-to-ceiling book collections, thick with heft, delicate pages yellowed with age. Another corner filled with three stacks of newer releases, all in alphabetical order. Charred oak sideboards crammed with all the foreign-language texts from every era. Neatness isn't something Taron bothers herself with either. Her desk is a testament.

Syrah eyes a teetering stack of Keeper logs. She has combed through so many already (and every day), though Taron presses her to do more.

There's also what in Rhiza passes for comfortable seating. Chairs half too tall for her but padded with moss and stuffed with recycled clothing. Bioluminescent light augmented by the flameless candle Syrah gifted her as a get-well gift.

The smell of paper, as welcome as the scent of baked cookies.

But there's one addition. Something necessary but out of place. A settee of sorts. A handcrafted, rounded thing overflowing with cushions. A makeshift workspace in the form of a longish desk that slides beneath the settee, the surface proving ample for working on. Taron sits there now. The bandages are gone, but the wounds are no less vivid.

The Keeper's face is drawn. By Syrah's estimate, since they don't measure such things in Rhiza, she's lost a good thirty pounds. One shoulder is noticeably more slumped than the other. Her eyes are sunken ships at the bottom of an endless ocean. The scar on her cheek, earned as her face smacked a rocky outcropping, is like an angry red vein living forever above the surface of her skin.

But there's still a quill in her right hand. The left one doesn't work as well anymore. In short order, the left-handed Taron has taught herself to write with the other. The glass inkwell stands at the ready. A journal open, the page half-filled with her impressive script.

Taron looks up at Syrah and, despite herself, allows a reluctant smile to stretch all the way up to her eyes. Unbidden, both their gazes float over to the desk where Taron has posted herself every day for the last two centuries. The desk is no less full, but the chair is ominously empty. When Syrah returns her gaze to The Keeper, the unspoken implication is clear. She means for Syrah to take up the torch, and soon.

"Time is not a renewable resource, you know," Taron says in her bossy voice.

"What you call dawdling, I call work," Syrah says, preparing herself for the volley.

"So I hear." Taron sniffs. "What are the most important duties of a Keeper?"

Syrah doesn't sigh. Taron would be on her in a minute if she did. She doesn't roll her eyes or drop her chin to her chest in resignation. She recites the words:

1. Lead the people in all manner of action and issue resolution;
2. Establish and sustain an enduring connection to The Mother;
3. Maintain the logs as Keeper of the scrolls.

And there are so many scrolls, she thinks as she finishes.

"Come." Taron waves her over.

Syrah settles herself into the space her mentor has made for her. She notices the strained exhalation of breath. "What are you working on?"

"Committing these to record." She taps a few loose pieces of parchment. "This week's duty reports: Scourge Suppression, Lattice Affairs . . . Blaze Brigade is here somewhere." Taron shuffles those aside and piles a bulky notebook on top. The cover is smooth, almost like it's covered in a fine layer of hair. "The winter is not officially over until May, but let us explore something new today. These are the season's snowfall figures. Tell me what you see."

"I mean, it is unlikely that we will see another snowflake this year, but anything is possible. Would it not make sense to do this in June?" Syrah pulls the notebook closer and scans the columns. The script is so fine and utilitarian that, at first, it's difficult to make sense of it. But soon enough, the outline of a table becomes apparent. "See, June 2042 was the last entry."

"Do you believe that I have lost the use of my eyes?"

"No, but—"

"Then can you just this once do as I ask without questioning it?"

Syrah swivels around, ready to give Taron a piece of her mind, until her gaze falls on that scar, and the hand that lies useless in her mentor's lap. It's the tremble in her lips that clamps Syrah's mouth shut. They're doing this now because there's no guarantee they'll be able to do it later.

"How do we measure how much snow has fallen?"

"Scourge Suppression." Taron slides back into teacher mode easily. "They place a simple board near Mount Whitney. Two marks measure new snowfall, what has fallen since the last recording, and the other notes the depth, a daily annotation of the total amount on the ground."

Syrah takes the nib-tipped quill when Taron waves it in front of her face. She studies the entries more closely. Meticulously straight columns, text somehow written evenly across the page, with no lines or other guide that Syrah can discern. Print that's clear, blocky, as if done by a divinely guided hand. Flipping back through the pages, more of the same. Not so much as one line scratched out or an extra blob of ink carelessly dribbled onto the page.

And Syrah is supposed to take over maintenance of this work? By the time she entered school, the keypad was queen. Some of her teachers were hard-line old school, insisting that handwriting be incorporated into the curriculum, but the effort, though noble, had largely fallen by the wayside. At first, her laugh is more of a chuckle. But in short order, she sets down the quill, shoves the journal aside, and full-on cackles as if a comedian has delivered their best joke.

"I fail to see what is humorous about this situation," Taron says.

After Syrah composes herself, she asks, "Have you seen my handwriting?"

Taron throws her hand up in the air. "Is that all? It is impossible to expect you to have a script as practiced as mine. To be certain, a Rhizan child is likely more skilled in penmanship than you are. That will come. What matters is the data. It is a most critical task of a Keeper."

"Can we address the elephant in the room?"

"Your constant reliance on these ridiculous sayings and colloquialisms is tiresome. Would it be too much to ask you to speak plainly? Have you not spent enough time with us to see the value in it?"

The last traces of mirth are zapped from Syrah. Taron may as well have called her an idiot to her face. "I've—"

"I. Have." Taron slaps her palm on her makeshift desk.

"Iiiii'vvvve"—Syrah draws out the contraction for as long as she can—"spent my entire life topside. To suggest that I can turn off everything about that experience in under a year? That just isn't fair." She exhales. "Is not."

"I will not live forever."

Now that strikes a chord, a nasty one. "Please. You are getting better. You will outlive me."

Sitting side by side, Syrah hasn't looked over, but she shoots a tentative glance at Taron now. Her breathing is labored. A bit of drool pools in the corner of her mouth, which she has trouble keeping closed. Syrah has to take off the blinders, another saying that she keeps to herself, since The Keeper would not approve. Taron isn't getting better. She's maintaining, holding on.

For her.

A chill tap-dances along her spine, and she reaches for the journal. Taron stops her.

"We will have time for that later," she says. "Your fungi. Show them to me. Now."

This she can do, with pride.

"Come." Taron is on her feet, staff in hand, taking slow, measured steps toward the door.

Chapter Six

Beneath Sequoia National Park
Rhiza on High
April 2043

If the eyes are the window to the soul, then books are the sovereign of the subconscious. Romelo knows that some learning is overt and some, the most important kind, is much more subtle. True knowledge, like a fine tea, must be given latitude, time to steep, so that later, at just the right moment, the planted seeds may be sown.

All the reading his adoptive mother tasked him with has shaped Romelo into the rootspeaker he is today. One seemingly innocuous fact, buried in the gilded pages and small print of a long-forgotten passage, will turn him into a legend.

When he discovered that passage that led him to the walled-off section of Crystal Cave, it provided him and his followers a place to amass and plan. Things did not go the way they should have. The word is as difficult to form in Romelo's mind as it is to let escape from his mouth. Failure.

He failed everyone who looked up to him and he failed the Giants. If his plan, Vice's plan, works (and privately, he entertains doubts that it will), Romelo must reunify their people by becoming The Keeper. If they are allowed to recover, he can combine and reopen all the shuttered fragments of the cave system.

That would require Rhiza's current leader to be no more. Not saying her name doesn't lessen the sting of what he must do. Taron still clings to life. They are both shells of their former selves, but she will never willingly step aside, so Romelo knows his next attempt on her life must be the last.

He meanders through the newly discovered section of the cave, comforted by the cool dark. There are not as many sconces here to light his path, but he already knows the way as well as he knows his own body. He studied the words and ways of it long before he ever set foot here.

He hears the steady tap-tap-tap of dripping water and senses the girth of a timeworn stalactite cluster. He lifts his hand. Moments later, his fingertips brush the spiky tips, exactly where he knows them to be. He wonders about the caretakers who once roamed these tunnels. How they lived, how different their time was. Did they see the shell that Rhiza would become?

There was a time when the directive to protect and serve the Giants was still thought to be attainable using the old methods. Taron is stuck in a reality born of her youth, long past. She does not want to accept the truth of things as they are now.

The humans are . . . winning.

More Giants have been lost under her watch than any of her predecessors', while she sits there in her library recording dates and times in her beloved scrolls like a machine. And when he, her son, devised a plan, she rebuked him. Denied him. The Keeper of the Canopy chose to protect the topsiders she claims to despise.

It is obvious, really. For all Taron's staff-wielding rough exterior and sharp tongue, she lacks the guts to command irrevocable change. His mother has simply served too long, has lost her way. Romelo has no such reticence. There is only one way to save Rhiza and the forest and, for that matter, all the trees.

Finding the abandoned offshoots of the caves was both blessing and curse. It pained Romelo to witness the true impact, to come to fully understand how many of the Giants have been lost. To raging, scorching fires that even seasoned blaze brigadiers struggle to contain. To putrid air that leaves them, enhanced lungs and all, breathless.

Each room Romelo scouted alone here had succumbed once again to nature's relentless, rightful advance. Layers of dust and damp coated everything. Unlikely vines clogged some of the walls. This section of Lattice Affairs had been shuttered, pods home to small animals and vermin after so long untended. The whole visage once shook him to his core—before he began to see the opportunity.

After he took his discovery to Ezanna, they hatched a plan. And once again, it has a chance to come to fruition.

Ezanna the teacher saw the seeds of hatred flourishing in Romelo and tended them like a shepherd to his flock. At first, he likely thought being assigned to educate Romelo was a punishment but soon must have known it for what it was: respect. So he took his young human charge under his wing and taught him all he knew. Shaped him to his vision for a world without humans—at least a California without them. Only then could Rhiza reverse the Giants' fortunes.

Once he and the others had broken through the blockade, they took care to restore it, lest Taron, her pet, Syrah, and their ilk track them down. And he took the book that had led him here. It stands defiantly on a shelf in his new quarters. But their isolation necessitated finding a new entrance and exit. It took weeks of tracking, backtracking, and dead ends, but eventually, his followers found the prize: a new entrance to a new Rhiza. At a higher elevation, miles away from the one that had been chartered before.

Pride swells in him as he strolls purposefully through the restored corridors. Pathways and dwellings swept clean. Thanks to a new colony of spotted bats, scratching and squeaking in the corner, the insects are kept under control. The sounds and sights and smells of life continuing as their ancestors would have intended. No, demanded.

A youthful gathering, playing at a game of stones. The whoops and shouts of winners and losers. Several entire families have joined as well.

They gather in groups nightly to engage in the telling, reciting Rhizan children's rhymes and stories. The one he hears as he passes is the new one, about The Breaking he caused, a few flourishes added on by the skilled young orator.

The most important resurrection of them all: his new Lattice Affairs center. Not as large as the one he left, but no less capable. It was here, months after the fire, where Vice first contacted him. He makes an effort to throw back his shoulders before he walks in.

Six of the ten pods are already occupied; whether here or in Rhiza proper, rootspeakers' first rule is to tend to the lattice, to the Giants. With a wave of his hand, one by one, they disconnect, nod their greetings, and leave.

"Is there something I can help you with?" Menhit asks. He is an exceptional rootspeaker. Almost as good as Romelo, definitely equal to Liesel, lost in last summer's conflict. Romelo feels a tinge of sadness, lets himself soak it in for a moment before letting it go. "I know you are planning something big, and I can help."

"Soon, my friend," Romelo says. "I need to test a hypothesis. If all goes as planned, you will have more than enough work to keep you busy. Our mission remains the same. Patience is called for now."

Menhit claps Romelo on the shoulder before leaving.

"No one must enter," Romelo calls after him.

"I will make sure of it," Menhit says, taking up a spot just outside to stand guard.

Romelo climbs into his pod. Early on, when he was first training, he tried to work in pods that had been designed for native Rhiza. Nearly a foot taller than him, it was Taron who pointed out the inefficiency. He was not letting pride get in his way this time. His people had worked tirelessly to tailor his pod to fit him perfectly. He uses the special hand grips they inserted to hoist himself upward, and with ease he slides in.

Snug. Mere inches above his head and chest, less between his right shoulder and the smooth granite wall. He pulls the lever and eases his bare feet into the opening. Moist, warm soil filters between his toes. He flexes his feet and breathes deeply. He feels Her presence immediately. The Mother. She has watched, if not condoned, his activities ever since he set up shop in the new space. She has not made a move to stop or sanction him. Romelo knows she is doing as she often does, waiting to see who will emerge victorious, he or his sister. She will intervene only when and if she believes she needs to.

It has taken great effort, but he and Menhit have worked to carve out separate pathways to the existing lattice. And they must mask their trail so that Rhiza's new head rootspeaker will remain unaware of their activities. Shansi must be even less skilled than Romelo thinks. He expected to have been found out by now, for someone to have tried to sabotage his new connections. Remarkably, he operates freely under the cover of the protections they have established.

Soon, the first feathery brushes make contact. He gasps as the tendrils fuse with the small hairs around his ankles and lower legs and sink beneath the skin. It is like turning on a radio to all channels at once. Once the noise has reduced from a roar to a slow, steady hum, he seeks out the one voice he needs. Vice. *His* tree.

Adrenaline shoots through him. It happens each time he is near the sapling, whether topside or through the lattice, feeling much more like his former self.

Oh, what it must feel like to have been forged in this forest and nurtured by wisdom and community. To be allowed to sit in decades' worth of contemplative silence, allowing centuries to pass without much notice. To grow a canopy and roots free and deep.

At times, Romelo wishes he were a tree.

Pondering aside, duty calls. First he checks Vice's overall health, things he cannot observe by sight alone. Growth is still accelerated. Roots strengthening and stretching out to four feet in circumference. Finding all well, albeit unusual, he turns his attention to his mission.

He sends a test command.

Stop transpiration. Do not absorb any carbon dioxide.

He waits.

And waits.

You are the breaker, Vice begins. *I am grateful for all that you have tried to do, even if what you accomplished amounted to a pile of dead leaves and loose ends. I will make this right. You need only remember that you live to serve me, not the other way around.*

Romelo is incensed by his willful charge. Much the way he suspects Taron thinks of him.

You speak true, but indulge me, dear one.

He tries again. Tries until he hears grumbling outside the door.

As much as he presses, Vice will not or cannot heed his command.

Chapter Seven

Rhiza
The Mother's chamber
April 2043

Syrah knows the path they walk in her heart. The Mother's hum, the arboreal song she first heard as a child, strikes up in her belly as if by a conductor's slim baton. Taron is taking her to see The Mother. Instinctively, Syrah guesses why. A panic overtakes her. She stops and takes Taron's arm. "No matter what Artahe cooks up and feeds me from that lab of hers, I am still human. How do you know I am ready to try to connect with Her?"

"I am not convinced that you can," Taron says, so casually it chafes. "It is long overdue that we make the attempt. What we learn either way will steer future efforts."

The Keeper pulls away and sets off again, led by the new leader of her honor guard, Yemaya. Syrah has no choice but to follow. The veins in Taron's already wrinkly hand bulge with the iron grip she has on her staff, which she's leaning on more heavily than before. Clumps of caretakers gathered here and there lower their gazes and step aside at their approach. Among one group, Syrah spots a familiar face. A caretaker who's somehow always near, always watching, but silent as a church mouse.

This time, though, he raises his eyebrows, gestures with a wide sweep of his hand. "A moment?"

Taron doesn't even stop, only tosses a warning over her shoulder. "Do not putter."

There's something about the way his eyes size Syrah up that is off-putting. Her curiosity gets the best of her. "What?"

"I am Inkoza," he says before bowing his head in the Rhizan way. "For a time, I was her most eager student. Did you know?"

Syrah casts a look at Taron's retreating figure. No, she's never mentioned having an understudy other than Romelo. It makes sense, though. "I will repeat—what?"

He tries to lean down, closer, but Syrah tilts her head in a watch-yourself angle. He gives her a conciliatory smile. "You will never be a match for what she has planned. Just like you will never be a match for Rhiza. I am born and bred. You are not."

Oddly, Syrah doesn't read anger in this, her latest obstacle. Only resolve. She chortles and walks off, not looking back over her shoulder as she hustles to catch up to Taron and Yemaya.

"Why did you not . . . Okay, that just sounds weird. Why didn't you tell me that you had another student? I thought Romelo was your pick for successor."

Taron makes a point of rolling her eyes before she glances down at Syrah. "Because it is of no consequence. Do not let that one get to you. There is a reason that I stopped teaching him. He has leadership qualities, that is undeniable. But like your brother, he is plagued by anger. Emotion comes second when you are a leader. You cannot keep it close at hand like a favored plaything. Neither of them quite understood that."

Syrah quells any other questions she has, but she knows an enemy when she sees one and commits herself to keeping an eye on this Inkoza.

As they get closer to The Mother, Syrah feels her steps faltering. Her legs feel heavier, and she has a sudden shortness of breath. Her stomach churns. She swallows it all down, though, and when they reach the entrance, Syrah takes a deep breath and, close on Taron's heels, steps through.

Syrah has not been to Her chamber since that time. When Ochai and the others were punished for their role in helping Romelo's insurrection. That animal attack had killed five people and injured a crap ton more. Ochai, who before his imprisonment slipped a note into her favorite book that told her what she already knew; he loved her as she loved him. Her breath catches in her throat.

The Mother is more than a living thing. She is an exquisite spectacle, a reckoning. A green goddess. Ten Giants wide and a canopy unmatched that stretches lower and higher than any other. That she lords over an island surrounded by a gentle sea is only fitting. The water is as clear and serene as a moonless night. Her awl-shaped leaves are a glimmering wildness like innumerable admirers.

"Will you stand there and gape, or will you come so that we can do what we must?" Taron makes her way down the stairs. Syrah, however, remains glued in place, overwhelmed by seeing this thing older than life, but also horrified that she once watched Her swallow Ochai whole. Watching his face, all those faces, imprinted into Her bark—no horror flick or book has ever topped that.

Reluctantly, Syrah swallows a massive lump in her throat and descends the earth-packed stairway. The steps are wide, tailored for legs much longer than hers, but she takes them at a gallop and soon stands shoulder to shoulder with The Keeper. Yemaya remains positioned outside, where she'll stay until they are done. Syrah can't help but think back to Taron's former guard, Dhanil. His betrayal surprised them both; at least he, along with those who helped him, is imprisoned right alongside Ochai.

The narrow walkway over the water is a piece of art made of salvaged California fir. Inexplicably, short stalks of meadow goldenrod are woven into the sides and handrail. Narrow leaves protrude all along the shafts, with feather-like shocks of yellow at the tips. Syrah read somewhere that Native Americans once used the flower for medicine.

Taron nudges Syrah with a sharp elbow. Together, they step onto the bridge that leads to The Mother. The crystal clear water that feeds all of Rhiza laps peacefully against both sides of the path.

The closer they get to Her, the more Syrah's mind quiets into awe. The feeling sweeps away everything else. It seems that even Taron's labored gait has improved since stepping inside these smooth, curved walls. When The Keeper lays a hand upon the cinnamon-colored bark, she exhales and rests her forehead there for a time.

Syrah is silent, maintaining a respectable distance for now. Artahe's words come back to her. She said aloud what Syrah has thought about a million times: if she is to lead Rhiza, her small but important family topside will become like ghosts, because she'll probably never see them again.

Inkoza annoyed her, but his words are no less valid. Is a human really meant to serve in this way? Syrah doesn't want to go down in the Keepers' logs as the experiment gone uncommonly wrong.

Her mind catalogs other candidates: Artahe is fair minded. Young enough to ensure a long tenure. She's a good healer and mycologist, a leader. She's even got better penmanship. Why not her? And even Inkoza. If he studied under Taron for so many years, that would give him a leg up on Syrah right there. Then there's Ezanna. Syrah has never met her brother's mentor, but that makes his reputation no less legendary. She's heard the whispers. He was a fierce fighter in his heyday, has read everything in the library ten times over. He was Taron's right hand for a time, until his ward twisted his mind into turning away from his people. He has the experience, the leadership qualities, but he's too susceptible to anger and manipulation. Of course, he also hates topsiders. And, strike three, he and Taron are very close in age.

"Come forward," Taron commands.

The first step is an impossibility. The others are like walking across molten lava. But Syrah takes each stride as if it were her last. Eventually, she is there and can't help herself. She lays both hands on The Mother. Her song pulses through Syrah's palms. The same sound that was the soundtrack to her childhood dreams where she would sit nestled in the crook of a giant sequoia's shoulder-like branch as, together, they walked through this very forest. She heard this same song on her first day at work in the forest.

"Will you stand or lay down?" Taron asks.

Syrah thinks for a moment before she answers, contemplating what Taron, what The Mother, would want. "I will stand."

"Suit yourself," Taron says. "The Mother's roots will connect with yours. Do not resist her. I can tell you nothing more of what will happen. Each candidate's experience is their own."

With that, Taron finds a patch of ground and gingerly lowers herself into a cross-legged seat, her staff placed beside her.

"That's it?" Syrah asks, panic rising like the sun at summer solstice. "I'm not Rhiza. What if—"

"Yet you are not fully human, either, not anymore." Taron rubs her chin. "We will bear witness together."

"Bear witness? That's your plan? No, we need to take some sort of precaution. You haven't thought this through, have you? How am I . . . ?" Syrah's protests melt away. Her vision goes blindingly emerald. She's surrounded, enveloped in color. When she opens her mouth to scream, a bitter spring pours down her throat, thick and viscous. Just when Syrah thinks she is full to bursting, she begins to ride the wave of it. And underneath it all are the root filaments. Moving like heat-seeking missiles. Probing her lower legs, roaming over her knees and thighs. Ranging over her middle.

Sinking through flesh.

A sensation like millions of hyphae.

Like ants swarming.

Like bees converging.

Like teeth.

Her lungs are an untapped, unpainted canvas. And the tendrils are mapping the boundaries. Probing, searching, and then . . . puncturing. Syrah's stomach and heart have retreated to someplace safe. Someplace not here with The Mother, who's trying to undo her. Unable to comprehend the pain, she squeezes her eyes shut and endures it.

Like a battering ram against a steel wall, the searching continues. It is as if those delicate tendrils are trying to open a door with the wrong key. Just when it feels like that key will break off in Syrah's chest and lodge there for all eternity, all the oxygen leaves her body.

Chapter Eight

There's no such thing as a hospital in Rhiza. Not so much as a walk-in clinic. Healing takes place in private, in one's quarters, with the help of Artahe, her staff, and a dizzying variety of fungus-based remedies. Poultices, powders, dried edibles, soups, and teas, their chemical offshoots the source of so many medicines, above- and belowground.

A whiff of one of those teas permeates Syrah's small room. A Chaga derivative, she thinks, blended with a *Helvella* variety harvested from the forest.

It's this scent, along with the blissfully successful gulp of air she drinks down into her lungs, that tells Syrah she survived the encounter with The Mother. Before she sits up, she scans her body, relieved that no traces of the invasive hyphae remain. She feels like someone took a rake to her insides.

When Syrah opens her eyes, she is greeted by the comforting image of her ceiling. The little birds that one of the Rhizan children carved into the earth to welcome her. There are two people in her room. She can feel them.

"Drink this." Artahe's singsong voice draws Syrah up onto her elbows. "And the rest here. In quick succession."

Artahe slides her a smile before she leaves.

"It is your lungs," Taron says as Syrah gingerly sets a foot on her step stool. "They are too small by roughly two pounds and four or five inches."

"No longer one hundred percent human," Syrah says, then stops to gulp down the first cup of tea. It's earthy, of course, but it has another, more subtle flavor. And a few rubbery bits that she doesn't chew. "But apparently I am not Rhiza enough either."

From her seat at Syrah's desk, Taron watches her, unblinking. "So it would seem."

"Does that mean I cannot become Keeper then?" Syrah asks. She's ashamed at how she wars with what she hopes the answer will be, at how some sliver of her subconscious hoped their attempt would fail.

Taron flicks her a look. "Based on all that you have come to know of me, of Her, you must know that we will not give up quite so easily."

Syrah *does* know. They are the most stubborn people . . . trees . . . Rhiza she has ever met. Had he lived, her brother would be the third she'd add to that list. "Strength, yes; connecting to the lattice, check. But unless Artahe has something truly special brewing in that farm of hers, I do not think growing extra lung tissue is going to happen for me."

Taron only lifts her chin. "An obstacle. Not an ending."

So it won't be easy. No surprise there. She, they, will try again, and somehow, Syrah will be ready.

"Quick succession." Taron taps her staff to the floor and gestures at the rest of the tea.

Syrah does as told and guzzles it down, gagging over the tasteless rubber bits.

"There is something else I want to let you know. It does not take a genius to see that our numbers are less than what they were even when you came to us. The members of Romelo's faction have not returned, and the last fire cost us even more. It is time to release some from their punishment with The Mother."

Syrah's heart is a shooting star. Finally, Taron has seen how wrong she was to punish Ochai for Romelo's crimes.

"Dhanil and those who sided with him and a few others who have served their time will be released later today."

Taron's words are like a blow to the chest. "Dhanil?" Syrah is incensed. "After what he did? He actually laid hands on you. Locked us up like criminals. Why him and not Ochai?"

"Ah," Taron says. "You are thinking with your heart again and not that sharp mind of yours. You will need Dhanil. He made an error in judgment. One he made for the good of Rhiza. That is the difference between us and the topsiders. When one's time is served, one's crime is truly forgiven. It does not continue for the remainder of one's life. That, even for humans, is inhumane."

"But Romelo was the one who orchestrated everything, and you know it. Ochai took the blame for reasons I still do not get."

"It was likely he and Ezanna who orchestrated everything."

"And you could argue that they did what they did for the good of Rhiza too."

"I would not argue that point."

"And what do you mean, I will need Dhanil?" Syrah says, growing angrier. "I would not trust him to tell me the time of day, let alone watch my back."

"When I am gone, you will need him. Inkoza will challenge you, and arguably, he should. Maybe others. Dhanil is wiser than you give him credit for, you know. You will need his strength and his counsel."

"Like hell I will."

"Dhanil was contrite. Apologetic. You must let your anger and resentment go. Focus on what is best for Rhiza, not your hurt feelings."

"Fine," Syrah says. "Then let Ochai go too."

"He will be released from The Mother when his punishment is finished. Until then, he stays where he is."

Syrah doesn't argue. She doesn't have to. She has a plan. "When do we try again?"

"When I am certain that your head is on straight. That you are ready for the task at hand. That you have your emotions and your goals aligned."

"You do not get to make all the decisions," Syrah says. "Not when it concerns me."

"You need some time to yourself," Taron says, rising with her staff. "Leave for now."

"I'd be happy to."

"For the Mother's sake speak Rhizan," Taron barks. "I *would*."

With more pep in her step than Syrah thought her capable of, Taron goes over and flings the door open. Yemaya's startled gaze takes them both in. She narrows her eyes at Syrah before turning and trailing after her charge.

Syrah strips off her Rhizan tunic and slacks and changes into her topsider gear. She grabs her backpack and storms out of the room and through the caves. She'll be back, though. And when she does, she'll take matters into her own hands.

Seeing with Ancient Eyes
A Time for Change

I am The Mother and mothers take little rest
My roots are bone tired
My canopy is not as lush as it once was
My trunk is less sturdy

The very air is a malignant blight upon an un-
    witting sky
Mine eyes dream of a world without humans
The unnatural lights that blanch the night sky
    will blink out of existence

51

Space litter will crash back to the earth
In time, vegetation and sand will overtake the
        hard edges of progress
Lush swamp creatures and habitat will consume
        the rest
An Elysium

The breaker has undone the caretakers and the
        Giants, my children
Split as if by a blade borne of his virulent resolve
To do good, to be good
A creature of flame and anger and grief
He may yet still be our savior

Two contenders, the breaker and the deliverer, at
        cross purposes
One of them will emerge victorious

I have not interfered
That may have been . . . unwise
An enigma, an outlandish and alien thought

Through the maneuvering of a mutation
The new sapling, offspring of the venerable one
        whom the topsiders called The President
It grows unnaturally
Consumes resources recklessly, without care for
        others
It takes notice of me with grumbling acceptance

Not the love and openness due to its Mother
The precipice of change is nearing
An ending and a beginning

Chapter Nine

Three Rivers, California
Syrah's home
April 2043

Syrah's heart sinks. She picks up the business card again, stares at it as if, in doing so, the letters will rearrange themselves into something less irrefutable. Dr. Baron Anthony. That hairline fracture of hope that the hairy-knuckled man with the needling eyes she met on her last debacle of a guided tour was a fake.

She stares at her virtual display. He's anything but. A new subdivision of the US Forest Service: the Bureau of International Investigations, or BII. There's an official .gov address, a simplistic logo. A sparse home page flaunts some indecipherable lawyerlike babble intended to tell you what the agency does and succeeds masterfully in doing anything but that. A stark contact page invites visitors to enter their messaging preference. She's heard about them; everybody who works for the National Park Service has. Theirs is a unit dedicated to research, species identification, and . . . unnatural phenomena.

Syrah guesses that would include incidents like bears hunting people in packs of three. Like dogs turning on their owners. Like when all the animals in the northern half of the state sought to replace people at the top of the food chain. All Romelo's twisted doings. That kind of thing raises all the wrong eyebrows. With all the time passed and news cycles swiftly moving on to the next outrage, she's convinced herself that Rhiza is safe.

Centuries, millennia, without discovery breeds a certain kind of arrogance. Understandable, though. It is one hell of a track record. But Syrah isn't so sure this time.

Her anger and angst surrender to worry. She cornered Artahe before she left and pressed her for the truth. The Keeper isn't getting better. She won't improve, nor will she hold steady. Taron's eyes have already told her as much, but Syrah couldn't acknowledge it. Taron is declining, fast, her impossibly long life cut short by her own adopted child. Syrah carries the guilt of it. She doubts Romelo has given it a second thought.

That's why she's being shoehorned into the role of Keeper. But how can she make this work? Last she checked, it isn't a part-time gig she can squeeze in alongside her tour guide duties with the park. She gives her head a quick shake.

Over the last six or seven months, Syrah has maintained a life both topside and beneath the veil. More of the latter, if she's completely honest with herself. Something she admittedly struggles with. She has developed an unhelpful tendency to try to ignore the things she doesn't want to deal with. Being Keeper will mean giving up her home with the sweet song of the North Fork River out back, her small but irreplaceable family, veggie burgers from the Gateway.

Her life, her humanity.

She'll have to deal with the wildlife biologist, even though he won't find anything. Rhiza has been hidden for as long as the world has existed. The flow doesn't linger in the air. Their camouflage is like nothing she's ever seen. No human has entered that place unless the Rhiza wanted them to, and in thousands of years, that number has been a meager three. Romelo, Syrah, and their ancestor, the only female buffalo soldier, Cathay Williams.

Dr. Anthony can look. He can have a team of a thousand swarm Sequoia and the caves. They can bring their tech and their tools. Scourge

Suppression will have a time of it cleaning up after them and all the trash that they'll dump along the way. Shansi and his lattice workers will have to repair any disturbed roots, trampled or subdued under the onslaught of too many pairs of boots. They work for the forest, but human stupidity is ever present, so the Blaze Brigade will be ready to help stamp down any fires inadvertently or purposefully started.

The Forest Service's bulldog will fail. Government resources and time wasted.

It'll all amount to nothing, Syrah promises herself, even as she hopes that she isn't once again dismissing that which makes her uncomfortable.

It's with this renewed, shaky confidence that Syrah is ready to return to Rhiza. As often happens when she is belowground for too long, her comms device has gone dead. She goes over and picks it up from the charger and turns it on. Ten calls, two messages. The first, after all the calls, is from her boss, the other her dad. She holds it, hoping for, expecting, a third—a call from Uncle Dane. His absence isn't mean spirited. He's just doing as she asked, giving her the space to sort out the fuzzy contours of her new life.

She showers first, thinking that there will never come a day when she gets used to the bucket-over-the-head variety of baths in Rhiza. Hot water, there's no replacement for it as far as she's concerned. She reaches beneath the sink and pulls out a jar of coconut oil, gone semisolid in the wavering temperatures. After taking care of her body, she looks in the mirror and frowns at the untwisted inch of new growth sprouting from her scalp. The last thing she has time for is a hair appointment for retwisting, so she settles for working the moisturizer into the full length of her locs. A silk scrunchie binds them back in place at the nape of her neck.

Dreading the first of her return calls, she pads back to her tiny living room, plops down on the sofa, and calls her boss.

"Carthan," Mr. Singletary barks. "What's with the radio silence? I've been trying to get a hold of you. Want to tell me what happened out there?"

No, Syrah thinks. She quickly calculates how much time has passed. Math isn't her strong suit. Twenty-four hours topside for every four spent below, so a day and a half, tops. "I let a couple of climate deniers get under my skin." No way she's going to mention the biologist from the BII.

"And you left your group?" Singletary's voice has an angry tremor to it.

How to explain? "I felt threatened," Syrah offers with a conciliatory softness. "I intended to just step away. You know, to clear my head and give them both time to either cool off or slink back beneath the rocks they climbed out from under. I did ask the group to wait for me, but I guess I was away longer than I thought, and they decided they'd be better off exploring on their own." Syrah has spun the tale fairly well, at least she thinks she has. The best lies have a seed of truth in them. "I'm sorry. I probably didn't handle that the best way. I'll be better prepared next time."

She lets the assumption that there will be a next time hang there in the balance while her boss considers his next move.

"Dane is going to take your next couple shifts. Give you some time to get yourself together. The updated schedule will be posted on our internal comms and at Wuksachi in the usual place. Let me know if that doesn't work for you."

"Yes, sir," Syrah says. So she isn't fired, but she is getting an unexpected break. Not a good sign. First the fire service, now this. Her career had been going well, promotions, a commendation. "Upward trajectory," Mama had called it.

All until she set foot back in California. She'd become the first Black female fire chief, then let the Manhattan-size chip on her shoulder ruin it. Her resignation is stamped on a digital file somewhere she hopes any record of her time there has been magically erased. It's taken her all this time to make peace with her decision to leave. And now, she's one agitator away from losing the only job she could get afterward.

The next call is to her father.

"Hi, Daddy," she says when he picks up, mindful to mask her sour mood.

"What's wrong?" he says anyway. She'd be surprised if he hadn't seen right through her.

"Nothing," she tries at first, then resolves to drop the ruse. After a drawn-out exhale: "I had a run-in with a climate denier during my tour. I got into this unnecessary back-and-forth with him and totally abandoned my group. The short version of the aftermath is, somebody else is doing my job for the next couple days."

"He didn't touch you, did he?" Dad asks.

Syrah contemplates her new body. Not only the fungi but how strong she's become. Physical intimidation ain't happening. "I'd be making this call from a place with bars if he had." She knows he wants to ask more questions. Her mother certainly would. Anissa Carthan was likely an investigative reporter in a former life.

"As long as you're okay, all you have to do is come up with a plan for the next time. 'Cause there will probably be a next time. I see these people on the news. Luckily we don't have to read their nonsense comments online anymore. The truth is just too scary for some folks. 'Cause that would mean they'd have to reconsider the way they live. It's easier to pretend the truth ain't smacking them every which a'way. Just be prepared is all I'm saying."

"Good advice," Syrah says, and she means it. And that's exactly what she'll do with Dr. Anthony too. Do her homework, alert Taron and the rest of Rhiza. Prepare. "Thank you, Daddy."

They go on to discuss her mother, who's considering going back to work as a physical therapist because retirement bores her. Then they slide over all the neighborhood goings-on. Her dad assures her that he got a clean bill of health during his last doctor visit. The effects of the stroke all but gone. She promises to visit soon but doesn't know when she can really make that happen.

When the call ends, Syrah feels better, ready to return to her other home beneath the veil.

Chapter Ten

Sequoia National Park
Moro Rock
April 2043

Instead of heading straight back to Rhiza, Syrah detours and takes Crescent Meadow Road toward the Giant Forest Museum. Her heartbeat does a two-step as she nears the already half-full Moro Rock parking lot.

She gets out, her vision swallowed by the towering granite wonder. A group of visitors, laughing and enviously carefree, move past her. Those overstuffed backpacks will have them bent over gasping for breath before they get halfway to the top. She isn't wearing her tourist guide hat today, so she doesn't warn them.

She falls in line behind the group before she can stop herself. Their giddy anticipation reminds her of what she felt the first time she was here. Syrah gets as far as the staircase but stops dead and watches as the tourists sprint upward, disappearing around the first bend.

Moro Rock once evoked that feeling of awe you get in the presence of things that exist in their own human-untouched grandeur. Like the Giants. Now it's the star of recurrent nightmares. A fleshy grief weighs her down like there are two of her now. One from before her world went all wrong-side up. And another, the one that surfaced after she witnessed Romelo send Taron careening off the side of this mountain.

The last time she was here, she let her rage fuel the fight with her brother, then hefted the plane wreck of his body onto her back. She slogged down those steps and laid him down to die. Syrah's grief is as heavy as tropical air after a rainstorm. Almost too thick to breathe.

Her face crumples and she squeezes her eyes shut. No tears come because Syrah has cried them all out, enough for two Rhizan lifetimes. More tourists move around and past her. "Are you all right? Everything okay?" She ignores them. She is far from okay and never will be again.

Syrah hightails it away from there, jumps back into her car, and rests her forehead on the cool steering wheel. She sweeps her pain into the brick-walled sections of her heart and mind. When she lifts her head, she's ready to get on with living again.

To ensure her car never draws too much attention during those long stretches belowground, she rotates between Sequoia's parking lots. Her lungs and limbs no longer protest at long, arduous hikes. Sometimes she has her uncle move it around or take it to his place. This time, she opts for her favored spot, Wuksachi Lodge. There's something tangibly peaceful about the stone and cedar building surrounded by evergreen conifers and the Sierras.

Despite the bristly conversation she just had with her boss, she heads straight for the schedule board. Behind a couple and their children, she scans the flickering digital screen.

Sure enough, for the remainder of the week, plus an additional day for good measure, all of Syrah's two-hour tour shifts have been assigned either to Dane or the Fresno Pacific University student who's interning with the park service for the spring semester. She swallows the bitter taste of reprimand, down where all her life's other disappointments live. Right alongside where her feelings about her complicated mother churn and roil. The place from where her longing to be a firefighter stirs every now and again. A tangled nook where a silhouette of remorse for killing her own brother rests. She suspects all the therapy and meditation in the world won't free her.

As Syrah turns away from the board, she catches sight of the man who disrupted her tour. He's at the front counter with a massive suitcase. Has he really chosen to vacation at a place he hates just to antagonize the people who love it? She agrees with Romelo on one thing: humans are so damned complicated. Syrah lowers her gaze and quickly makes for the exit. It's well past time to check on Taron.

On foot, she starts at the Congress Trailhead and then veers off into a thicket of forest. Early on, she tried to take some of the creature comforts from her Three Rivers home back to Rhiza. Overstuffed blankets, a back pillow, socks. Taron and Artahe had given her looks, then spoken plainly. If she was to become one of them (at that point she had not committed to any such thing), then she would have to learn to live as they did. There were no lines to be straddled. So aside from a refashioned lattice work pod that fit her height better and the extra bed cushion she refuses to part with, she has done just as they said and, for the most part, come to appreciate the simplicity of it all.

Her senses, more finely tuned than those of the woman who first came to this park, pick up the sights and sounds of nature. She welcomes this delicious respite every time. It's spring, and Sequoia's entire landscape bursts with color. Virescent emeralds, rich brown barks and roots, many-hued wildflowers fighting for their place in the sun. She trails her finger along their tops, and she imagines they lean in to meet her.

Warm, dappled sunlight trickles through the breaks in tree canopies like water from the falls. A fox darts into the path and stops. It tilts its head and stares at Syrah like it, too, recognizes she is something different, something more than other humans. Artahe and Taron are unsure when and if that evolution will stop. What she will become. Part of her is horrified, but the other part, the one that in a previous lifetime relished the study of flora and fauna . . . *she* is curious enough to see it through.

In no time, she's there. It's early in the season and not many campers have invaded this section of the park, but Syrah still gives a cursory check over her shoulder before she slips into the gaping hole in the Giant and begins the descent to Rhiza.

The slow trickle of water accompanies her footsteps. Stalactites that before had bruised her forehead, scraped a cheek, are easily navigated now. And The Mother's pulsating bass beckons her forward.

Soon, Rhiza's other chords strike her. Their singsong voices. Bare feet slapping against the hard-packed earth. As she emerges into a corridor flooded with the bioluminescent mushroom wall sconces, she is met with both the traditional greetings and nods, but also the eyebrows raised in disapproval of her hiking boots. She'll remove them when she gets to her room and not a moment before. She has accepted things about the Rhiza, and they'll have to just deal with this oddity about her. For a woman who had set aside time during every shower since she was a teen to pamper her feet, the barefoot thing is one aspect of living belowground that she still struggles with.

It is no accident that Syrah's room is not more than a few paces from Taron's. The Keeper wanted her close at hand, and Syrah doesn't mind. Just as she does when she walks through the door of her home topside, she relishes her space here. She lets her shoulders relax, allows the feeling of calm to wash over her as she opens her door.

And, not for the first time, she curses the fact that locks are not a thing in Rhiza.

There's a sharp, desperate silence before her mouth opens to scream. Nothing comes out but the tears that flood her eyes and spill down her face. Syrah glances over her shoulder and then back inside her room. Instinct says to run. Another feeling that she refuses to name won't let her.

She scrubs her face with the back of her hand, steps inside, and closes the door behind her. Her heart is pounding, and she seems unable to take in a breath. Squeezing her eyes shut and opening them again doesn't change a thing. Romelo, alive and well, is still there.

Chapter Eleven

Rhiza
Syrah's quarters
April 2043

Syrah is bent over, trying not to be sick, refusing to be sick. The bastard hasn't lifted a finger to so much as pat her goddamned shoulder. He just stands there looking at her with that flat expression.

The wave of anger recedes just enough for relief to wash over her. She did not kill her own brother. But he has let her believe it.

Something snaps inside Syrah, and she lunges at him, pounding her fists against his chest and lashing him with a string of profanities. Romelo blocks the blows easily because, as much as Syrah wants to, she just can't muster enough energy to put anything solid into it. Her fingers dig into his shoulders, his arms, as if she is trying to ensure he is real.

She pulls away from Romelo and goes over to sit at her desk. "How?" The question comes out in a whisper.

Romelo ambles over to stand beside her bed, but he still angles himself so that he can keep an eye on the door. It takes him a long time to answer. "It was you," Romelo says, and Syrah arches her eyebrow, waiting for the rest, because he isn't yet making any sense.

He takes his time looking around her room. Pats the extra bedding on her bed. He goes over and runs his hands along the books neatly lined up on her shelves. He restocks one that's been left on its side. He nods as if giving his approval of the life she's established here.

Then, in his own time, like always, he finishes his thought. "I underestimated you," he says. "I thought you would put family above our minor philosophical differences." He nudges her step stool out of the way with his foot and hoists himself up onto her bed in one swift movement. He crosses his ankles and stares at her with something uncomfortably like hate. "You fought well. You bested me. And then you somehow carried me down three hundred and fifty steps and into the forest. I guess your strength gave out only after you deposited me in the only place you knew that I would have a sliver of a chance of connecting to the lattice, of being saved."

I didn't murder my own brother. The thought crashes against Syrah's skull over and over, like a rock skidding across a lake. "You survived," she says, and she immediately feels silly, stating the obvious.

"I did," Romelo says. "I am grateful to you."

Syrah doesn't know what to say to that, and the room falls into a weighty quiet. Only her own breathing and the cacophony of life, of help, on the other side of her closed door break the silence. "You let me walk around with that guilt all this time. Do you have any idea what I've been through all these months?"

"Do you have any idea what it feels like to have everything you believe in destroyed?"

Syrah thinks back to her prescribed burn gone horribly wrong. It is so like Romelo to think that he's the only person in the world who's suffered. "Yeah, I do."

Romelo lifts an eyebrow. It hits Syrah then too: there's something different about him. A sadness. He's still got a bit of that haughtiness, but he's diminished, a little less himself.

"Why are you here? Why now?"

"Like The Keeper, I needed time to heal."

It is only then that Syrah begins to scan his face, every inch of exposed skin, to comb the memory of everything since she opened that door, looking for signs of injury. He appears unmarred. No hitch in how he walks. No slurred speech. Only a bit less self-assured. The mention of Taron stokes her anger. "What happened . . . all that did not have to go the way it did."

Romelo inclines his head. "It was not my intent to harm her, but I could not allow her to stand in my way either. Our mission is to protect the Giants. That is still my mission. Hers is to protect the humans."

"There is a way to do both," Syrah counters. "It's what Rhiza has done for centuries."

"And lost thousands of Giants in the process."

Syrah's chest rises and falls with indignation, but he's right. Part of him has always been right. "What do you plan to do now?"

"Do you still fear the monsters, little sister?" Romelo asks, sidestepping the question. He lifts an arm and points to the crook of his armpit. "I do not remember much of our lives topside, but I do remember that this is where you used to sleep when you feared the monsters in your room. They are topside, always have been. You were right to be wary of them. They have done more damage than I fear we can fix at this point."

This again. "You could have sent word," Syrah says. "A sign. Something to not let me wallow in a cesspool of guilt."

"You were not ready, nor was I. Our anger, our commitment to our sides of the coin, were too fresh. I had my own scars to heal. You were prepared to kill me . . . for the woman who treated me like an inconvenience."

"I was not the aggressor. It is so much like you to forget that part of it. Basically, you started something that I had to finish."

"I am curious. Why do you protect them? You know what they have done, and you know there is only one way to save the Giants. If you could so easily decide to take me out, when I have done nothing but to survive and to try to fulfill a mission that will save the planet for the very topsiders you love so much, why not them?"

Each word is a blow. Syrah doesn't have an answer. "The last thing I wanted . . . ," she begins before choking back a sob. "The last thing

I wanted was for any of that to happen. I had just gotten you back; you think I wanted to lose you? It didn't matter that we were at odds. I mean, I didn't even disagree that something had to be done. But wholesale slaughter isn't the way."

"In the time that you have had to reflect, have you come upon another solution? One that will save the Giants? The forest? And Rhiza?"

Syrah swallows the lump in her throat. She has done little more over these past months than tread viscous, murky waters of regret. She's tried to learn the ways of being Keeper. In that time, she hasn't been able to make a real decision about her life, let alone come up with a way to save the world.

"You contacted Uncle Dane," Syrah says as the thought occurs to her. "And, as you expected, he forwarded your demands to his superiors. That message ended up in a section of the NPS, on a particular scientist's desk."

"The one that rattled you during your tour the other day?" Romelo perks up, his relaxed posture gone.

Syrah should have known. Prickly skin, that unsettled feeling, her fungi reacting. Of course he's been watching her. Has probably been watching her for months, and she didn't sense a thing. She still has a long way to go to become as Rhizan as Romelo. "One and the same."

"You are not planning to tell me that he has agreed to all my demands, are you?"

Syrah blows out a breath. "You do not poke a bear, then get mad when it shows you its teeth." Immediately, she regrets her words. Everything that happened last fall began with the bear attack at the campground.

Unlike Taron, Romelo doesn't chide her for using an idiom. He only waits, as is his way. As if his expectations are known and he is simply giving you time to give him what he wants. "He is heading up a team, a government-backed team with deep pockets, that is going to look into what happened," Syrah says. "They plan to research what made the animals do what they did. They will be combing the park—"

"And trampling the roots, leaving their trash in their wake, and generally making a nuisance of themselves," Romelo says. "But they will find nothing."

"How can you be so sure?"

"Because there is nothing for them to find. What will they do? Interview the forest creatures one by one? Knock three times upon Rhiza's door and be welcomed with open arms?"

Despite herself, Syrah feels relief. Romelo's thinking mirrors her own, as unsettling as that is. But then, there's always been much they've agreed on. Still, something in the biologist's eyes doesn't quite allow her to dismiss him so easily. "I just think we all need to be prepared."

Romelo jumps down from the bed. "And there is no better way to guarantee nothing ill will befall us than to reunite our people."

He is right. Again. "Your room," Syrah says. "All of your rooms are just as you left them. We have a new head rootspeaker, but I think it would make sense to keep the other lattice outpost you've established operational. We can work something out. Of course, Taron . . ." Syrah can't say the words.

Romelo watches her, his expression unreadable. This time, Syrah decides to wait him out.

"There can only be one Keeper," he says finally.

"We agree on something."

"One that has more days ahead than behind. Sound mentally and physically."

"I—"

"I know that Taron is not getting better." Romelo walks over to Syrah. "She will not get better."

Syrah wonders who has been keeping Romelo informed. The Mother . . . or . . .

"After she's gone"—Syrah considers her next words carefully, then stands to face her brother—"I will become the next Keeper."

"Oh." Romelo's calm visage shatters, and his voice takes on a dangerous edge. "I think not. Perhaps you believe that I have what you would call a 'soft spot' for you. I did, once. But you stopped being my sister the moment you chose her"—he stops to jut his chin upward—"and them, over me."

Syrah tenses. This is it. He's only stayed away long enough to rebuild his strength so that he can have another go at Taron.

"I won't let you do it." She comes to stand directly in front of him. "Try again and see what happens."

Romelo reaches for Syrah's face, but she pulls away. "The next time we meet, if it is here in Rhiza, and you are anything more than a lower-tier member of the Blaze Brigade, I will kill you."

With that he steps around her and strolls out into the corridor without a care in the world for who sees him. Syrah is left to stand there gaping and hating herself for not going after him and taking him out first. But she can't. How can she be redeemed from being a murderous bastard and turn around and commit the crime as if she just hadn't gotten it right the first time?

Love comes at you with an axe, not some timid invitation. And she hasn't the will to fend it off.

Chapter Twelve

Rhiza
Outside Taron's library
April 2043

Syrah is still standing there trembling with rage minutes later when something in Rhiza snaps. She sneezes as dust and dirt cascade down from the ceiling. The books that Romelo righted earlier tumble from their shelves. And with the snap comes a heaving moan, a dread that seems to bleed from the walls. Syrah clamps her hands over her ears, but the terrible ululation finds those spaces between her fingers and wedges them wider. That hard note plunges into her body.

Who or what can cause such a reaction in Rhiza? It crosses her mind that perhaps Dr. Anthony has already returned, that he and his team are blasting their way through. But as quickly as the thought comes, the rumble deep in her chest dismisses it. Because she knows now, knows who the only living thing capable of such a sound is.

The Mother.

Only a handful of situations would warrant such a powerful response. Each almost empties Syrah's bladder. She forces her legs to move and is quickly through her door, into the hall, and buffeted by the bodies running every which way. "What's going on?" All she hears are shouts and howls. She rushes left, heading toward Her chamber . . . but no . . .

Taron.

Syrah reverses course and darts off in the direction of The Keeper's quarters. Trepidation dogs her every step. Though the distance between them is less than the space between three topside houses, it feels like it takes hours to get there. Around a bend, Syrah's heart nearly stops when she catches sight of the crowd, wailing and wide eyed, gathered outside the entryway to Taron's library.

Still a head and more shorter than the average Rhiza, Syrah can't see anything. "Move," she screams at the top of her lungs. "Get out of the way!"

She barrels through the bodies, and when others see it is her, they actually make way. "Move aside, The Keeper's protégé is coming through."

Syrah makes her way to the door. *Shit, shit, shit!* Taron's new guard, Yemaya, lies sprawled at her feet, bearing all manner of cuts and scrapes, blood dripping from multiple wounds. Someone is untying her hands and feet, which have been bound behind her.

"Yemaya," Syrah says, dropping to her knees beside her. But she is out cold. Just then, Artahe appears at Syrah's shoulder. She pulls her up. The terror almost keeps Syrah rooted in place. Too afraid of what she'll find just on the other side of that archway. "What happened?"

But Yemaya's eyes are unfixed, and she coughs up a glob of blood.

With Artahe beside her, Syrah enters the library.

Papers are strewn across Taron's desk and on the floor. Books yanked from the shelves, some lying open on the ground, other spots empty where books have clearly been taken. Syrah advances. The first thing she sees is the overturned inkwell on the desk. Dark liquid spilling across the smooth wood.

Flowers, the kind that Taron sometimes wears braided into her hair, lie torn and scattered on the ground.

From the corner of her eye, she sees the tip of Taron's staff. Her gaze travels as she moves to the far side of the desk. There on the floor lies what she already knows is Taron's lifeless body. Both she and Artahe scream then. And those on the other side of the doorway join in.

"No," Syrah sobs, leaning into Artahe. "God, please, no."

She sinks down and crawls over to the body. She first touches her leg, still warm. Then she feels for a pulse at her wrist and yanks her hand away when she finds none. Blood pools at the side of her head and soaks the ground. The wound, a red-and-white turmoil. Syrah takes in Taron's open eyes, staring up at the ceiling. On the other side, Artahe reaches out to close her lids. It's such a human gesture that Syrah is momentarily taken aback.

She takes Taron's hand in hers, and for longer than she is aware, she cries. Syrah yearns to hear one of Taron's smart-mouthed quips or her deadpan sense of humor. To have her show her another Keeper duty. To watch her wield that staff like an expert once again.

But Taron is gone, suspiciously right after Romelo left Syrah. Her brother resurfacing after all these months and Taron's sudden death are no coincidences.

That fact dries Syrah's tears like she's flipped a switch. She's alone now, but she can feel the Rhizan presence outside, waiting for her. Their need, a palpable albatross in the room. She places Taron's hands on her chest, lays her cheek atop them once, and rises.

When she steps back through the archway, it's as if everyone is holding their breath. Yemaya has been freed of her binds and is finally able to focus. "They wore masks," she says. "One distracted me long enough for the others to come up from behind."

"I saw something," a voice calls from somewhere near the back of the crowd.

"Come forward!" Syrah yells.

"I may be mistaken, but I think I saw Ezanna fleeing," a thin-faced Rhizan woman says.

"Are you certain?" Artahe asks, once again by Syrah's side.

"My eyes are not as sure of anything as they once were," she says.

Whispers of outrage flitter through a crowd that has grown to stretch out as far as Syrah can see in the corridors in either direction. And they are all watching her. Including Artahe. Dhanil is there, too, looking well and truly stricken. Taron had gone ahead and freed him and his fellow traitors then. Her last act as Keeper.

Syrah nearly buckles under the weight of their expectation. She wants nothing more than to slip through the gathered Rhiza like a whiff of smoke and run. Go topside and forget she ever stumbled upon this world. But something in her feels Taron's presence like a hand in the small of her back, urging her forward.

She steels herself, lets her gaze travel the length of those gathered around her. She moves away from Artahe. She can't rely on her friend for what comes next.

"The Keeper of the Canopy is dead."

The caretaker's resolve is as shaky as a house constructed from brittle November leaves. Syrah's pronouncement is like a splash of ice-cold water, and they dissolve into a frenzied misery.

"Murder!" The cry from an unseen figure is wild and desperate.

A young one, not yet half her height, begins banging his head into the sharp edge of a stalactite. By the time his mother yanks him away, his forehead is split and blood pours from the wound.

Others fall to their knees, hands clasped, eyes squeezed shut.

A man whom Syrah recognizes from the rootspeaker crew begins chewing off the thick ends of his own hair.

Their grief is like an open wound.

"A Keeper has never died by the hand of any foe except time." This from a lanky scourge suppressor who occasionally brings Syrah things she might like that they've collected in the forest. His hands are clasped together, tapping his lips. He's thinking about whatever he plans to say next. "Ever since you came—" Syrah's glare breaks off that line of thinking like it is a thin branch beneath her feet. The scourge suppressor recovers smoothly. "It simply does not happen. It cannot be. The killer may still be among us. Right in these very corridors."

Syrah has faced down the flames enough times to know the slick feel of panic greasing her spine. She is aware of it now. The same thing is reflected in the hysterically blinking eyes, open mouths, and heaving chests of her people. They're shouting over each other, throwing out all manner of conspiracy theories. They are bees who've lost their queen. They're directionless and afraid. And so is she.

"Okay, stop!" Syrah tries to corral them. She sniffs. Someone has soiled themselves. A rustle and shift of bodies, and a few of the supposedly benevolent caretakers have gotten into a shoving match. Others are sobbing loudly. A young couple sinks to the ground, clinging to each other while they rock back and forth, blubbering incoherently. Syrah hikes her voice up a few notches and adds some bass. "I said everybody needs to just calm the hell down."

"Ezanna did not act alone," a rootspeaker whispers in the ensuing quiet. "The Keeper's son lives. Romelo was also here today."

"But he is dead," someone behind Syrah murmurs, and it is like tinder, spreading through them like wildfire.

Artahe shoots her an imploring look. Syrah scrambles for what to do or say next. She's heard mention of Ezanna but never had the chance to meet him. He was, *is*, Romelo's closest ally, aside from Ochai. Could he have done this? In her mind, the answer is swift. Of course he could. The question is, Did he do it, or is there yet another turncoat among them?

For a moment, the caretakers are pensive. Was Romelo's visit a distraction so that Ezanna could finish Taron off?

Artahe and an injured Yemaya close ranks around Syrah. "We must gain control," Artahe growls under her breath, but then corrects herself. "*You* must. Taron chose you to succeed her, so act like it." Artahe, who's just heard that Romelo lives and doesn't so much as blink. And why not? Can she really be loyal to Syrah and Taron and still care for that fanatic? Cloaked in complexity, the utmost wingman. Or woman. Or Rhiza.

"But Taron was wrong." Inkoza slinks forward.

Syrah wastes no time. Suddenly the job that she scoffed at has replaced fire chief as the most coveted role in her life. She certainly won't yield it to Inkoza, not like this. "We have just lost The Keeper. Look at your people." Syrah pauses. With effort, her opposition turns his usurping gaze away from her, and she takes in the grim faces staring back at them. "You want to challenge me, fine, but right now, I have to do what Taron wanted. We do not have time for chest bumping."

Inkoza flicks a look at Artahe, then Yemaya. He skims the mass of canopy keepers still crowding the corridor outside Taron's library. "Later, then." He fixes his sights on Syrah, the venom in his gaze plain, before he steps aside. Syrah flashes a return glare. Backing down now won't do. Then she pushes her way forward, into the midst of the chaos. Inexplicably, her fungi flare. Do they, too, know the despair of loss? The blooms are many but a little less vibrant. The sight of them ushers in a hush.

"She was chosen by The Keeper." The whisper flits around the passageway like a wraith.

Syrah clears her throat. "The unthinkable has happened. We must mourn Taron, and we will. Right now, I ask that you all return to your rooms, to your work, if that is what gives you comfort. The Keeper did not leave us unprepared. Our work has not changed, and that is what we will continue to do. I do not have all the answers, but know that we will persevere. For now, allow me time to chart the way forward." Syrah pauses, turns slowly, making sure to make eye contact with as many of them as she can. "First, we have to lay Taron to rest." She realizes she has no idea how they do such a thing in Rhiza. There are certainly no underground cemeteries. This is a lesson Taron had yet to complete with her. "And then we will continue our mission, under the leadership of a new Keeper."

She braces herself for the inevitable questions about who that will be. It seems the apprehension hangs there on the tips of tongues in open mouths. She can't say she blames them; her pledge feels like it has all the weight of a grain of sand.

She stands there with her chin raised, fists to hips, until the crowd begins to disperse. Alone, in pairs and small groups, Rhiza's citizens return to wherever they need to in order to process their unprecedented grief.

When they are gone, only Artahe and Yemaya remain. "Come," Artahe says. "You will need all the allies you can get now."

In pockets here and there as they navigate the belowground world, they are greeted with tentative nods. Syrah turns away from the tear-streaked faces.

They make their way to Artahe's fungal farm and pass by the entrance. "Where are we going?" Syrah asks just as Artahe stops a couple of doors down. She knocks. And when Dhanil opens the door, Syrah immediately seethes. He looks more subdued than the self-assured care-taker conscripted to The Mother. There's a little less bulk to his frame. Those wide shoulders, however, haven't slumped an inch.

The way Dhanil sizes Syrah up reminds her of the first time the two met, when he far too easily wiped the floor with her and then carried her like a sack of potatoes into Rhiza. A prisoner. A reviled one at that. But then something in his expression and posture shifts. His face is a mask of contrition. He drops his chin and presses his lips together before he regards her again. Syrah crosses her arms to stop herself from reaching out and slapping him.

"Time," Yemaya says, cradling an arm that's probably broken, "is a thing we cannot forget. We must bury The Keeper and appoint a new one. Must you two stand here pouting like infants?"

To know something is right and to then do the right thing are not one and the same. Syrah struggles, but soon the bigger picture barges into her mind's eye. Yet she can't admit to them that she doesn't even know where to begin.

"You will need a champion," Dhanil says, throwing Syrah a much-needed lifeline. "I have served my punishment. In Rhiza, if not topside, that stands for something. I did not challenge the sentence; I did not deny my wrongdoing. And I have emerged even more sorry for what I have done than after I committed the treason. That I was not here—my apologies, Yemaya—is something I will never forgive myself for. She is dead because of me. I say that not in a manner of disrespect."

If Yemaya takes that personally, Syrah is thankful that she doesn't choose that moment to voice it. She takes the hem of her tunic and mops away the blood dripping from her forehead into her right eye.

Dhanil is right, though. In a way, he has contributed to everything that happened after his little coup attempt. What he says about crime and punishment makes sense. "If I am to restore Rhiza and help move us forward, I will need the help of all of you." Syrah gulps and looks away before she continues. "Yemaya, you mentioned that there is some sort of time clock surrounding the burial. I am ashamed to admit, I haven't got a clue." She quickly kicks herself for the lapse in language. "The Keeper and I did not cover those practices yet. How does Rhiza bury her dead?"

The three members of Syrah's crew exchange a glance. Syrah's pulse rises. Artahe breaks the silence. "It will require a connection to The Mother. Have you achieved that during your training?"

Chapter Thirteen

Beneath Sequoia National Park
Rhiza
April 2043

The short answer is no. Syrah recalls the failed attempt that Taron guided her through so recently that her body still feels strange. The problem is with her lungs; they're enhanced enough to let her streak through the forest for hours without batting an eye, but nothing else.

Not only did she fail miserably, but she also has no idea if she'll ever be fit, physiologically speaking, for the task. She looks up, around, anywhere but directly at them. She starts plucking at a loose thread in the arm of her tunic. She shifts her feet nervously. When she finally blows out a frustrated breath and is just about to answer, someone else delivers the blow for her.

"Is it not obvious?" Inkoza bulldozes right through the door they've neglected to guard. "She cannot."

A kick to the jaw or a well-placed punch to the throat would silence him and wipe that patronizing look off his face. But he's right. Only she can't bring herself to say the words aloud.

"Is this true?" Artahe asks tentatively. Syrah can see it in her eyes, how much she hopes that it isn't.

Syrah catches herself fidgeting and brings that to a sure stop. "Not yet."

"But what if the answer is 'not ever'?" Inkoza suggests.

"Syrah was Taron's choice." Dhanil speaks up for her, and Syrah whips around to make sure she's heard him right. "That is not up for debate. But we must return to Yemaya's point: time is of the essence."

"For you, topsider," Inkoza says, "that means that when a Keeper dies, tradition calls for an immediate burial. The Mother cannot be without one for more than a sun's full rotation. And we do not know how long Taron went undiscovered."

Syrah can't help herself. She doesn't have time to comb through Taron's books. "Are we talking minutes or hours here?"

He sneers but before he can answer, Artahe saves her. "A little more than what you consider thirty-six hours," she says.

Inkoza swoops in. "I would be remiss in my duty if I did not point out that we—most of us—are aware that a quick burial will reduce our suffering." Silence, then he blurts out, "Everyone here was a witness. I studied with The Keeper. I know the ways to connect with The Mother. Between us, I believe that I am the only one who can. I will perform the final rites."

"You know the ways," Artahe says. "But have you been successful in an attempt?"

Syrah's eyes dart over just in time to catch the hitch-shrug before the answer. "Not yet."

As much as Syrah wants to protest, she can't. There's no argument she can counter with. Even if Inkoza is more boastful than anything else, he has a better chance at connecting with The Mother than she does. Maybe she shouldn't have resisted Taron so much in the beginning. Maybe she should have taken what The Keeper was trying to teach her more seriously. Maybe if she'd made a choice about where she wanted to be, one way or the other, and not waffled and whined her way through the past six months, she wouldn't be in this situation.

She sighs. "Send a rootcast. Have everyone assemble at Her chamber."

Without needing further direction, Artahe and a badly limping Yemaya head off to Lattice Affairs. With Dhanil trailing them, Syrah and Inkoza make their way through the passages. "I have nothing against you personally," he says, glancing down at her.

"I do have something against you personally," Syrah says. "You originally sided with my brother."

"So did Ochai," Inkoza says. "That does not seem to trouble you as much."

Syrah winces inwardly at the truth of that statement. But she keeps her face placid, her steps steady. "I will grant you that."

"Do you want to do what is right for Rhiza?"

"More than anything."

"Then you must admit that having a native-born caretaker makes the most sense," he says. "You will always be welcome here for as long as I am Keeper, but you have your life topside. Your brother is different. He joined us when he was extremely young, has been with us since. He is more Rhizan—"

"Than me," Syrah says. "Where do you stand now? After The Breaking?"

"I stand on the side of Rhiza."

"Rhiza with humans or Rhiza without?"

Inkoza is quiet for a moment. "There was a time when I thought Romelo's plans made sense. However, I would not welcome all the attention that a wholesale slaughter would bring. We have not been discovered for this long, and I do not anticipate we ever will be, but—"

"But that has not stopped so many things that we did not think possible from happening anyway." Syrah finishes his thought and thinks about Dr. Baron Anthony. She didn't even get a chance to tell Taron, and she has to clue in someone besides Romelo. But she isn't sure yet if she can trust Inkoza. She isn't even sure if that feeling of challenge in her gut is real. Does she really want to be Keeper, or is she just fighting him because he's trying to push her out?

When they arrive at the chamber, they march down the stairs side by side, Syrah struggling with the abnormally high steps. The differences between them keep adding up, becoming more stark. They both stand beside The Mother as the rest of the canopy keepers shuffle in. There isn't a dry eye among them.

When Dhanil signals that everyone is present, Syrah takes a step forward, but it is Inkoza who speaks. She bristles, but what would she have said anyway?

"In light of physical differences between The Keeper's chosen successor and our people, I will be performing the Return to the Earth ritual."

Though Syrah reads confusion, some unsettled, nobody speaks up. It is with great effort that she keeps her own tongue tied in its current knot.

Inkoza somehow is both the picture of hero worship and confident leader. He practically floats over to The Mother, while Syrah stands there trying to figure out what to do with her hands. She feels ridiculous. If every eye weren't already plastered on her, she would tiptoe out of here. As it is, she can only shuffle off a ways and clasp her hands behind her back, the effect being that she looks only slightly less useless.

The Mother's cacophony has settled into a strangled hum, and Her leaves begin fluttering. They brighten as if a backlight has been implanted in each. Her bark rumbles, and Syrah feels that hum again; from the way hands fly to everyone's chest, the others feel it as well.

At that point, a group of caretakers begins the walk down the right stairway. On a pallet, they carry a body, Taron's, wrapped in a plain sheath. At the base of the steps, they bring her as close to The Mother as they can without disturbing Inkoza before retreating back among the onlookers.

Syrah will not let this ritual pass without saying something, and the sight of Taron's unmoving form has unlocked the words. She steps forward. "The price of life is death. Today we bury one of our own. A Keeper unmatched in tenure, in accomplishment, in knowledge. It is a loss from which we will not easily recover. She served for two hundred and ninety-eight years, guiding us through the worst climate disasters the world has ever witnessed. And she did it without a single complaint." Syrah stops, then adds, "Maybe a sharp word or two, but never a complaint. Taron is irreplaceable. But we, The Keepers of the Canopy, will live on, and her through us."

Syrah steps back again and allows Inkoza to do his part.

Filaments erupt through the earth. Inkoza throws his head back as they connect with him and vanish beneath his skin. Syrah seethes with envy. She wants to turn away but forces herself to watch. To learn why it all seems so easy for him.

And the earth gives way. Taron's corpse is absorbed, and the earth knits itself back together. When it is done, only the cloth remains, and someone swoops up to remove it. Syrah notices when the filaments, one by one, remove themselves from Inkoza. When he steps back, he shoves his hands into the air.

Great rivulets of water stream down The Mother's bark. Her canopy trembles. Tears. She cries, and everyone gathered, Syrah included, joins Her. It is a keening that emits from Her, the leaves and open mouths.

They mourn Taron until eyes are dry and throats are raw.

When the last trickle of moisture trails down the great bark, the mourning ends. Everyone ambles out of the chamber. Inkoza stops to spare her a pat on the shoulder before he, too, is gone. There's no gloating in him, and for that, Syrah is thankful. She sinks onto the spongy earth at The Mother's base and places a palm on Her bark.

How? she wonders. How can she make this connection work?

Long after everyone is gone, Syrah wipes the last tear from her cheek. And she resolves to figure it out. Never again will she stand idly by while the work of The Keeper is handled by an interim selection.

The Mother cannot be without a new Keeper for more than one full rotation of the sun. Syrah will honor Taron, and she will do the work she charged her with.

And she will sit here until she figures out how.

Seeing with Ancient Eyes
An Ending

Is there such a thing as a favored child?
Of course there is
A mother loves all of her children the same, but
    likes them differently
Such is the way of things for time immemorial

I cannot call Taron a favored child but I feel her
    loss all the same
My caretakers will suffer the void
A tree is but as strong as the forest that sur-
    rounds her

So the heart at the center of my growth ring beats
    with less vigor
My many-furrowed bark blanches
My canopy wilts and weeps

The deliverer is stubborn, indecisive, and yet a
    pathfinder, a force
The breaker is a formidable creature, purpose
    warped by revenge and madness and a twisted
    sapling
And then there is a third contender, learned and
    capable but of questionable leadership
Until reconciliation
A maleficent imbalance

Chapter Fourteen

Ultimately, sitting and staring at The Mother does not provide answers, but it does solidify Syrah's resolve. For now, that's got to be enough. Her foot is on the top step of the chamber when she senses someone or multiple someones on the other side of the archway.

Syrah braces herself, lightens her steps. All she feels is a slight itch beneath the skin. She passes through the archway, and there he is, Dhanil. And Yemaya, more bandages than bare skin. The pair raise their eyebrows in unison. Protection. They've stayed behind to look after her. "Thank you," she says to them both. As she heads toward Taron's library (what will become her library), she hopes that it is still intact.

A distinctive woodsy fragrance fills the air. Syrah follows the scent and then spots some of the fungal farmers angling small bowls into the natural nooks and recesses that make up the subterranean world's irregular walls. She stops and goes over. They're using some kind of tinder to light them. The bowl of fungi goes up in tiny flames before they're blown out and the smoke wafts off like an incense.

"Chaga mushrooms, right?" she asks. The smell isn't unpleasant, but if a scent could be characterized as mournful, this would be it.

"Think of them as funeral pyres," Dhanil answers. "They will burn until a new Keeper is installed."

They continue through corridors that are eerily quiet. Between their work and their active social lives, Rhiza is a buzzy, lively place. The complete absence of activity casts an uneasy pallor over everything. Most of the doors that they pass are closed, and Syrah imagines the mourning taking place. But a few are open, revealing the sequoia caretakers in repose: sitting at desks, staring off blankly, children clinging to parents.

"How long will they be like this?" Syrah asks without stopping.

Dhanil answers in his baritone, "Under normal circumstances, when a Keeper dies, a day or two, no more. Assuming a successor is installed."

But these circumstances are as far from normal as one can get. It won't do to let them linger in this state for too long.

When she gets to the library, she pauses. Someone has cleaned up Yemaya's blood already.

The mental imprint of Taron's lifeless body slides back into her reality. She braces herself and steps inside, only to find Inkoza already there, lording over Taron's desk as if it were already his own. Why didn't she think to post someone here to keep him out? He has the nerve to look up at her like she's the intruder.

With a flick of her head, she gestures for her new honor guard to wait outside, then rushes in like a storm cloud and slaps her palms on the desk.

"You are overstepping," she says, narrowing her eyes at the papers and books he's laid out. "You are smart enough to know that, but you did it anyway." Inkoza leans back and interlaces his fingers behind his head, a gesture so similar to what she's seen Taron do a million times that she wants to leap forward and rip him out of the chair herself.

He stands, crossing his massive arms. "Why do you believe that The Keeper saw fit to train two people to take up the mantle in the event of her passing?"

Syrah refuses to answer his questions. She will not answer to him at all. "Does not matter. One was done in secret, the other in the open. You know why? Because she wanted to make it clear to everyone who her first choice was. Even you. How about honoring that?"

"That must mean that you are prepared to conclude your affairs? Gather everything you will need from topside?" Inkoza presses. "Abandon or sell that home you retreat to when you tire of us? Are you ready to say goodbye to the park ranger and your parents, then? They will never be welcome here, and The Keeper does not keep topside hours. They never leave their people, Rhiza's caretakers."

Syrah feels cut to the core by every word. Of all the things she discussed with Taron, these uncomfortable truths were the worst of them.

"You may marry, though Ochai will never be yours alone," Inkoza continues. "But you may not bear children." He stops to give her a forced chuckle. "Just look how an adoption turned out for Taron."

As hard as she tries, Syrah's mind and her normally ever-ready tongue aren't prepared to respond to this onslaught of truths. She feels Yemaya and Dhanil just outside the door, probably bearing witness to every word and to her inability to address them. "You have had your time here," she says instead. "There are things that Taron asked me to do in the event of her passing, and so, if you would get out of my way, I have work to do."

With a jackal's grin, Inkoza moves away from his perch, towering over her. "My quarrel is not with you. Do not center yourself as if it is. That Rhiza continues in its mission with a leader capable of performing *all* of the required duties is all that matters."

"We are in agreement," Syrah says. She knows he's talking about her inability to connect with The Mother.

"You will need my help either way," Inkoza continues. "Let us not forget that a murder—the murder of a *Keeper*—has been committed. That cannot be left unsettled. The perpetrator or perpetrators must be brought before Her for punishment."

Why is he taking the words out of her mouth? He's really playing into the role of leader, and it grates that he's right. "If you will leave me to my work . . ."

He inclines his head.

"Dhanil, Yemaya," Syrah calls. When they appear in the doorway, she says, "Please see Inkoza out, and you have my permission to pummel him if he tries to come back in."

They curtly nod. Thankfully Inkoza leaves without another blistering word.

Syrah looks around Taron's library, *her library*. Scrolls and logbooks, sheafs of paper. Inkwells and quills, plus the fountain pen Syrah had coerced The Keeper into using. Teetering stacks of books. Mounds of them shelved and in every spare nook. The truth is, Syrah has no clue where to begin. She feels like if she so much as places a fingertip on one crew report, everything will collapse, burying her beneath the responsibility of it all.

She hasn't even had the time to sort through her complicated feelings about Taron. In some ways, their relationship mirrored that which Syrah has with her own mother.

Nobody would mistake Taron for the overtly emotional type. Yet hadn't she shown her true feelings in the way the corner of her mouth quirked when she looked up from her desk and saw Syrah walk into the room? Wasn't there always a bowl of Syrah's favorite fungal chips suspiciously close at hand during their lessons? Those tears that fell from her eyes when she heard the news of Romelo's death—those were real.

Blink and you could miss it, but in her own way, Taron cared for her. Romelo too. Affection then, maybe even love, carefully guarded and doled out. The feeling, Syrah admits to herself, had been mutual.

A sharp wave of unexpected grief moves through her. For the first time, she allows herself to sit. The chair is barstool height, so her legs dangle. She'll need another footrest.

She sorts through an inch-thick pile of papers and plucks out a report from the new head rootspeaker, not so new after half a year, but she can't break herself of the habit of referring to Shansi as such. Her eyes glaze over, and she drops the paper to the desk.

Despite what Inkoza thinks, she has taken her lessons seriously. She has made a cheat sheet of sorts, and she rummages through the papers on Taron's desk, looking for it and wondering if her opponent has swiped it to further hamstring her.

After making a mess of the desk, she ends up finding the document in a drawer. She hops down from the chair and pads over to the oversize chair to read. Maintain the logs, review work crew reports, and on and on. All important tasks, no doubt. Irritatingly enough, though, Inkoza is right about something else. Nothing will return to normal in Rhiza until they find and punish those responsible for Taron's death.

A thought slips into Syrah's mind. If she had been successful, had killed Romelo at Moro Rock, his band and his rebellion would have been broken. She isn't proud of herself for thinking it, especially after the relief she felt when she found him again, but she knows it to be true. He was only biding his time. His sick mission is still the same, and he has proven that he is willing to kill to get what he wants.

She'll stop him. Whether he or Ezanna actually delivered the final blow doesn't matter; they're equally guilty. This time, her brother has to be brought to justice. Everything else will have to wait.

The Keepers' log
Rhiza
Taron Keeper
March 2043

To lead is to welcome with a lover's open arms, the brutality of an infinite loneliness. A setting aside of one's self. A separation from all that you may have held dear, or aspired to. A sacrifice of whatever else your life may have become. Your dreams. If you are lucky enough to have had them.

These are the dens and hollows I contemplate as the end of my life grows perilously near. Three hundred and twenty-three years of living, two hundred and ninety-eight of those as The Keeper of the Canopy. Rhiza's leader. The Mother's servant, Her pawn.

There was a time when I felt a call to serve Rhiza as a scourge suppressor. A caretaker to the gentle forest and all that rightfully call it home. To wash away traces of human waste and carelessness. The delight of collecting and recycling those things that have come to their natural or forced ending. A chance to spend time equally aboveground among the giant sequoia and below, beneath the veil. Noble work, that.

And there would be a family, perhaps. A suitable mate, at the very least. A woman of strong character, a man of virtue and respect. It wouldn't matter which, only that they build a life that includes those quiet moments, exchanged glances, and intimacies you develop with one you allow yourself to love openly and fully.

Of children, I was uncertain. If the right mate required it, I would have considered. But to be a parent does not require direct lineage. There are many children in Rhiza for whom a kind word, a stern look, or a bit of wisdom would be welcome. Any creature can have offspring, after all, but the virtuous soul chooses to support all children, regardless of their blood ties.

The end of those many other potential lives is no one's fault more than my own.

My parents took an early notice of my interest in Rhizan history. They sat me at the then Keeper's willing knee. Without knowing, I began my training in those early days.

I was an intent student, asking what my mentor called "thoughtful" questions, sometimes obstinate, like Syrah, the deliverer. She dodges acceptance like a woman who has options. She has none and will succeed me whether she wishes it or not.

As the years progressed, I assumed responsibility for the smaller tasks: managing the work rotations, carefully maintaining the sacred scrolls. I documented figures and weather conditions in the daily logs when he said his fingers would not allow it. I took the most pleasure in arranging the literature carefully upon the shelves that I now savor with great affection.

Most important of all, I attended him when he visited Her. The Mother.

It seems my curiosity, under other circumstances such a coveted trait, sealed my eternal fate.

I turn my ear now to the activity just outside the ornately carved library archway. The winsome peals of laughter and gaiety. The rolling carts of a gaggle of scourge suppressors passing by with their topside flotsam. Scraps that will be refashioned into useful things for the caretakers.

Ezanna, the flamboyant fool, used to pass by during my lessons and fling his envious glare at me.

If I had not been so determined to best him, I would have invited him in for a good laugh. You see, the joke is on me. Ezanna had choices. The chatter on the lattice suggested he would become a rootspeaker. Indeed he has, and no doubt he has been a good one, but his arrogance prevents him from becoming great, like his charge, my son, the breaker. Romelo Thorn.

I wish I could step away, take a cart and go and collect the downed branches and tender fallen leaves of the forest. Tend to them with loving hands and give them life anew. All except for the bones. The remains of the human I struck down in anger in my reckless youth buried in the room where, for an ill-advised moment, Dhanil imprisoned me. The topsider's crime was so trivial as to be irrelevant, but by then I had nursed a dangerous hate for them. Remorse is memory awake.

So scourge suppressor was not to be my path. I know it now, just as I did then. I remember the day; The Keeper filled the doorway with his bulk. He spared me the slimmest of smiles. You are ready. *I recall his words so clearly, even though by then, his voice had grown soft with sickness.*

I stood at once, ready to protest, but held the words fast.

As he stepped into the room, he collapsed. Like an arrow loosed from a quiver, I ran to him and knelt where he lay prostrate, watching life and love fade from his eyes.

I am ready, I told him. *The last words he heard in this life.*

His expression carried the full weight of the relief that ushered him into the next realm.

It was then that I felt the solemn tether of that pledge settle deep into the furrows of my skin and bones. Everything that I would have become no longer mattered. Those other potential lives died in an internally lit flame. The time was upon me, and with welcome melancholy, I gazed into the mirror of my decision.

And I became The Keeper of the Canopy.

Chapter Fifteen

Beneath Sequoia National Park
Rhiza on High
April 2043

Ding-dong, The Keeper is dead.

Romelo also bore The Mother's terrible tremor. From the new segment of the Crystal Cave, they, too, endured Her teeth-clenching declaration of Taron's demise. He braces for an avalanche of sorrow to rain down upon him, only it is more of a trickle, a thin stream of regret. More than anything, Taron was an allegory of a real mother; she never openly expressed love for him, nor he to her. Yet he would be lying if he said he did not already feel the absence of her strong, steady presence. For that alone, he mourns in silence.

He also does not admonish those who grieve openly. A Keeper's passing is significant. It is the end of an era that began long before most of them were born. Many of them are gathered now near their subterranean lake. A triangular-shaped basin where time and erosion have withered away limestone and granite. They could not have established themselves here without it.

Ezanna sits tight lipped and triumphant across from him. Aside from a few scrapes on his knuckles, he bears no visible scars from the altercation with the formidable Yemaya. The grimace he tried to hide when he lowered himself into the chair, however, is a sign of some internal injury, something beneath the folds of those elaborate robes of a generation past that he still favors.

Romelo's makeshift office is a lackluster replica of the one that he will inherit when he returns to Rhiza proper. Only this one has a door. Their planning has been of the most delicate nature, and though he is confident in himself as a leader—has in fact drawn more to his cause over these months—slips of the tongue with former friends and relations are inevitable.

There is no lock, there being no need or concept of shutting anyone out so completely in Rhiza. A primordial reality that may also bear examination and consideration for change.

His mind has wandered, but it returns, groping for specifics of Taron's ending.

What kind of blow ultimately felled her?

Did she fight well?

How long did she hold on, given her current state of infirmity?

Did she ask about me?

Instead of these queries, Romelo focuses on the mole on Ezanna's face, just beneath his right eye, and simply asks, "We helped her, did we not?"

Ezanna eyes Romelo. He knows his charge well enough to recognize the fissures, the omissions between his words. Those concerns he will never voice but feels no less. "She would not have survived the year," Ezanna confirms as if he has Artahe's experience with such things. "Whether or not she was grateful that I sped her to the afterlife is another matter. From the way she fought, I can say with confidence she was not."

She did fight well. Romelo wants to tug on that thread. Unravel it in a play-by-play retelling of his mother's final moments. And Ezanna knows it. Yet his mentor would rather see him beg for these final crumbs than graciously allow him the dignity of not having to ask. Romelo will find a time to make him pay for the affront. For now, there are other things to put in motion.

"Any word of other successors?"

Ezanna shifts his bulk and grimaces again. "We know who she had chosen. Your sister." He watches for a reaction from Romelo and, rewarded with none, continues: "But a challenger has emerged."

Romelo sits up. "A challenger, you say?"

"Indeed. Inkoza Blaze."

Romelo thinks back and recalls the name. "One of Ochai's subordinates." His mind is flooded with thoughts of his friend then. He stepped up and took the blame for Romelo with only the slightest of hesitation. Once he is freed, and Romelo will see to it that he is, he will be honored for his sacrifice.

"Why him?" Romelo asks.

Ezanna raises his hands in a helpless gesture. "'Lack of options' is at the forefront. Apparently he also sat at your mother's knee for a time and was a quick enough study."

They are waiting, Romelo thinks. To see what the fallout is between Syrah and him.

"The job is all consuming," Ezanna continues. "There was a time when a long line of successors would have been vying for the privilege. And make no mistake, this position is a privilege. But our young people are succumbing to change. Taron never wanted to accept the fact that the topside world is infecting us. It is a blight that must be wiped out." He pounds his fist into a palm.

"And were you fifty years younger," Romelo says with a quirk to his mouth, "you would have challenged me for the post."

"Twenty years," Ezanna corrects him with an emphatic finger tap on the desk.

The tension Romelo is holding melts away as the two share a chuckle. He is not bothered; rather, he appreciates the honesty. Something he could never count on had he been successful in one of his many attempts at running away and going back topside. He is grateful to Taron and Ezanna, the both of them, for never allowing him to succeed.

But there is something needling him. What Syrah said about the wildland biologist who will descend upon Sequoia. He has not changed his stance. They will come away empty-handed.

One of the many challenges for a leader is to decide which information to share and what to keep close. Focus is key. And for now, he has to secure his leadership.

He stares at Ezanna, again thankful that his mentor allows him to think without interruption. Trusting him. Challengers, his sister or this Inkoza person, nothing but bumps in the road. Caretakers he can handle. Rhiza's citizens will fall in line once they have been sidelined.

There is, however, a critical next step. Something he has to do before he can fully stake his claim. Someone whose approval and assistance he will need, aside from that of his baby Giant.

"The Mother," Romelo says, and Ezanna nods in agreement.

Chapter Sixteen

Rhiza
April 2043

It's late. Syrah knows this not because of the sun or the moon. Human tech doesn't work this far beneath the earth either. Time here is guided by the bells and chimes that announce the work crew and food schedules. The evening meal bell dinged what she thinks was hours prior. For what she has to do next, she wants quiet, no interruptions, no witnesses.

With Yemaya recovering from her injuries, Syrah is accompanied by Dhanil. He has bounced back to his surly, albeit somewhat subdued, self with a speed that has impressed Artahe. Syrah opens her door and pokes her head outside. The stench. There he is. Warrior stance: feet slightly spread, shoulders bunched and poised for a fight, head atop a thick neck, on a constant swivel.

Unsurprisingly, his presence gives her about as much comfort as having a horde of scorpions at her back. Syrah isn't like other people, topside or below. She's always had trouble with the whole concept of "forgive and forget." Nobody talks about what Rhizan prison is like, so how is she to know that he's even suffered enough?

Syrah has taken every brain-rattling blow he's hit her with, both mentally and physically. She has never been under the delusion that he likes her or wants her here, but never in a million years did she anticipate him backstabbing Taron. No way he gets the chance to turn on her. She'll have to have a talk with Yemaya once she feels a little better. She's going to need someone else besides Dhanil whom they both implicitly trust.

"You should consider moving your quarters to a more easily defensible location," Dhanil advises. "I am adding to my staff. Increasing the honor guard is a grim reality that I must face. I realize I have difficulty adapting to change. It is a mistake I will not make on a Keeper's watch again."

Syrah mutters her agreement. There's little enthusiasm there. She doesn't have a lot of time, so she walks ahead of him and can hear and smell him following. She wonders at his distinctive scent, like a mix of the smelliest of cheeses and damp soil.

"You do not trust me." Dhanil's voice sounds more tired than challenging.

"How can I?" Syrah inclines her head to one of the caretakers, who scoops bioluminescent mushrooms from a pouch slung across his shoulder and refills the sconces that line the pathways.

"It is a human failing," Dhanil starts and then stops as Syrah spins, eyebrow raised. She's sick of his talk, "human" this, "human" that. Always negative.

"It is my belief, as it was The Keeper's, that topsiders are in such pain because they rarely, if ever, truly forgive others, while at the same time yearning to be forgiven for their mistakes."

Syrah refuses to reply that he has a point.

"If you are to lead us," he begins again, "and I believe that you will, you must learn to balance what will likely always be the two halves of yourself. Topside, those released from incarceration are still stigmatized, labeled, rejected. As if the punishment were a mere formality, a red carpet to a lifetime of punishment. But here, slights are addressed. Apologies offered and forgiveness granted. Those of us released from The Mother never hear of it again. We are not labeled and judged lesser for our transgressions for the remainder of our days. Such negative feelings are the undoing of a society. We cannot have that here."

God damn it, he makes sense, Syrah thinks. She hates to admit it, but every word he's spoken is true. And if she is to lead, she'll have to do exactly what he says: lead not with her topside prejudices but by embracing the customs and traditions of the people right here. But just because he's saying all the right words doesn't mean there isn't a knife waiting for her on the back end. She slows down so she can walk beside him and watch his reaction, then asks, "Recidivism. Is that a thing here?"

Dhanil looks down at her and then blows out a breath. "0.125 percent."

Syrah knows this is recorded in a logbook somewhere and vows to check, even though she senses the certainty of it. "Not impossible then," she says.

"Barely," Dhanil counters. "And I will not be among the few."

That remains to be seen.

Though the corridors have been largely empty, one of Rhiza's citizens stops her. She recognizes the kid who challenged her to a fight when she was walking this same path with Artahe.

"Shouldn't you be in your room?" she says.

He pulls her away from Dhanil. To his credit, Dhanil steps back, looking both ways like he's her personal sentinel. "It was Ezanna," the boy says.

"How can you be so sure?"

"I rounded the bend near The Keeper's library. Yemaya was already trussed up like a swine. It was from the back, but I saw him leaving the scene. You ever seen anybody else prance around here in that ridiculous stuff he still wears? Nobody but him and the breaker wanted her dead."

"Thank you . . ." His name escapes her.

"Rhett," he supplies. "Someday, I will be Rhett Rootspeaker, I just know it."

He blinks at her with such certainty in his eyes. "Why them?" Syrah asks. "Why not the Blaze Brigade or the fungal farm even?"

Rhett scrunches up his face. "You think I would be better suited to growing mushrooms? I would barely get to spend any time topside. I would become all pale like them."

Pale? Artahe might be lighter than most, but topside, she'd still be Black. "Let me see your ankles," Syrah says.

Rhett grins and makes a show of lifting his legs and showing off. "Very strong, you see. And I already know how to do hands-on root knitting."

"I think you will make a fine rootspeaker. Now, off to bed."

The kid grins and sprints off in the other direction, and Syrah continues on her way.

Soon she and Dhanil are at The Mother's chamber. Syrah moves forward alone. Determination quickens her steps. As her feet land upon the spongy, mossy understory, she tenses.

"Mother," Syrah says and then immediately feels silly. Taron often told her, one does not speak to Her audibly. "I know you can hear me. You know my heart; seems like you always have. I know it was you that came to me in my dreams when I was a kid. I'm here now because you called me. I will not abandon Rhiza. I will learn how to connect with you because I know I have to if I am to become Keeper."

The Mother's humming response is enough for Syrah to take as encouragement. She concentrates on that drumbeat in her chest and sits with her back against the trunk for support and drapes her legs over a thick cinnamon root. With one last glance at the doorway, she closes her eyes and slows her breathing to match The Mother's lovely murmur.

There's no place she has ever been that felt more peaceful. The Giants aboveground, in the forest when there's nobody around, that had been what she thought was the ultimate. Aboveground it still is. But nothing compares to this.

Syrah feels as if she is floating on the surface of a calm sea. So relaxed is she that she dozes. It is only when she feels the root filaments traversing her legs and continuing up to her arms, where her fungi have flared, that she wakes up.

She gapes as barely perceptible hyphae spring from the full clusters on her arms and stretch out to meet The Mother's.

When they touch, starlight strobes beneath her eyelids.

Syrah is lost in a time and space diffused with all the colors of nature. She floats on a windless current, propelled by her arms, treading air, not water.

The Mother's deafening thrum has been overthrown by jazzy birdsong. She cannot see a sun, nor a moon, for that matter, but the warmth on her skin is no less present. The air smells sweet enough to eat.

But something is wrong.

Syrah tries to sit up, to stand, to do anything but hover, and finds that she can't. Her weightless limbs are no longer under her control. What has she done? A cold sweat breaks out on her forehead, and panic twists her stomach in knots. She strains against whatever is holding her but can't break free. It is like the worst of nightmares. The ones where you're fully conscious but can't move a muscle.

"Mother?"

No answer.

She fell asleep in the chamber. That has to be it. Even as she thinks it, she knows it's nothing more than a rationalization. A wrong one. Waves of sound rise and fall, sounds like the forest. No voices or clumsy human footfalls.

"Is anyone there?"

Nothing.

Maybe on her journey to meet The Mother, she took a wrong turn. It occurs to her then that this could be a holding place. A cell dressed up like paradise. That stubborn tree has to know that Syrah is stuck here. "Mother!" Syrah screams again, though even her mouth doesn't move. In her mind's eye, Syrah is thrashing, kicking, trying to free herself.

Every decision she could have made that would have put her back in Three Rivers taunts her. She should have handed the reins over to Inkoza and left. Tears pool at the corners of her eyes. *Is this what it's like for Ochai? Is he also here somewhere?*

Syrah's failure is a sentence, then, one that will see her go completely mad. She calls out again, "Is anyone there? Mother, can you hear me?"

In response, a wisp or an essence—that is the only way that she can describe it—whizzes above, circles, and passes her. "Hey!"

"What do you want from me?"

"I'm only trying to do what Taron wanted."

Syrah is alone, and she is five years old again, clinging to Uncle Dane's hand while the social worker's open car door waits to take her away.

Her tears have progressed to full-on sobs. She has no perception of her body back in the chamber. And she wonders if this is it. Maybe Romelo or Dhanil sabotaged things so that she will be trapped here forever. Out of the way. She shouldn't have trusted him, and she knows it.

Syrah screams and cries and tries with everything she has to move. She hates this feeling, of not being in control of her own body. Time goes on and on. *That's it then,* she thinks. *This is how it will end.* Neither her parents nor her uncle will ever know what happened to her. And it fills her with a rage like a cloud she cannot hold on to. Perhaps she should have died in that fire with her parents, both her and Romelo. Their presence here in Rhiza has caused nothing but trouble.

In a way, Syrah accepts her fate. When the last whimper sounds in her head and a tear falls from the corner of her eye, she exhales.

And like a rocket, she is catapulted.

Chapter Seventeen

Dane Young is a lucky man. He has the only job he has ever wanted, more of a calling than work. Most days it feels he's trying to fight a battle that's already been lost. He knew what he was signing up for.

One day shy of his thirtieth birthday, he was appointed the next in a long, admirable line of Sequoia National Park rangers. He is of the rare breed of person who actually loves his job, soup to nuts. Even if, as the years have passed, all the things he's tried in order to make things better have amounted to a pile of beans.

At first he was happy to have Syrah here with him again. There was a time when guilt had tugged at him every time he saw his niece, because it was her mother's—her birth mother's—face that stared back at him. That part is over now, but the universe, in her infinite wisdom, has decided to replace it with something no less irksome. Worry. This new life of hers, where he has to go and knock on a tree like some kinda fool just to reach her. He wonders when the day will come that somebody spots him and then runs and tells his boss that his renowned park ranger has finally inhaled too much smoke.

He heard his mother complain about the people she worked for most of his life. He shakes his head, thinking about how she'd barely be through the door before she'd rattle off a string of the day's offenses, holding him and his father captive until she was through.

Yeah, he's seen his fair share of eyebrow-raising decisions come down through the ranks, but NPS leadership isn't what fuels his complaints. Fire and pests and people, that's what gets him worked up. If only he had someone to tell it all to.

This life ain't for everybody; a handful of potential partners have told him as much. Thing is, Dane can't imagine doing anything else, crammed into some cookie-cutter neighborhood or condo with the overhead footfalls of people instead of sky.

Dane makes his morning rounds, driving through the park checking for anything out of place or any damage done overnight by campers. He's navigating Highway 180 near the border between Sequoia and what used to be Kings Canyon when his radio beeps. Most comms devices are iffy out here, but a good old-fashioned radio never fails.

"Officer Young, got your ears on?" His boss's voice is pre-morning-coffee gravelly. The man doesn't so much as check an email before he has his first cup from the office pot. Dane steels himself. This must be important. He reaches for the radio and thumbs the button. "Officer Young here. Do I need to pull over for this?"

"I've got some hotshot secret agency poking its head around. When you finish your rounds, stop by the office and I'll fill you in." No "good morning" or small talk. He didn't end with one of his legendary dad jokes.

"Copy that," Dane says and then puts the receiver back in place. A secret agency? Somebody really wants to go forward with the investigation they hinted at last year and dropped? Nobody likes it when outsiders start digging in your backyard. You don't have to be a man of science to get why animals gone mad would raise some necessary questions, but why bother looking into it after so many months gone by?

Snowfall is nowhere near what they were hoping for this past winter, and at least a decade of winters before that. Enough had fallen that the spring thaw brought out the mud; surely any so-called evidence would be long gone by now. Syrah was so sure there wasn't anything to find anyway. Those Rhizan folks have been covering their tracks since . . . since forever, he guesses. Why now? If they've got money to burn, he's happy to chat them up about how he can put it to good use in Sequoia.

He finishes up his survey of the park and heads to the office. Not the headquarters up in Fresno, but the satellite building they set up just outside the park. When the fires and emergencies became more prevalent, leadership made the decision to move closer to the site. Dane doesn't mind. If anything, he's glad to have more interest in the park than less. He and his supervisor get on well; he pretty much leaves him to do his thing without looking over his shoulder.

Dane pulls his truck in alongside the only other car in the small parking lot. The office, as it were, is nothing more than a hastily built log cabin, not all that different from the one he calls home. A panel of triple-paned windows front the building. Two posts frame the teakwood door. A peekaboo stained glass cutout near the peak. He gives the door a rap with his knuckles and then enters.

"How many times do I have to tell you . . ." His boss comes to his feet and extends his hand for a fist bump. Like Dane, one pandemic too many has convinced him to give up on handshakes. "It's a public building. You don't have to knock."

"Old habits die hard," Dane says, returning the gesture and taking off his hat. Despite the logs on the outside, the inside of the building has been plastered and painted a government-standard dull off-white, ruining the whole effect, in Dane's opinion. A small kitchenette sits off to one side, complete with tiny fridge and the infamous coffee maker. A large wooden desk that has the dents and cuts worthy of its age and hand-me-down status. A bathroom that has to grudgingly be shared with the public, tucked away behind a false wall in an attempt to not make it too obvious.

"Coffee?" Mr. Lee says. When Dane declines, he points at the two chairs in front of his desk. "Take a load off."

Of the two "guest" chairs, Dane picks the one on the left. Experience reminds him that the other one has a broken front leg. "What do the government folks have for us now?"

"It's that damned animal madness from last year."

"Again?" Dane asks, not as shocked as he makes himself sound.

Lee runs a hand over his head. His eyes are tired. "Don't think I didn't try to put them off it either."

"I trust you did," Dane says, and he believes him.

"Wish it was otherwise, my friend, but you'll be the point person."

"What do they want with me?"

"Who else?" Lee shrugs. And he's right. Ranger numbers are half what they were just five years ago. And in the last eighteen months, one ranger has retired early, another has quit due to injury from a fire. For Sequoia, now it's only him.

"What is it that they're going to need?" Dane asks.

Lee picks up a pen, fidgets, then tosses it back on the desk. "Someone to once again spin up some kind of story about what happened. A tour guide? Who knows?"

Dane takes that all in with a curt nod of his head. "Basically, I'm to make myself available for whatever they need; all the other work I have to do will just have to wait." He can feel his blood pressure shooting up ten points. "That and to help speed them along to the conclusion of this bogus investigation as quickly as I can."

That earns a smile from Lee. "As usual, we're on the same page."

"You know they'll probably end up doing more damage than good, right?" Dane tells him. "And how many people are we talking about?"

"I've got no idea."

Dane has a thought. "I never take vacation."

"And now wouldn't be the time to change that," Lee warns. "Let them do what they need to do. That's all I'm asking. If anything gets out of hand, then call me. The whole team is coming in tomorrow. Today, you meet the leader of the pack"—he picks up a Post-it Note—"a Dr. Baron Anthony."

Dane takes little comfort in that. He stays a moment or two longer, passing the time with his manager, but his mind is already elsewhere. After the meeting with this Dr. Anthony, once he's got some sort of idea about what this investigation entails, he'll call on Syrah.

Lee hasn't mentioned it, but Dane thinks back to last year, that message he got. It listed all kinds of demands about how people had better change or they'd suffer some unnamed consequences. He even laughed out loud when he read it. He wonders if that note he forwarded, thinking it would end up in some bureaucrat's trash bin, has come back to bite him.

Has he inadvertently exposed his niece to scrutiny she does not need? If only he weren't always so by the book. He'll meet with the man and figure out just what he's got planned. If it's what Dane fears, a warning is probably all that he can give Syrah and the Rhiza.

Chapter Eighteen

Three Rivers, California
River View Café
April 2043

Once they've decided on a late-morning meetup, Dane picks the place. The River View Café is not only one of his favorite restaurants; its outside patio with a view of the Kaweah River makes it one of the places he feels most comfortable. Dane is the kind of man who likes sitting with himself, alone in the park, on the porch of his little cabin, just staring out at the trees. He's got everything he needs . . . almost.

Then his niece went and discovered an entire world beneath the paths he's roamed for thirty years this June. The fact that he has yet to actually see those people doesn't mean he doubts their existence. She tries to sidestep it whenever he brings it up, but the young woman he half raised has changed. *They* have changed her. Even when she's with him, she's someplace else. She is stewing about something, and not just her brother's death either. He likes to think that she still values his counsel, but she's been particularly tight lipped these past few months. The distance bothers him, something he admits only to himself.

It's a bit too chilly outside, so Dane is seated in a booth at the back of the restaurant. It gives him a view of the entire place and, most importantly, the door. Three Rivers has been his home for the better part of his life, so he knows the locals and can spot a tourist ten miles away. Dr. Baron Anthony, though, this dude has an entirely different look altogether. It's not just the government-issued car that gives him away.

Through the picture window marred by only the blinking name of the café, Dane watches as Dr. Anthony pulls into a parking spot closest to the road.

He wears a fleece zip-up against the morning cold and pants that indiscriminate color of tan that those who work outdoors favor. Sneakers instead of boots, so he's not heading out to the park today, Dane surmises. Maybe after they get through the biologist's little fishing expedition, Dane can convince him not to waste his time or taxpayer money.

He barely hears the bell tinkle when the door opens above the roar of activity in the diner. Conversations, the cook shouting orders, a blender whirring somewhere behind those double swinging doors. Dane holds up a hand and waves the biologist over. His walk is more ex-marine, less Dr. Doolittle. Not the mad scientist Dane was expecting. The man's gaze sweeps over the diner and everyone in it with each step he takes.

"Dr. Baron Anthony," he says, extending his hand.

"Dane Young," he answers and then offers his closed fist. "I'm sure you understand."

A hint of a smile before Dr. Anthony returns the fist bump. "You'd think we would have done away with the practice after that 2020 pandemic." He slides into the booth and ignores the menu the waitress has left there for him. "Thanks for meeting with me."

"No thanks necessary," Dane says. "Food first or talk first?"

Dr. Anthony seems to notice the menu then. He glances up at Dane, then says, "I can walk and talk at the same time, you?"

"I can practically recite everything on that menu," Dane says. "Take your time."

Dr. Anthony uses his forefinger to point to something that apparently snags his attention. Dane waves over the waitress. Once their orders have been taken, the scientist unzips his jacket and reaches into a shirt pocket. He pulls out a stack of field notebooks stuffed in a leather cover, outfitted with a pen loop. He flips the notebook open and slides the cap off the pen—a fountain pen. When he looks back at Dane, the congenial scientist is gone. Deep green eyes, almost unnaturally so, have taken on an intensity that has probably scared many folks sitting on the opposite side of them senseless. Dane swallows it like a glass of sweet tea; he's faced down bears and snakes, and hellish wildfires.

"You know why I'm here?" Dr. Anthony holds the pen in front of him, kind of like a shield, then fingers the cap a few times before he catches himself fidgeting and stops.

"Mr. Lee briefed me," Dane says, keeping his own hands clasped in front of him. "But I'd like to hear it directly from you." Dr. Anthony's sigh tells him he's had to repeat this story one time too many.

"That message you forwarded to your supervisor last year." He taps a page in his notebook but doesn't look down. "February. It sounded like the ravings of a madman. Why not just trash it? That's what I would have done."

Dane doubts that. "When you work in one of the country's largest national parks, you see and hear a lot. There seems to be an equal number of people who love us and an equal number who think of us as nothing but a bunch of people-hating tree huggers. The latter group can get pretty vocal."

The waitress appears then and pours them both cups of coffee. Dane takes his black with sugar. He pours a generous amount into his cup and takes a sip before he finishes his thought. "Point is, threats are a routine part of the job. I learned long ago to take all of them seriously. I'm lucky in that, you know? I don't have to judge them. I concentrate on my job." He stops to point west. "I try to be a good caretaker to that park. It's not your regular nine to five, you know. I have to leave the rest to somebody else."

"You were on the scene when the bears attacked the campers at the campground?" Dr. Anthony asks.

"I was."

"Walk me through it, and add the parts that weren't in the report." Dr. Anthony flips to an empty page in the notebook, pen at the ready.

Dane thinks about the question and sips his coffee before he responds. He gives him a rundown of the sequence of events. Of course, he'd only happened upon the scene during the aftermath. "What's not in the report is the smell. The metallic scent of blood. The survivors' screams. The looks of absolute horror on the faces of everyone there."

"Speaking of those present, I understand your niece, one Syrah Carthan, was witness to the entire thing."

It isn't a question, so Dane has nothing to say. He merely keeps his hands folded around his cup and waits, something he's exceptionally good at. During the standoff, the food appears. Plates overflowing with eggs and bacon and hash browns. The smells make his mouth water. Coffee cups are topped off. Dr. Anthony surprises Dane by uttering a few words of prayer before he pushes his notebook aside and tears into his food.

"What do you think caused the bears to attack that way?"

Dane finishes chewing before he dabs his mouth with a napkin. "I could name a hundred things that have changed in the park. Things that go totally against nature. The animals are trying to pivot, to adapt, same as us. There's less food. Bears, for instance, don't hibernate how they used to. They're off kilter and hungry, caught up in the effects of a climate that doesn't make sense to them anymore. That's the only thing I can, in my most unscientific way, attribute their behavior to."

Those eyes again. Evaluating every word, every gesture. Dane feels like he's a speck under a microscope. They eat in silence until their plates are empty. When the waitress offers to refill his coffee, Dane declines. So does Dr. Anthony.

He opens the notebook again and scribbles some notes. Dane doesn't bother trying to read them, but it's his turn to ask a question. "What do you hope to find after all this time?"

"I won't know it until I see it."

"You understand the importance of this park?" Dane asks.

"I'd like to hear it in your words."

"The Giants mean everything. Without them, there's no us, and I'm not overstating that."

"I couldn't agree with you more."

"If you and a team will be out there, the first thing is, do not get too close to the Giants. The root system is delicate. Pick up after yourselves. There are bins all over the place for trash—use them. And watch out for the wildlife. We don't want another repeat." He doesn't mean that as a threat, only stating the obvious.

"Good advice," Dr. Anthony says. "Thing is, we will have to get close to the trees, and despite those barricades you have up around some, we've got the clearance. What I will tell my team is to be mindful of the root system."

Dane checks his pocket for his keys, a habit he's had ever since he left them in this same diner when he first got the post. He makes to move out of the booth. "I'm your point person. If you need anything . . ."

"There is one thing." The scientist closes the notebook and puts it and the pen away. "Syrah Carthan was present at both the bear attack and the animal attack in Three Rivers. Quite the coincidence, wouldn't you say?"

Dane doesn't hesitate before speaking as he normally does. And later, he would realize, that was his mistake. "Not at all. She works in the park and lives in town."

Dr. Baron Anthony gives him an almost imperceptible shake of his head. "I'll be interviewing the firefighters and first responders as part of the investigation. And I'll also be talking to your niece," he says. "I already met her, you know. Good on you to get her a job as a . . . what was it again?" He pauses, then snaps his fingers. "A park guide for kids and retirees. A former fire chief, one who has worked at top stations all over the country. There's a story there. Something more than that prescribed burn gone wrong. And I look forward to hearing it."

With that, Dr. Anthony slides out of the booth and leaves the River View Café without a backward glance. He didn't even offer up his half of the check.

Dane settles that and hops in his truck. He makes a beeline for Sequoia and to one of the Giants. After checking over his shoulder to make sure he hasn't been followed, something he's never done in his life, he delivers the knock. One . . . pause . . . one quick rap, then another in succession.

Now, he waits.

Chapter Nineteen

Rhiza
The Mother's chamber
April 2043

It is Artahe's rich, mushroomy scent that rouses Syrah. Her brain feels as dull as a butter knife.

Slowly, she hacks through the fog and bolts upright. Relief that she once again has command of her body floods through her. Artahe is on her feet, but Syrah waves her off. First, she scans her body, groping around for any injuries. Finding herself pretty well intact, all things considered, she gets to her feet and takes a few tentative steps. She stretches and flexes her limbs.

"You did it, did you not?" Artahe's face is positively alight with excitement. She gestures behind them. "You connected with Her."

"For now, it stays between us," Syrah says. Her back is to the great tree. She's almost afraid to look. There's a question in Artahe's raised eyebrow that she ignores. Reluctantly, Syrah turns around to face the queen of the Giants. Goose bumps erupt, along with a shiver. And then it fades. Syrah isn't afraid, only has a healthy reverence. She knows at that moment she'll try again.

"I will respect your wishes, but there will be talk."

Syrah purposely chose to do her experiment after everyone had gone to bed, yet Artahe is right. There are few secrets in Rhiza. They have a totally different concept of privacy than the rest of the country. "I know you're right, but I'd like to keep this quiet for as long as I can."

Artahe takes her arm and guides her to one of the benches at the front of the chamber, where they sit. They gaze up at Her. Syrah feels like she's being watched, assessed. She won't tell her friend the whole truth. The Mother did not fully open to her.

Syrah squeezes her friend's hand but can't seem to draw her gaze away, not yet. It occurs to her that she hasn't a clue how old Artahe is, has always assumed they are close in age. As soon as she's resolved to ask, she knows it doesn't matter. Time and age are difficult concepts to wrap your head around here belowground. "What? No questions?" From the corner of her eye, she can see Artahe shake her head.

"There are only two groups of people who enter Her realm. Keepers and those who need to be punished. I will never be the former, and for now, I am not the latter. Those who have the privilege do not share anything about the experience. It is the way it has always been."

Syrah has read as much in the Keepers' logs, but it still surprises her to see that the missive is as true on the page as it is in real life. Two other things catch Syrah's attention: that Artahe said "for now" and that bit about the way things have always been. Since she arrived—in fact, since Romelo arrived—she knows how much has changed. How much things are not the way they have always been. What she's just done proves it.

"You are unharmed, then?"

After a quick mental check, Syrah confirms that she is.

"And your fungi?"

This she hesitates at. But who, if not the master and orchestrater of her change, can help her? "They are the key. I just need to work out a few more of the details. Is it possible that I am still evolving?" She feels Artahe watching her; then her long fingers prod at the space on her arm where she flowers.

"All fungi have phases of development. Of course, none specifically like yours have been studied. From the spores come chitin and the hyphae. Then their network forms."

"The mycelia, like with the lattice," Syrah mutters, as a theory she can't quite put to words, stirs. "And what then? What's the next step?"

Artahe's eyes widen. "Typically? Propagation. Reproduction."

But Syrah is about as atypical as it gets. She remembers how beautifully they flowered the first time she saw them. After she'd gotten over the fear and the revulsion, that is. Human beings have long been hosts to all manner of symbionts. Some unknown and as invisible as a quark, others, like hers, clear as the day is long. It has taken every bit of the last six or seven months, but now she considers them as much a part of herself as her fingers and toes. But reproduction?

"Please tell me that does not mean that one day my entire body will be covered and I will turn into some walking, talking five-foot-eleven-inch mushroom cap."

Artahe shrugs. "Who can say?"

"You say that like—just, never mind." Another thought occurs to Syrah. "What would stop reproduction? What are fungi sensitive to?"

"Not much. Air pollution."

Hmm. Over the last few years, the air quality in Southern California has risen up the charts to overtake New Delhi as the fourth worst in the world. And her parents wonder why she doesn't visit much.

Syrah pulls her hand away, pulls a leg up onto the bench, and turns to face Artahe. There's something they've been avoiding, and she's tired of carrying it around like an overstuffed backpack. "We cannot dance around it. Romelo is alive, and you are a hu—" Syrah catches herself. "You have feelings. It is perfectly normal that you would want to see him. Even I was conflicted about seeing my brother. I still want us to be what we were meant to be before that fire destroyed our family."

Finger fiddling. Looking away. A subtle shift, moving inches away. Creating separation? Simply uncomfortable? *All of them,* Syrah thinks. And why shouldn't she be?

"You topsiders abandon each other, how do you put it? Like hotcakes. We cannot dispense with love as easily as you do." Artahe is looking down at her hands as she speaks. Syrah feels the slight and accepts it as a return volley for all the ones she's delivered over her time here. Maybe there isn't a slight there at all. Last check, the divorce rate was hovering around 65 percent. And that's for the people who bother to get married in the first place. "How was he?"

Syrah shrugs. "Surprisingly well, at least physically. There is something changed about him, though."

Artahe looks over at Syrah then. "You know that brings me so much joy. And anger. I have grieved for him all this time, and he did not reach out to me once during the previous months."

"I suspect he had a fair bit of healing to do." Syrah says this not to brag but as a matter of practicality.

"His ego likely took the biggest hit."

Syrah sighs. "I wouldn't argue that."

"He did not kill The Keeper," Artahe states. "I am convinced of it."

"I am really surprised you can be convinced of anything when it comes to him," Syrah says. "It is not like he never tried before."

A flash of annoyance passes over Artahe's face. "Do you think I have forgotten? Well, I have not. I am only saying that it is impossible to be in two places at once. In your room, where you did not raise an alarm, and in The Keeper's library."

"But that does not put him totally in the clear." Though she has a point, Syrah is nowhere near ready to completely concede. "If Ezanna did indeed kill her, it was at Romelo's direction."

Artahe inclines her head. "A point *I* would not argue."

"How come you never ask me about my family? My topside family?"

"Because they do not—or soon, they will not—matter."

"How the hell can you say that?" And then Syrah knows. If she is to become Keeper, they will have to become nothing more than fond memories for her.

"What were my parents' names?" Artahe stands and plants her hands on her hips.

"Touché," Syrah concedes, then adds, "I am no happier about any of this than you. The first thing we have to do is to figure out how they slipped in and out of here so easily. Once we find them, then we will figure out who killed Taron and bring them to justice. Get Yemaya, Dhanil, and Shansi together. I will meet you in the library, but first, I have to go topside to make a call. Give me about an hour."

Something is off about Artahe. Syrah recognizes it because she feels the same way. It's conflict, plain as day. But how can either of them be conflicted? Romelo is a monster. He plowed headfirst in the opposite direction from everything Taron tried to teach him. The malevolent truth is that if it serves his twisted purpose, he'll take them both out.

So why the hell does she, do they both, still love him?

Because love is as irrational as it is inconvenient.

Dhanil grumbles about leaving her alone, but she hasn't had a moment to herself to think and is badly in need of time. And she knows her brother. He's made his move, and now he'll give her time to think about what she wants. He won't act again so quickly. Heaven help her, she's starting to think like him. Maybe she always has. She feels the same way about people's blatant disregard for the environment, for the Giants. Hasn't she made a flippant comment a time or two about how the earth would be better off without them? Genes are strange that way. You don't have to grow up with someone to be so much like them it grates. The difference between them, however, is that she would never act on it.

Syrah is on her way to her room when the new head rootspeaker rushes up to her from the opposite direction. With Romelo defected and Liesel dead because of him, Shansi has stepped up to the plate and proven himself more than worthy.

After Syrah took down the lattice, he helped to get it back online and has maintained it well ever since. The hems of his tunic are slightly dirty, a sign that he has just come from Lattice Affairs. Taron would have frowned on this, and Syrah tries to muster up the same indignation at his less-than-pristine appearance, but she abandons the effort.

"There is an incoming rootcast for you," he nearly whispers. He's what Syrah would call a low talker. "From topside."

This gets Syrah's attention. Unless something has gone terribly wrong, Uncle Dane is the only person who would send a message. Has something happened to her father? Her mother? "What was the message?"

"It was the knock," Shansi confirms with a sideways glance. Oddly, the caretakers are reluctant to acknowledge any connections she has topside.

"Thank you," Syrah says. "Artahe should be looking for you—"

"She has already found me. We will await your return." With that, he touches his palm to his heart and leaves.

Fear propels Syrah through the corridors. Her uncle would only call on her if it were an emergency. Another, added to the long list of emergencies building up. She navigates around rocky outcroppings, leaps a little stream. At just the right moment, she dips her head to dodge the stalactites hanging from the ceiling. She knows Rhiza's passages as well as she knows her own home. She's spent more time here than there in the past half year.

She exits the veil with her heartbeat barely above normal. What she judges to be a flaming-orange midday sun temporarily blinds her. She blinks away the spots behind her eyelids and makes her way through the forest and to the trail. Long ago, she figured out it was difficult to explain to others why her car sat alone for such long intervals. So sometimes, Dane drops her off.

Since her comms don't work in the caves and because the canopy keepers frown upon it, she often buries her fully charged device beneath a group of rocks a few meters behind Lodgepole. Each time she wonders if it will be there when she returns. As she shoves the rocks aside and claws through the dirt, she is relieved that her luck has held. She powers it up and checks the connection. Too low. Even after all the advancements of the last couple decades, it is almost as if the forest refuses to yield this one thing. She moves here and there until she gets a better signal and then speaks the words: "Call Uncle Dane."

For a while, Syrah hears nothing. "Come on, come on!"

Four staticky rings later, he picks up. "I don't think I'll ever feel less foolish when I knock on a tree or more surprised when it works."

Syrah notes his tone. Not light but not too heavy. Her parents are okay. "You and me both. What's going on?"

"Give me a second."

While she paces, Syrah picks up the sounds of voices, wind whistling, and feet shuffling.

"First, everybody is fine," Dane says when he comes back on the line. "I don't know if anything will come of it, but there's this biologist from some big shot secret agency, and they're going to look into last year's, uh, events. It's everything we hoped wouldn't happen."

Syrah groans. "Dr. Baron Anthony."

"You met him?"

"He ambushed me during my last tour." Syrah kicks angrily at a rock in her path.

"Well, my manager hauled me into the office and told me in no uncertain terms that I was to assist these people in any way I could. That means this is official, and we're not going to be able to stop it. I couldn't even get back to the park before he called."

"Already?" Things are moving way too fast.

"Yeah, we had breakfast in town. I couldn't get him to give me anything solid about how on earth he and this team of his hope to conduct this investigation, not yet. But I did ask what he hopes to find after all this time."

"And what did he say?" Syrah stops pacing.

"About what you'd expect. They want to know what made the animals turn on us like that. Winter held them off, but now there's nothing in the way. And you know, he mentioned you directly. You have to get your story straight because, a guess? That first visit was just a primer.

He isn't your typical government drone. There's real intelligence there behind those eyes. So you have to get yourself ready."

Syrah is quiet for a time as her stomach roils. Her fungi flutter strangely, but she stuffs them down. "I'll figure it out," she says finally.

"Listen, I gotta run, but you're going to have to spend some more time aboveground," Dane advises. "Make your life look as normal as possible, at least until this is over. Oh, and Syrah, call your folks."

The Keeper is dead.

Neither she nor Inkoza is ready to succeed her.

Romelo has returned from the dead.

He and Ezanna have to be found and punished.

Spending more time aboveground is exactly what Syrah cannot afford to do.

Chapter Twenty

Sequoia National Park
Lodgepole Campground
April 2043

Syrah is wearing a path in the wooded area behind Lodgepole. Chills despite the sun blanketing everything with warmth. Car doors slamming announce people arriving at the visitors' center. Snatches of their clueless conversations ride the wave of a biting wind. She squints, then blinks a few times. There's something glimmering so weakly she can't make it out.

It's the flutter and tingle on her forearms and lower legs that provide the answer. Fungal spores. Artahe said there were thousands of them in the air at any given time, but why is she just sensing them now? *I'm evolving into whatever this next phase is . . . reproduction.*

"Great, just freaking great," Syrah mumbles.

She thinks back to when she first heard she'd landed the job at Fire Station Ninety-Three. She was so excited that she'd positively floated every mile of that cross-country drive. Sadness about coming back to the place where her life had changed so much rode right along with her, but the awe she felt the first time she saw the forest, and the Giants, was right up there on the list of the best moments of her life.

The awe is still there; she feels it every time she's here. But crisis on top of crisis has plagued her ever since she arrived. Is that a sign of something? Is the universe telling her to get her behind back in that car and floor the pedal until she's back east?

To what? Eroding edges of the country. Toxic wildfire smoke drifting down from Canada? A long list of lost loves that she has no intention of revisiting.

And she thinks that somehow, The Mother wouldn't let her. Syrah is convinced that, from the time she and her brother were children, that tree has interfered with and forever altered their lives. She knows why, though: so that they could come to this very moment.

Syrah has slogged to another area of the park, looking for more solitude, when her comms device's chirp disintegrates that hope. The promise of trouble is all she has now. She expects the message to be from her parents; Dane told her to call them. Only, when she puts the device to her ear, it's her former coworker Alvaro's voice. She's pleasantly surprised.

He was her biggest supporter and advocate for her all-too-short tenure as fire chief. She had briefly allowed herself to skirt the edges of her attraction to him, her self-professed Afro-Cubano champion. Although he was incredibly handsome, she knows she mainly felt gratitude for the solidarity.

"Hey, Chief . . ." Syrah smiles: all the times they've talked since she quit her job, he's never stopped calling her "chief."

"Just calling to check in. Well, that ain't all. I'm calling to see if you want to come back to service. No sugarcoating it: things are rough. Have you read about what's going on with the wildland firefighters? Hit me up when you get this."

She hasn't read anything. Another crisis? She welcomes the excuse to put off calling home. Syrah holds her device up to the sky, checks the connection, and finding it oddly sufficient, taps the screen.

"It didn't take you a week to call back this time," he says. There's noise in the background, voices, clanging and banging. He and the crew are probably cleaning and servicing the equipment. "Hold up."

When he comes back on the line, all Syrah hears is birdsong. "How you doin', Chief?"

Syrah grins like a fool. She has a lie, the one she practices all the time, all ready to go. It's a burden wearing two faces, and for some reason, she feels like it's okay not to. "I've been better."

"If that's because you miss being here, we can fix that up in the time it takes to lace up your boots."

That's only part of it. She does miss being a firefighter, but that's the smallest part of her worries now. "What's going on at the station?"

"One retirement, two people that had kids quit and moved inland, and our recruitment efforts are in the toilet," Alvaro rattles off.

Syrah is at a loss for words. Finally, she blurts out, "Why?"

"Things ain't getting better." Alvaro confirms her first thought. "The last few fires we've fought charred so much of the forest. We haven't had a prescribed burn since yours, and guess what's predicted for this summer? Hotter temps. Outreach and education are doing fuck all to change how people see and do things. Technology is all directed at social shit. The promises they made us about AI that would help how we fight fires? Where is it?" Alvaro stops then, the typical lightness in his voice gone. "The fire crews are tired—so many of us are feeling the effects of too much smoke, *and* they're scared as hell."

It doesn't take a climatologist to know that the words Alvaro speaks are true. Syrah saw the beginning evidence at the stations she worked the years before Sequoia. She's just starting to forgive herself for her error with the prescribed burn; she contributed to the park's loss, and hurt her only friend in the process. As much as she'd like to be back in the front passenger seat of that engine, her life's other priorities won't allow it. Even if her fear would.

They fall silent after that.

"You gonna make me spell it out?" There's an edge to Alvaro's voice, not quite razor sharp, but there nonetheless. "The chief's chair is filled with Lance and his ego, but even he won't be here forever. Come back. Work your way up again. We need you."

Syrah's entire being responds to that call. Her heart both revs up a million beats and hurts at the same time. Her scalp tingles. The memory of scorched earth singes her nostrils. Her toes flex in her boots, ready to dig into the earth. Her muscles tense. Being a firefighter is all she's ever wanted, and she lets the full effect of how much she misses it wash over her.

But then she picks her gaze up off the forest floor and looks around her. Takes in that sign that leads to the trail back through the park and back to Rhiza. And she knows that she can no longer have what she wants. The Mother took that away from her when she invited her beneath the veil.

"Hello?" Alvaro prompts. "Please tell me you're not still nursing guilt."

When crafting a lie, it's best to start with a nugget of the truth. "I'll never get over the guilt," she tells him. "And there's no way I can work in that station with Lance as my boss. We'd be at each other's necks, and that's not good for the station or the crew. You may trust me, but I have to learn to trust myself first."

"Everything in me wants to call you a selfish baby, but I can't, 'cause I know that's not right. And as much as I'd like to think I'd handle it different"—he blows out a breath—"who knows until you're in the same situation. Think about it, though, okay?"

"I promise I will," Syrah says. That much isn't a lie. It doesn't change the fact that she may never find her way back.

Syrah leans back against a blue oak tree and taps the back of her head against the trunk. Not hard enough to hurt, but enough to inflict some level of punishment. She'd taken an oath and then walked away from it like she'd spoken in an unrecognizable tongue.

Each call has been worse than the last. She's about ready to shot put the thing away when she remembers Dane telling her to call home. Why not, she figures. She'll go three for three. Then it's back to the caves.

Device in hand, she's about to call her father when she stops. She doesn't know why, but she surprises herself by saying, "Call Mom."

"Is your father's device on silent mode again?" Her mother's voice, even and warm. It sets her on edge and gets her guard up anyway. Dad often switches off his alerts by accident. Still, there's an undercurrent in that seemingly innocent question. She almost never calls her mother first. They both know it. It's not something she's proud of, but she's got her reasons.

"I don't know," Syrah says. "I didn't call him. I called you."

"Huh," Mama grunts. "How are you, baby? Something wrong?"

"God, Mama, does something have to be wrong for me to call?"

"Yes, when you usually only reserve that hot minute between when you're done talking to your father and when you're ready to hang up for me." This isn't going the way Syrah wanted, but has anything today? "And you better watch your tone too."

"My tone?" Syrah is incensed. She tried, and what does Mama do? Bite her head off. "You . . ." Syrah glimpses a little girl, maybe five or six. Running as fast as her little legs will take her, her expression one of pure joy. And then a woman—her mother—is on her heels, swoops her up and tosses her over her shoulder. Their laughter trails them back toward the parking lot. "I'm sorry. I was thinking about you and just wanted to call to see how you were doing."

Anissa Carthan is nobody's fool. In the seconds before she speaks, Syrah knows her mother is trying to decide if Syrah is just placating her. "That's the nicest thing you've said to me in months. My hip hurts when I walk too much, and this gray hair is obnoxious—battles even the stiffest of gels and mousses—but other than that, especially since I'm hearing your voice, I'm good."

The door is open. Syrah can and will walk through it. "What do you do when you have an impossible decision to make? When two sides need you equally?"

"Are we talking about men?"

Syrah blows out a breath, loudly. "No. We are not."

"Fine then. I guess you're not ready to give me any of the details?" Mama asks.

"Can't," Syrah says. "Not yet."

"Some people will tell you to make out a list of pros and cons. Waste of time, you ask me," Mama says. "All you need to help you make that decision is your gut. Stop all that endless running you do and just listen to it. Bring up each side, think about it, and let your gut tell you what to do."

Syrah is stumped. It's surprisingly good advice, and she doesn't hesitate in telling her mother so.

"Of course, if you could give me a little more information, the second-best thing is a mother's viewpoint. Nothing is more rock solid."

"Thank you, Mama," Syrah says. She envisions her mother passing out right then and there as she tries to explain the existence of a subterranean species. "Really. This helps."

"Okay, baby. Despite what your father says, I'm learning when enough is enough. Wanna speak to him now? He's outside lecturing old Mr. Greenwood about water waste."

Normally, she'd say yes. Normally, she'd have asked his advice instead of Mama's. This time, Syrah says, "Tell him I love him. I'll talk to you both later."

Syrah slips her device in her pocket, then turns and plants her forehead against the tree. There was a time when she thought of tree bark as rough and uneven. But living in and becoming more Rhiza has opened her eyes. Beneath her fingertips, the roughness is just texture, beautiful centuries-old character. Like wrinkles on the skin, they tell a story.

She does as her mother says. Instead of two, there are actually three things she has to consider: rejoining the fire service, returning to Rhiza as simply a caretaker, or returning as The Keeper. She holds each consideration up for inspection and weighs it. She listens to her gut.

The decision crystallizes from the ash-streaked tatters of her world.

Chapter Twenty-One

Beneath Sequoia National Park
Rhiza
April 2043

Syrah comes back to Rhiza more determined than when she left. Topside, all the calls and pacing consumed more than an hour. Belowground, the time slip is the few minutes it takes to jog the circumference of the exercise room.

It's the absence of the sound of water that strikes her first. The main rivulet near the entrance and then two others that she passes are stilled, mute. She bends down, narrowing her eyes, and just makes out a clear water line, a good inch lower than what it was before she left. Syrah makes a beeline for her office, where she finds her team assembled.

Dhanil is stationed outside the door, along with someone else whose name she can't recall, but she assumes he must be a member of the new honor guard Dhanil mentioned building. She gestures for her foe turned friend to come in with her as she passes. Inside, Artahe and Shansi are seated in the chairs around the long table. Syrah ungracefully climbs into what used to be Taron's chair.

She glances at her small team and worries that they, that she, are not enough. They have a lot to accomplish, though, and in very short order, so she will have to set any feelings of hurt and betrayal aside.

"Two things we need to do first," Syrah says. "Find out how Romelo and his crew slip in and out of here so easily. That will take care of the next: finding the killer."

"I could not agree more," Dhanil says. "I have to admit, this is unprecedented in Rhiza. We do not conduct investigations. We are an open and direct people, and eventually, the accused steps forward. There may be some dissent, but The Keeper makes the final judgment, and we agree to whatever punishment is decreed."

It's so ridiculous that Syrah almost laughs in their faces.

"Before we do that," Artahe interjects, "we must anoint a new Keeper. You cannot deny that you have noticed. The decline has already begun. We are not at a critical juncture yet, but each day it will worsen."

Syrah wasn't aware of this. "Our drinking water—"

"Cleaning, maintaining the fungal crops, everything," Artahe says. "And the caretakers are afraid. I do not know how long they can maintain the status quo without clear leadership in place."

"And I do not know how long The Mother can survive without a Keeper either," Syrah adds. This last bit earns uneasy looks from her team. This is for her to solve, and everyone at the table knows it.

Dhanil clears his throat and meets each of their gazes before he speaks. "My priority will be the breaker and his followers. As our numbers reduced, we withdrew, and for safety's sake, our ancestors walled off those other entrances."

Nods and murmurs of agreement all around before Syrah adds, "So this is not a matter of trekking through the cave system. They could literally be hiding behind any one of our walls."

Artahe crosses her arms and looks positively piqued before she chimes in: "Nobody living today knows the full extent of those other sectors. Only Taron . . . and probably Ezanna."

For a few moments, they're all lost in their own thoughts.

"There's obviously one other person," Syrah says. "Romelo."

Artahe averts her eyes. Again. If Syrah is capable of not taking it personally that her brother is behind this, then Artahe is going to have to get over it as well. She can't go flinching every time his name is brought up.

"I am reluctant to add to our already considerable obstacles," Shansi says. "However, the lattice is also suffering."

Syrah barely suppresses a groan. "How?"

Shansi is one of those people who rubs his hands together while he speaks, and it takes him a few seconds to gather his thoughts. "Think of it as a blackout. There have been intermittent silences, periods where rootspeak fades and then vanishes completely."

Syrah imagines this as an emergency akin to losing all communications coverage topside. "I know what I have to do."

"My team will begin scouting missions, and I will use my tracking methods," Dhanil says.

Syrah agrees with this; then trepidation raises another question. "Best guess. How many are with him?"

Hand-wringing, sighing, shrugging.

"If our total number was around five hundred, then I estimate that through death we have lost six and through defection"—he expels a breath—"thirty."

So the numbers don't bring Syrah an ounce of comfort or relief, but at least they don't send her scurrying for the hills. "There is something else I have to tell you. I wish it was good news."

"As if we could take anything else!" Artahe throws up her hands and dramatically slouches back in her chair.

Everyone leans in, almost imperceptibly. "While I was doing one of my park tours last week, a man approached me, asking questions. He is a wildland biologist, appointed by the topsider government."

"What does he want?" Artahe blurts out, her face a blotch with uneasy eyes.

"If you would let me finish . . ." Syrah stops herself. They're all on edge, understandably. She takes a deep breath and then starts again. "He and a team are poking into the animal attack."

"A full season ago?" Shansi says. He has been his quiet self so far, but now he's agitated. "How many of them? We cannot tolerate them trampling the roots and filaments. The lattice is already sputtering. I cannot even fathom the repairs we will have to undertake if a full army descends on the forest."

Beneath his protruding brow, Dhanil watches Syrah so intently that she fidgets. He clasps his hands in front of his chin. "You are worried about them finding Rhiza."

It isn't a question. It's a statement that couldn't be more true. Syrah knows it should be impossible. Every single thing she's experienced in the last year should be too. Had she mentioned any of it to anybody other than her uncle, they would have suggested she seek mental health counseling, stat. And there's another wild card that she's been pondering, hesitant to mention to the others. Keepers have their secrets, after all, but this one she can't keep. "You say that the other areas of Rhiza have been sealed off, right? If they are sealed off so well, then what is to stop Romelo from leading topsiders right to us? Ever heard the phrase 'the enemy of my enemy is my friend'?"

Artahe slams her hands on the table and shoots out of her chair. "You knew him for exactly four years before you pushed him out of that tree. The child I met and the man he grew into would never do that. He would not invite topsiders beneath the veil. He could not . . . sacrifice us . . . that way . . ."

Artahe trips and stutters over her last words, her outburst like an engine running out of gas. She sinks back into her chair and buries her face in her hands. As her friend, Syrah wants nothing more than to comfort her. But she's more than that now; she's going to become their Keeper.

The others watch her, waiting to see how she'll react.

"I hope not," Syrah says. "And for what it is worth, despite the fact that he has upended everything belowground, I agree with you. It would lead to his own demise, and my brother treasures himself more than anything."

"But we must prepare, nonetheless," Dhanil says.

"They will not find anything," Syrah says with a conviction she mostly believes. "They will waste taxpayer money poking around, and in a couple weeks, they will go away."

"We will send a message on the lattice," Shansi says. "With your permission."

Syrah grants it and then stands. "You know what you have to do. I am returning to The Mother."

Chapter Twenty-Two

Rhiza
The Mother's chamber
April 2043

Why? When the simplest explanation is right before your nose, why must we always look right past it in search of something more complicated? Syrah wishes that knowing a thing and being able to change it were as easy as they should be.

As she stands before The Mother, a small shudder ripples through Syrah's body. Only a practiced eye would see it, but Her branches, once elegantly uplifted toward the cavern ceiling, are more limp and bowed. In spots, Her bark is washed out and drained of color.

When Syrah lays her hand against the trunk, The Mother's hum is still there, strong, but the tone is somehow not as full. The feeling in Syrah's gut doesn't resonate at half the pitch it used to.

She hasn't allowed herself to see it before, but her willful blindness can't hide the fact that the cracks in Rhiza's impeccable veneer began as soon as Taron was injured. And that unfortunate vulnerability paved the way for dissension.

At first, there were only a couple dozen, but one morning after the next, they discovered more caretakers turning traitor. Throwing their lot in with whomever they thought would ultimately win the battle for The Keeper's seat—her brother, not her. Not even Inkoza.

That lighthearted cheer that originally drew her to this underground world is all but gone, right along with the proud determination with which they go about their lives. Everything here is in a symbiotic relationship with the other: Mother, Keeper, caretakers, fungi. It comes to Syrah like a pale sun emerging from the cover of a full eclipse. None of them can exist and flourish without the other. It makes what she has to do all the more important.

She needs Her. Both Romelo and Syrah have Rhizan strength and their own versions of the flow. He has evolved to become their most gifted rootspeaker. Through the lattice, he can touch Her.

Fungi are Syrah's gift. They've got a network all their own, and when they joined with the trees, the lattice was born. That's it, then. Those perfect blooms are not just decoration. She's been searching among the branches for what only appears in the roots.

Syrah immediately drops down on the spongy earth. She settles into a comfortable position. Then, with a deep breath expelled, she waits.

Purpose and clarity unlock the door. In her mind, Syrah calls to them: *Bloom.* Tiny stems move aside the fine hairs on her forearms and poke through the skin.

As they elongate and fill out, the caps form over the ends. Syrah runs her fingers over the delicate flowering. They bend and spring back beneath her touch.

The Mother's root filaments erupt from the confines of the earth and snake toward her. Their urgent tips encircle both her wrists as if binding her in place. Urgent tendrils form that symbiotic relationship between tree and fungi. They speak without words, a sophisticated and implicit language of electrical impulses.

Syrah enters the in-between place again. Her entire body feels interwoven with history. The fungal colonies were the first. Their spores dispersed on a zephyred wind and settled into the earth and the sea. It is as if they see her, take her face between the innumerable branches of their hyphae, and *Yes, we see you, we are you.*

Next, she feels The Mother come into being as a sprout in the center of her chest, the Giants birthed from Her shed cones. Syrah senses the formation of the Crystal Cave and Rhiza in the extension of Her limbs, the canopy keepers, Her heart.

The battle for resources raged between the fungi and the trees. She put a stop to it, and their union was born.

Syrah gulps in something that is not quite air, more like time unfolding. The sound of water, first a slow trickle, then a great wave, and she is swept up in the current. Her thoughts are wild and random, intangible.

She fights, struggling to understand. And then she realizes the futility and releases. Like a gentle hand, something, someone, takes her by the wrist and sweeps her off the current.

She touches down on a grassy knoll. Her thoughts are like slime, gooey, shapeless. Coming to her feet, she is drawn by the sounds of water. As she walks, her mind knits itself back together, and the contours of the place slowly unfurl in layered complexity.

Aside from herself, there isn't another soul in sight, but she hears the echoes of movement. She wiggles her toes in the soft emerald grass, slightly warm beneath her bare feet.

Instinct or The Mother, she's not sure which, but something compels her to turn north.

The basic landscape doesn't change much. Her nostrils delight at the sweetest smells, stalks like sugarcane, fragrant wildflowers kindled into delicious color with a cadre of bees drunk on their overflowing nectar.

If she concentrates, she can see pheromones wafting off the tree trunks. Oaks (*genus Quercus*), bay trees (*Laurus nobilis*), and firs (*genus Abies*), all varieties living side by side. More than she's ever seen in any forest she's ever worked. But other things become apparent. A flock of birds soars overhead. Small animals dart across her path and among the trees, the hint of larger ones lurking in the shadows. Only, there is no sense of danger. Just everything existing in harmony, one with the other.

"Mother?" she calls tentatively after a time. Her voice carries through the air and dissipates without any response.

Her march continues, and she notices a subtle rise in the terrain forming a few feet ahead. Minutes later, her thighs confirm she's walking up a hill. She isn't tired, doesn't even feel much of anything in her body. No fatigue. She isn't really even conscious of breathing. In a setting so beautiful and serene, she can't help but wonder where the imprisoned are. A millennium's worth of people entrapped somewhere. The place where Ochai is unjustly held with them.

The incline grows sharper, and Syrah almost feels as if she'd do better walking on her hands and knees for fear of falling backward. Everything in her says to turn around, and when she does, she's staggered by how far she's climbed. She nearly loses her balance before she turns back around and presses onward.

If time is slow in Rhiza, it is almost nonexistent in The Mother's world. At one point, Syrah started counting her steps, but she has long since abandoned the attempt. She stopped at fifteen hundred. Just as she's about to stop for a rest, she crests the hill.

Before her is an island with giant sequoias lining the circumference, save for what appears to be a gap, an entrance. Syrah rushes down the hillside, onto the path, and through the opening.

Then she sees Her. Instead of the towering Giant that exists in Rhiza, The Mother is small and sturdy looking, but wizened. Though no less beautiful. The bark is a rich cinnamon kiss, Her canopy brilliantly full and sparkling with dewdrops of light. The Mother sits on an incredibly lush meadow, surrounded by concentric circles of lightly lapping water, crystal clear—three in total.

What is before Syrah is a miniature, aged giant sequoia.

———— ≈◦◦≈ ————

You have come. The Mother's voice is a symphony. A collection of wild-land instruments that spill out over the earth and buffet Syrah's body, then sink into her.

"Better late than never," Syrah says aloud with a forced chuckle.

Does it appear to you that we have time to waste? This, bossy like Taron, only multiplied by a thousand.

Syrah realizes her attempt at sarcasm has once again fallen flat.

Yes. That flippant tongue of yours is useless here. Think it and I will hear it.

Everything? Syrah hates the thought. It is said that mothers can read minds; here, apparently, that is true. Syrah's second thought is to try to shield her thoughts, clear her mind so as not to give away some of her deeper feelings. When she glances at the tree, she all but abandons the attempt. "Where are we?"

Is it not obvious? You have already discovered a world different from your own. Is it so unlikely that there is a third? That there are more?

This is The Mother's realm. Where really doesn't matter, at least not yet. "I guess what I mean is, I know that there are people imprisoned here. Where are they?"

She shimmers, pinpricks of light that momentarily blind Syrah. Wrong move.

Command yourself to flower.

Flower? Syrah is at a loss. Then it hits her. *Bloom.* She wonders momentarily if it will feel differently here. Then her taste buds flood with flavors, like rain on the tip of her tongue, like wood and grass and sun. Behind squeezed eyelids, stars wheel like the universe in ecstatic motion. Her arms quiver, from shoulder to fingertips. With a velvety sigh, like the turning of old pages of parchment, her fungi burst through her skin into full glorious bloom.

There. Now you are more like my children. More than human.

Like a child, Syrah beams beneath Her approval. No matter that she put down being human in the same breath. The beginning buds of acceptance are present within her. Pride at what she has become. Really relishing in her enhancements. "Is it enough?"

That is a question you should be able to answer for yourself.

Syrah can't help herself; she rolls her eyes. Taron was the same way. An expert at dodging questions with the precision of a football player. "Just tell me what I need to do to become The Keeper. I am ready," Syrah says.

Are you, child? The Mother quips. Her trunk oscillates and wobbles as if she's laughing.

A hand flies to Syrah's hip. Her temper almost forces her to say something she'll regret. Instead she stands tall, inhales the fragrant air. And holds it, her Rhiza-strong lungs accommodating the extra.

Then she exhales and retracts her mushrooms. Syrah holds her arms up in the air, turns them so that her forearms are facing Her, then calls and silences her blooms so many times that it's as if she's turning a light switch off and on.

The Mother's branches lean toward her, Her canopy bristling as if clapping.

Syrah lowers her arms, her demonstrations done. "You know already, probably more than me. But a good number of the caretakers are ready to follow me. And I figured out how to get here, didn't I?"

As has your brother.

Syrah's legs go watery at that. "What? Why? How could you allow it? Are you on his side? Do you sanction every crazy thing he's—"

Syrah's voice is cut off midsentence. Her mind has gone dangerously blank. She opens her mouth. Her lips and tongue move, but she has no words. The Mother's trunk has gone rigid, sparkling a deep dangerous green. Syrah's thoughts are like sand. She has a vague sense of self, but everything else is gone. She's free-falling into nothing, and it's the most terrifying thing she's ever felt.

I am The Mother. I hold the entire world on my shoulders. In your realm and mine, you will show me the respect I am due, or you will be reminded of your place, child.

When Syrah regains her ability to think, to speak, she is mollified and unsure. "Which of us will become Keeper?" she says haltingly. "The choice is obviously, rightfully, yours."

There is something else you wish to ask me.

So she does know every corner of Syrah's mind. She wonders if that uncomfortable ability translates to the real world. "In order to make it through this summer's fire season, we will need the very best on hand."

Both questions, the spoken and unspoken, are true. And the other half of the story is that you petition me for Ochai's release because you care for him.

"I will not bother denying it. But I will tell you that my feelings for him will not get in the way of my duty."

Keepers may occasionally take a lover, but they do not mate for the long term. There will be no children. It is not cruelty but a necessity. A Keeper's decisions cannot be compromised by her feelings for the few. It is the same reason that my caretakers are no longer paired to one Giant.

That and the fact that so many of them are gone, Syrah thinks. "I understand," she responds, but in her heart, she wavers. The truth is, she isn't sure she wants some long-term thing with Ochai anyway, despite how she feels. But no children? That's not something she's planned for, but to have the option taken away?

Every person who has taken up the staff has had the same concern. It is a natural thing.

"But you have children." Syrah's tone is a decibel above respectful, and she has no desire to go back to that space The Mother put her in before, so she dials it back. "Does it interfere with your decision-making?"

See.

Syrah blinks, and she is in an entirely new part of the realm. She walks barefoot through a field. The terrain couldn't be more different. Not one blade of grass. No wildflowers or weeds. No trees. Barren. If despair had a scent, it would be whatever the stink is that is clogging her nostrils.

The ground is still moist beneath her feet, but the texture is all wrong. It's like a marsh. She doesn't think it could rain here, but if it does, she'd be buried up to her waist in mud in short order. She bends down to run her hands through the muck, but what she sees . . .

A belly-deep shriek explodes from her open mouth.

And doesn't stop as she turns and sprints in the opposite direction, but moments later, she's back in the same spot. She doesn't want to see it again. Can't fathom. But she glances down, and there it is. A wide, rheumy, dark-brown eye. Staring back up at her. It blinks and Syrah wails again.

"What is this place?" she shouts into the void.

An invisible force shoves her forward. In another spot, a full hand is visible. Another push. To her right, a protruding shoulder blade. On her left, a sun-dark foot. While she's gaping at that, her own foot lands on a fully visible face, raised several inches above the dirt. It is a face full of hate. It sneers at her. Holds her gaze in a tug-of-war, losing, sinking. She is submerged, frozen in a vat of solid ice. With effort she yanks free and runs.

She asked for it, and now she's here. This is the Rhizan prison. It's more horrible than Syrah could have imagined. Again, she's struck by how very human they can be in their cruelty. And she doesn't care if The Mother hears her think it.

Ochai is here, somewhere. A stronger shove. Syrah tiptoes around the field, careful not to step on anyone again.

Her eyes land on something familiar. She would know his topknot anywhere. She's found him. But how is she to free him? Claw through the earth and wrench him out?

Think like a Keeper, with only your abilities.

To be a firefighter, one must have incredible endurance and strength. Her lungs are double what human capacity should be. Her eyesight much the same. But her true gift is her mycelia.

Bloom, Syrah calls to her fungi, and they answer.

The caps flare and emit hairlike tendrils that extend all the way to the ground. They stab through the earth, latching on to the full length of him. They lift. Ochai is pulled out inch by glorious inch.

His eyes watch her every step, and Syrah melts a little. Once he is held fully aloft, her mycelia retreat, and he is released. Before Ochai can hit the ground again, he is gone.

Chapter Twenty-Three

Rhiza on High
April 2043

Lattice Affairs is where Romelo feels most comfortable, most confident. Here is the place where his most-honed skill shines. He became head rootspeaker because he earned it. He was—and, in spite of the usurper sitting in his rightful place in Rhiza proper, he is—the best there ever was.

Or will be.

He knows that at some point, when he ascends to the role of Keeper, he will have to step away from the pod, but not today.

With a wave of his hand, the other rootspeakers abandon their stations and exit with lowered heads. One, a particularly ambitious youth whom Romelo has vowed to keep an eye on, stops him as he passes.

"I am ready and able to help you in any way that you need me, Keeper." He makes a move to touch Romelo on the shoulder, but the look in Romelo's eye wards that off.

Romelo does not need dissent at this point, so to mollify the ambitious one, he says, "You have proven yourself worthy. Be ready."

The brightness of the suck-up's face annoys him. He smiles and, none too soon, leaves Romelo alone to his task.

If Vice's plan is to have a chance at succeeding, they will need Her. The Mother's assistance would be a welcome assurance, but all they really need is for Her to turn a blind eye to what is to come. Sneaking into The Mother's chamber undetected proved difficult. Romelo does not like to have the word "impossible" infect his mouth or mind. But because he is who he is, he has found another way.

In the end, it proved to be so simple that it made Romelo laugh. A thing that only his dear friend Ochai is often able to elicit.

He kicks away the step stool that someone, likely the ambitious one, set in front of his pod and hoists himself up into the narrow opening. These earlier versions are different, smooth all the way around, with no back support or headrest, and so he has made adjustments.

Romelo inhales the smell of earth and, with it, thoughts of Artahe. He is not ashamed to admit that he loves her. That he misses her. But her constant rebuffs, even at this, his lowest point, have angered him. The thing that first attracted him to her—her spirit, having her own mind—has since turned into a grating annoyance. But that is the way of love, is it not?

You are forgetting yourself. Romelo bristles at the momentary loss of concentration. He understands now what he has read in the rules outlined in *Lives of Imminent Keepers.* Keepers cannot have life partners. Has he not proven the ancients right? But as Romelo has discovered, things do change. When he ascends, he will rewrite the rules. One must become master of one's own mind. Reliance on outdated rubrics will not be his crutch. He and Artahe will be life partners. They might even reproduce, as he will need a successor. He will rebuild a family. And he, not that draconian book, will be the ruler of his reign.

With that decided, Romelo pulls the lever and waits.

Soon, the soft hairs on his lower legs tingle in anticipation. They sense the approach of their brethren. There is no way to see down to the end of the pod, but if one attunes one's senses just so, a true root-speaker can hear the lattice, the mycorrhizal network at play. When those lacelike strands brush across his feet and traverse his ankles, he holds his breath.

This is almost the best part.

Almost.

When they touch, his hairs and the roots, every time, it is like a most delicious first kiss. When they twist and knit and braid, it is a mingling of tongues. When they sink beneath his skin, it is an electric rhapsody.

Romelo's body stirs, which he allows before he settles. Already he is flooded with information from the lattice. Roots in need of repairs. Giants that have suffered wounds from humans or beasts or insects or all three. Gripes and joys. A wealth of things that need doing, that need tending. It is not that these things are no longer his concern but, as much as he hates to admit it, that the new chief is managing them well enough. Were Romelo truly needed, he would intervene. In fact, his staff has done so, all without the others knowing, such is the level of his ability to conceal their tracks. But today, he has another mission.

Romelo erects all the protections he's mastered. And then he calls out to The Mother. He knows that she is watching. She always does. Like all busy mothers, however, she does not respond at his whim. Romelo's thoughts are lazy and heavy with fatigue by the time he feels Her charged acknowledgment. It ravishes his spine and travels through his limbs before it dissipates. Romelo thought this through before he connected. True speech can only come when you connect to Her as a speaker does. But, through reading, testing, and his own wit, he has discovered something else.

He begins the communication by sending Her an image of himself kneeling at Her roots as he remembers them in Her great chamber. It is the most accurate sign of respect he can think of.

No message comes back to him. A door not quite shut. He proceeds. The next thought he conveys is risky but necessary. It is of himself, walking through the blackened remains of Kings Canyon National Park. Then the scorched earth, the stubs where Giants once lived. He ends with a thought of his own chest torn open, his heart bleeding into the blackened ground.

This time, she responds. Through the lattice, Romelo feels it first; then a thought coalesces in his mind.

Wrong.

Yes, he agrees. *Unforgivably wrong.* Next he thinks of a city, the largest he can imagine, Los Angeles. San Francisco. His sister does not believe it, but Rhiza knows. He has read their news, seen them scurrying to and fro in their cars and trains and buses. All intent on goals that make little sense. They aren't even sure why they do these things.

Millions of them.

And their willful, blind destruction of everything natural.

Then Romelo thinks of something different. The humans are gone. Their skyscrapers and yoga studios are empty. Their planes and rockets grounded. Their communications streams silent. Nature takes note and encroaches on it all. Weeds sprout from cracks in the concrete. Animals pad through the streets. Roots extend and thrive.

The Giants redouble and clean the air of all human filth.

The connection between Romelo and The Mother is vibrating. And then, Her thought.

How.

And then Vice inserts itself. Vice senses the carbon dioxide in the air. It feels the instinct to take it in, to clean it and to give the humans back what they need in the form of pure oxygen. But it resists that urge.

As do all the other Giants.

At first, the humans have minor respiratory illnesses. But then their symptoms worsen. They choke. They attempt to compensate with their machines and technology. But, all too late, they realize what Romelo has been trying to tell them all along.

Without the Giants, they cannot survive.

And they succumb.

When they are gone, Rhiza and the Giants thrive. The rest is up to nature.

Romelo waits. Vice's plan is a bold one. And it involves something he knows will change the course of history. But is that not what she knew might happen when she took him in in the first place?

After a time, Her response comes. Again, a word.

Nature.

With that, Romelo can feel their connection break in half like a twig beneath large feet. But what does she mean? That is neither a yes nor a no.

Frustrated, Romelo turns his attention away and then goes on to his next task.

He shields himself deeper and reaches out to his new tree, Vice. The nascent Giant is still technically a sapling, but like none other before it. Infused with the very best of its father, and Romelo's own blood, it grows and thinks beyond its years.

Through the lattice, Vice responds.

It has the beginnings of a nasty fungal infection that Romelo will go topside to attend to. Beyond that, his tree is in good health, good cheer. And then Romelo feels it through the lattice. The excitement, the growing anticipation. His sapling, it appears, is ready. He communicates his appreciation and then covers his tracks and disconnects.

Romelo doesn't know how much time has passed, and it is of little concern. He believes that The Mother is with him. He has to get back to the task of becoming Keeper now. And he must deal with this Dr. Anthony. He will not interrupt Romelo's plans, nor will he be allowed to harm the forest.

If the beginning is a first kiss, departing is a brutal severing.

Chapter
Twenty-Four

Rhiza
The Mother's chamber
April 2043

The sound of water trickling down the walls rouses Syrah. She did it. She connected with The Mother. It's an incredibly tough feeling to put into words, Syrah thinks as she returns to herself, that her body remained here, in this chamber, while her mind, or at least some part of it, traveled to Her realm. It has always been so easy to dismiss it when people talk about having an out-of-body experience. Until this very moment, those were words that she thought existed only in overactive imaginations. Books are great, mentors even better, but firsthand experience is the world's best teacher.

When Syrah saw her parents after she moved back to California, she picked up little things about them that didn't come across on video. A few new lines on their faces, a scar on the hand—the result of a gardening snafu. How her mother's formerly brisk walk had slowed a bit. A reintroduction of sorts.

And it's the same for her. It lasts mere seconds, but in that time, she becomes reacquainted with herself—with her fingers and toes, the aches and pains, the itch of a scalp in need of a good scrubbing. The problems she's tucked away for later. Her body. Her self.

She comes to her feet and glances up at Her. She feels even smaller in Her presence, now that she understands what she's built. How she seems to exist everywhere at once. And what of Syrah now? Does what just happened make her the new Keeper of the Canopy?

Not yet.

The answer comes immediately. Only, Syrah doesn't know if the thought is her own or something that's been implanted. Didn't she say a bit of Her would remain?

Voices, not raised, drift in to her from the corridor. Either way, there is work to be done. Syrah lays a palm against Her trunk and then turns away. When she walks through the archway, Dhanil and Yemaya are there, their expressions full of relief.

"Are you the new—"

Syrah silences Dhanil with a shake of her head. Apparently the connection is one of an unknown number of steps. There's one thing she knows is missing and she didn't think to ask. Taron—and, as far as she knows, every Keeper before her—had a weighty, tall staff they learned to wield with the skill of an ancient swordsman. Syrah's got her six-inch pocketknife.

"Artahe awaits," Yemaya tells her.

Syrah's heart leaps. She knows why. Running is out of the question, but a fast walk, nobody would raise an eyebrow at. Her guards fall in line behind her. She goes not to the fungal farm but to the room that Ochai once called his own before he left and joined her brother.

The door is open, and she steps through. Ochai's legs dangle from the side of his bed. Nearly his entire face is buried in the bowl of soup. The aroma is different from the concoction that Artahe gave Syrah and continues to feed her. Also different from the various ones she fed Taron during her recovery. Artahe is a master mycologist. Her friend is seated in the chair, one arm lying on the desk, inches away from a large colander, a long spoon poking out of the top.

Ochai tilts the bowl up and drains it. "Another," he says to Artahe before he stops, swiveling his head so fast he appears momentarily dizzy, and those amber eyes take in Syrah. He passes the bowl to Artahe and stands.

This is no film. This is real life, and things are different. She can't run into his arms like some lovesick Hollywood starlet. She is, or will be, a leader now.

"It was you that negotiated my early release?"

A nod, then: "The coming fire season." Syrah pauses. "The predictions are not good. We will need every hand we can get, especially the leader of the Blaze Brigade."

Syrah feels like she's melting under the intensity of his gaze as he waits for something more, something personal. But she can't give it to him, not yet.

"One more bowl and not another spoonful more," Artahe says, stepping into the tense space between them.

As she makes to leave, Syrah stops her. "No, you stay. Look after him. I have to . . . I have to check in with Shansi and Dhanil about what we discussed."

While both of them stumble over themselves trying to convince her to stay, Syrah just about runs through the door and slams it shut behind her. Dhanil and Yemaya are all sideways glances and raised eyebrows. "Where is Shansi?" she asks. "I have lost track of time."

"On shift." Yemaya tosses a thumb in the direction of Lattice Affairs.

Around every corner, nestled in alcoves, passing by open doorways, the corridors are alive with heightened chatter and the scent of that obnoxious incense. Either through one of her guards or the lattice, the Rhiza know she's connected with The Mother. And they also know that she came back with Ochai in tow. Expressions of wonder trail her. A few bowed heads. She wants to tell them that she isn't Keeper. Not yet, anyway. But she likes it, the deference. Finds herself getting full on it.

The bell tolls for the end of shift just as they make it to the post. Some rootspeakers are still disconnecting from their pods, while others are already at the refreshment station, downing cups of water and tossing back fungi chips. There are a few knowing gazes among them. She greets them and makes her way to Shansi, who is washing his feet at the bowl next to what used to be Romelo's pod.

He looks up at the sound of her approach. "You have another summons from topside," he tells her.

This is the last thing Syrah needs right now. While she stands there contemplating whether to answer, Shansi adds, "Two of those knocks, about five human minutes apart."

Syrah finishes the unspoken thought and curses under her breath before she says, "It's urgent."

Chapter
Twenty-Five

Sequoia National Park
Wuksachi Lodge
April 2043

After Uncle Dane told Syrah her supervisor was looking for her, she called and was reminded that, in no uncertain terms, she is to meet with Dr. Anthony. Why this pawn of the forest service is here to conduct some bogus investigation into an incident covered over by a thin layer of snow and a thicker layer of mud, windswept and animal trampled, is beyond her. He isn't going to find so much as a broken Rhizan fingernail after all that. This whole thing is another headline-grabbing, bureaucratic farce. Another waste of taxpayer money.

She refused his offer to meet at the Gateway restaurant. That is the place she and her uncle favor, their special place. Instead, they agreed to meet tomorrow morning at Wuksachi Lodge. Now is about the most inconvenient time to leave Rhiza, but Dane was insistent. He couldn't cover for one of her extended absences.

The night spent at her home in Three Rivers wasn't bad. The warm shower and coconut-scented bodywash sluiced off what felt like dirt and grime three layers deep. Artahe's concoctions were tasty, but nothing like the chai tea she keeps in her very own cupboard. And the fresh change of clothes from her closet was long overdue.

As she drives through the town, everything is quiet and pristine: the very thing that drew her to this place, aside from wanting to work in the national park. Wuksachi's parking lot is still mostly empty. She pulls her car in among the handful of those brave enough to face the frigid temperatures common at this early hour.

Syrah waves to the two workers behind the service counter. The dining area is a Northern California time capsule. A chair cushion or two may have been replaced and the bleached-out window coverings are long gone, but everything else looks exactly the same as it did when she first began perusing Sequoia's websites years ago.

Her gaze travels over the table and snags on the only person who doesn't look like they're here for a fun-filled vacation. He gives her a small wave, which she doesn't return.

"Dr. Baron Anthony." He actually stands. Without the distraction of the climate denier, Syrah gets a better look at him. He sports the look of a man who wears middle age well, like a piece of fine jewelry.

She takes a seat opposite him.

"Thanks for meeting with me." Dr. Anthony's voice is gravelly, like he guzzles rocks for sport. "Care to order something?"

"I've already eaten," Syrah says at just the moment her stomach growls loud enough for the couple three tables over to hear.

"Chief of Fire Station Ninety-Three to part-time Sequoia park guide. Care to tell me that story?" Dr. Anthony watches her like a hawk. The man doesn't blink enough. His eyes must be dry as the desert.

Syrah crosses her arms and struggles to hide how much of a sore spot that is for her. "I thought I was here to assist you with your investigation into the events of last fall. I'm not interviewing for a job with the forest service."

"Not a fan of small talk," he says.

"Not a fan of you sneaking up on me during my tour either. Why not go through the proper channels?"

"I'd heard about you, you know." Dr. Anthony repositions himself. He, like most humans, can't stand the hard wooden chair. Syrah chuckles inwardly. "I heard about how you revamped that program. Adding in those bits of history. I can't deny, there's an almost reverent passion you exhibit for the Giants and the forest. Those people were hanging on every word. The talk is, you're making a difference. You've taken a job that most would sleepwalk through and turned it into something that matters. I wanted to see for myself."

Syrah is dumbstruck, and just a little angry at herself for appreciating the praise from this figurehead. She's really got to work on her ego. "And I've read about you as well. You've gone from the person who discovered hundreds of new species in Thailand to the one conducting a baseless investigation six months too late. Care to tell me *that* story?"

That self-important expression on the man's face is gone. "No more than you care to tell me yours."

Syrah pulls her comms device out of her pocket and checks the time, an exaggerated movement that she hopes gets her point across. "What can I do for you, Dr. Anthony?"

"You know why I'm here, so I'll move on. One of the campers, the survivor of the triple bear attack, reported hearing another voice out there. He thinks you were conversing with someone else, trying to get them to stop. This was before any of the rescue teams arrived on the scene."

Romelo. So someone did hear her trying to tell her brother to call off the attack. "No," Syrah answers. "He'd just witnessed and survived a bear attack. The man was in shock. There wasn't anybody else out there."

Dr. Anthony slips a leather-bound traveler's notebook from an inside pocket. This time, *he* makes a show of removing the small pen from the loop and jotting down some notes. Syrah has said all of two sentences, but he writes for what feels like a half hour. Finally: "Why were you there? At that campsite, at that time?"

Whoa. Syrah isn't prepared for that one. She hasn't prepared at all, thinking his questions would be more of an accounting of what she saw.

She wishes she had ordered something, even a cup of tea, that would give her time to think. "Honestly, I can't remember," she says. "I spend a lot of time in this park. Walking the trails, you know. I was probably just out for one of my strolls."

"Coincidence, then?" Dr. Anthony says.

"An unfortunate one," Syrah adds.

More scribbling in that notebook before: "When the survivor left to go for help, what did you do in the span of time between then and first responder arrival?"

Dammit. What can she say? That she and a bunch of underground absurdities used the flow, their version of pheromones, to battle for control of the bears? "I did what I was trained to do. I screamed and waved my arms like a maniac. I tried to divert their attention."

"Unfortunately, you didn't succeed."

"I don't think I like your tone, Dr. Anthony."

A hand flies to his chest. "You'll have to forgive me if I don't have time to waste being polite, but three people died out there. Three bears also lost their lives. I'd think that you would be as interested in finding out why as I am."

Syrah leans forward, seething. "I am interested. Or rather, I was. Almost half a year has passed—you're not going to find anything out there or in here by peppering me with these useless questions. The truth is, we'll never know what made those bears act that way."

Dr. Anthony eyeballs Syrah, his left eye twitching. He leans back, smooths his face like a river stone, and drums his fingers on the wooden tabletop. He goes for the notebook again and flips to a page at the front. "You studied botany at UCLA. Top-notch grades, a little over a semester away from graduation, and then you quit. I'm seeing a pattern here, Ms. Carthan."

Syrah just waits. He's trying to rattle her. A timeworn tactic, thinking that she'll get angry enough to say something she'll regret. That Rhizan patience is useful for something.

"While you were at school, I'm assuming you spent at least some time studying trees. So you'd know that under specific circumstances, they can emit pheromones."

Syrah nearly falls out of her chair. Her gaze darts around the lodge, hoping for a rescue, an interruption of some kind. A lifeline that she can grab on to. The bathrooms. She can excuse herself, but to do it now . . . no. "They do. Those pheromones can do things like change the flavor of their leaves to ward off unsuspecting deer from nibbling them," Syrah says and then laughs. "They certainly can't orchestrate a bear attack."

"Thirty years ago, I would have agreed with you," Dr. Anthony says, dead serious. "But I've been studying the effects of climate change on wildlife, and I'm not saying that a tree would be able to do this on purpose, but I have to explore the possibility that some wires, that is, some pheromones, could have changed. That the message could have been misinterpreted."

And you'd be wrong, but oh so right, Syrah thinks. "So you want to get samples and examine them? Hopefully you don't plan to incite another attack."

Dr. Anthony ignores her while he scrawls more notes in his damned notebook. A whole page full.

"How many people are on your team, and how long do you plan to be here?"

"You can check with your superiors for all the details," Dr. Anthony says, standing. "I'll call on you again. Your supervisor has given me permission to call you directly, and when I do, I expect not to have to get your uncle to help track you down."

As Dr. Anthony strolls out of the dining area, Syrah wants nothing more than to give him a quick and thorough demonstration of her Rhizan strength. He's close. Dangerously close, and The Mother will not be happy about that. Nor, if he finds out, will her brother.

Suddenly, Syrah fears for Dr. Anthony, if Romelo should get wind of what he's doing.

Chapter Twenty-Six

Rhiza
The library
April 2043

With an overnight stay and half the day wasted topside, about five hours have passed. Syrah combs through the Keepers' logs, hoping to find something, anything that will help prepare her for what's coming. So far, nothing. Dr. Anthony has shaken her. She's underestimated him. Despite what Uncle Dane said, she doesn't think he could possibly find out anything about what happened.

Pretty underhanded of him to come at her that way during the tour; he had to know she would be off her game. Then the slick bastard circled through her uncle and boss. That his questions focused so much on her was an unexpected eye-opener. All in all, she thinks she handled herself well enough, for what little it might matter. He so quickly homed in on the pheromones—damned impressive.

Still, it's not possible. Unless he's gifted with some powers that no other human being has ever had, there's no way he'll find out about Rhiza or its people.

Unless.

Three times the veil has been lowered for someone from topside to walk through: her triple-great-grandmother, her brother, and now her. The first two because of need. Cathay Williams had been found out, dismissed from service, and cast out when she most needed medical care. She spent her last days here and now rests somewhere in The Mother's realm. Romelo was brought here to save him from the fire that stole their parents.

Syrah was in no immediate danger. In fact, she's pretty sure the only reason she's here is because the markings in her blood were so similar to her brother's that the tree where she shed blood during her run with the fire crew made a mistake.

So only The Mother can decide when the veil is lifted. And the one thing she will not do is put this world and herself in harm's way.

A good theory as far as theories go, but she can't be sure of anything.

It was late when she returned to Rhiza, and though her feet, her legs, wanted to drag her to Ochai's room, she wound up here, in Taron's library, instead. How long, she wonders, until she starts to think of it as her own. There's something The Mother is still waiting for, though. Taron didn't tell her everything. No surprise there. Syrah thought that once she entered the realm, all would be revealed. There's a saying about making assumptions that she hates but should have heeded.

Syrah's senses are different from what they were—that is, when she remembers to concentrate. So this time, she knows that Artahe is approaching before she hears her greet Dhanil and stroll through the entryway. "What happened?" she says as she comes in and takes a seat in front of Taron's—or rather, her—desk.

"Dhanil," Syrah calls. He pokes his head inside. "You'll need to hear this as well."

"I'll get another guard to stand outside." He turns.

"Don't bother," Syrah says. "This will only take a minute."

He looks like he's ready to protest but holds his tongue. He doesn't sit, though, only posts himself just inside.

"His name is Dr. Baron Anthony. He is a wildlife biologist who works for the government. I will cut to the chase."

Raised, quizzical eyebrows. Syrah envisions Taron pursing her lips and shaking her head at her topsider speech patterns.

"What I mean is, I will skip over inconsequential details and tell you the most important part of our conversation. I do not know how large his team is. And I have no idea how long they will be here. He has a theory." Syrah pauses. "A good one. He believes that the trees may have altered their pheromones and that by doing so, they affected and somehow drove the bears and all the animals to start the attack."

Syrah can barely look at them while she speaks. When she finishes the last word, the looks on their faces are enough to send her gaze back into her lap.

"Even if he is on the right trail, it will lead nowhere," Syrah says with surprising confidence.

"You are correct," Dhanil says, coming forward. "But I think it wise that the caretakers limit our movement to the bare minimum for the time that they are here. Our camouflage protects us from sight, but we are still flesh and blood. Physical contact could still make us vulnerable. It has happened before."

"Makes sense," Syrah says and then turns to Artahe. She's unusually quiet.

She glances around the library and shakes her head. "Too much has changed," Artahe says. "So quickly."

"Everything changes," Syrah replies. "Even if you do not want to see it. Even if it makes you uncomfortable."

Artahe narrows her eyes and scoots to the edge of her chair. "You connected with The Mother," she says, glancing around. "Where is your staff?"

Syrah can feel Dhanil watching what has turned into a very tense exchange. "I do not have one, yet. This is not some 'snap your fingers' kind of process."

"Are you as certain as you appear that this topsider poses us no threat other than that outlined by Dhanil?"

Far from it, Syrah thinks. But she casually interlaces her fingers in her lap and lifts her chin anyway. "I am."

That seems to mollify her. "Ochai cannot be trusted." This comes completely out of the blue, and Syrah stiffens. "Do not forget who he allied himself with. There is a reason he was punished."

Syrah is ready to jump back on her soapbox about how he took the blame for what Romelo did. It's all a joke, though; he was with Romelo every step of the way. He isn't innocent of anything except good sense. That doesn't mean that she can change his mind. "What about all this 'forgive and forget' talk? I thought once someone served their time, all was forgiven? Didn't the two of you just tell me that?"

"He did not serve his full sentence," Artahe points out.

Syrah flicks a look at Dhanil. "She is correct," he says.

"We will need to send out a rootcast to all caretakers and to every tree in the forest," Syrah says. "Prepare for the human onslaught. It will be short, and we will make it through; we only need remain vigilant for a short time."

With that, they leave, and Syrah is left to wonder about Ochai and the staff she doesn't have, and what, if anything, will go wrong.

"You are up and about," Syrah says as she strolls into Ochai's room. He's standing in front of his desk, a book open. Her peripheral vision confirms what she already knows: not one book, not so much as a journal, graces the shelves on the walls. He is good at his work and, according to some, a master at other things, but a reader he is not. At least not before his imprisonment. Syrah's thoughts go to Artahe. She is so sure about people. She thinks that who they are is who they will always be. But this, among other things, proves that she is wrong. *See,* she thinks, *things and people can change.*

"Your friend is a master of healing," Ochai says. He grabs the cup sitting near the book and takes a sip before walking over to Syrah and offering it to her.

She drinks and walks past him to set the cup back on the desk. She can't face him. The flutter Syrah feels when she looks at him is pathetic. She has no time for this. Yet. Yet. "On a scale of one to ten, with one being 'I feel like I need to sleep for another week' and ten being 'I am ready to take on the world,' how would you rate how you are feeling?"

She recognizes the book as one from Taron's library. Curious. It's not like that room is locked—there isn't even a door—but people rarely remove a book without asking.

And then he's behind her; she can feel him. Syrah turns.

Ochai stretches his arms out, then curls his fingers into fists and releases them. He steps back and does a few impressive stretches, all the while keeping those eyes of his fixed on her. A small grin at the corners of his mouth. "I would rate myself a twenty."

"Good," Syrah says. "We are going to need you." She goes on to tell him about the predictions for this summer's fire season. How it's already too warm.

"I have not been sitting here just sleeping," Ochai says with an odd bite to his words. "I have been in communication with my team and am well aware. We will be ready."

"I was not implying . . . ," Syrah starts and then stops herself. She is The Keeper, or at least she will be soon. She doesn't have to explain herself to anyone. "So you must also know about Dr. Anthony? The biologist?"

"You know there are few secrets in Rhiza." Ochai moves back over to his bed and sits down. He pats the space beside him. Syrah takes the chair at his desk instead.

"Then you know that we have two things to worry about."

"And a third." Ochai tilts his head and regards her. "You are to become the next Keeper, are you not?"

Syrah nods.

"Your brother lives," Ochai says. "Despite the fact that you nearly killed him."

"I was not aware until recently, but yes, he is alive and still plotting somewhere."

"After what you have just told me about what is going to happen topside, has your mind not changed?" he asks. "Not at all?"

That question gives Syrah permission to step back. "Am I angry at what is being done to the world? Yes, it pisses me off. But if you are asking if I have decided that killing every human being in the state is the answer, then no." She wants to ask him about his allegiance. If, after what happens, he will still follow Romelo, or if he'll be willing to stay here with her and be . . . what? Her concubine?

"You think that I am angry at him?"

Syrah fiddles with her hair. "You took the blame for something he did, and he showed no remorse. I know he can communicate with Her. I did not see *him* trying to get you out of that place." She wants to ask what it was like, but she knows that is not their way. She'll find out, either through those stacks of Keeper journals or by asking at another, more appropriate, time.

"Why did you have The Mother free me?"

"I told you," Syrah says. "The fire season. We will need you."

Ochai grins again and stands. He walks over and takes Syrah's hand, pulling her up and close to him. She cranes her neck to meet his gaze. Everything in her body is firing on all cylinders. He leans in close, his lips brushing her ear. "Is that the only reason?"

His breath curls around her, smelling of the woods and everything fresh. Syrah's heart hammers in her chest. She wants to pull away. With effort, she does. Putting as much distance between them as the small confines of his room will allow.

But Ochai isn't easily dissuaded. He marches up to her. She retreats until her back is against the wall. He places both his hands on the wall beside her, effectively closing her in. He leans down and kisses first one cheek and then the other.

Syrah trembles. She finds her own hands rising and settling onto his chest. She is surprised to find his heart beating as hard as her own. She meets his gaze, drinks in the obsidian beauty of him. Those flecks of amber in his eyes. The intensity of his gaze nearly melts her. When his lips touch hers, she welcomes it. In an odd tangling of angles and other misfortunes of their height distance, the kiss lingers and Syrah loses all sense of the world outside this moment, the two of them.

Syrah has not thought too much about how this will be, even as she pulls her tunic over her head and drops it at her feet. She didn't dare. Reason, probing questions, have a way of ruining things.

Ochai pushes the garment aside with his foot as he comes closer to her. The sweet, smoky smell of him fills her nostrils. "Are you sure?" he asks in his playful voice.

Sure? Syrah can't remember the last time she's felt sure about anything. Except, except, that she cares for this person. Maybe the feeling that stirs so violently within her whenever he is near, whenever she thinks of him . . . some people might call it love.

"I'll tell you after," she says, and Ochai throws back his head, and that waterfall laugh of his pours from his mouth.

There have been other lovers. Not more than a handful, mind you. Syrah has left them littered from one side of the country to the other. The last, in Florida, given time, she might have loved. And she ran from him as fast as her feet could take her. In her quiet times, alone at night, it is him she thinks of most often.

Ochai takes both Syrah's hands and kisses the knuckles, then slides her trousers off. The wall sconces provide just the right amount of light. Not harsh enough to showcase the scar on her thigh, the bits and pieces of her imperfections. He steps back, as if he is ready to put on the grandest of shows. He removes his own clothing, and Syrah is pleased that, yes, Rhiza are very much humanoid.

In two short steps, he lifts her and carries her to the bed. The weight of him is solid, not uncomfortable.

"I have waited for this," he says, and she is lost in his amber eyes.

"So have I," Syrah mutters as he enters her, her body parting around his. Slowly he moves, and she easily finds his rhythm. She wonders idly what topsiders would think of her. Her parents and uncle. Her neighbors, former colleagues. A woman who cannot keep a boyfriend longer than a year, who has fallen headfirst for a traitor from an underground world who can never be part of her own.

And she finds that she doesn't give one rat's ass about what they think. In this moment, all she can see and feel is how much Ochai wants her and how she returns it in kind. A pressure is building, a long-held dam that is about to break loose of its constraints. It starts in her breasts, where his lips and tongue feast. Her hips, and then her middle.

As his movements quicken, the pressure builds. Her release, their release, comes in a series of poetic grunts and moans. A melody of wildflowers.

Ochai plants a final kiss on her lips and wraps his arms around her before he tumbles to the side and wedges himself into the small space closest to the wall.

Syrah's fingers long to touch his chest, run a trail across his broad shoulders. But she is afraid to move. Because doing so might break the spell of how perfect this moment is. She fears that she will wake up, back in her little house by the river, and find that the past year of her life has been the most outrageous of dreams.

Ochai shows her how very real this is. His hands are between her legs, his fingers working her up to a second, powerful, lovely release.

"Are you sure?" he whispers directly into her ear, his face so close to hers.

Syrah's answer is the sweetest, deepest of kisses.

A knock at the door ruins it all.

And the murderous look on Zehra's face when Ochai's former partner enters, without waiting for anyone to invite her in—well, Syrah knows that she has another enemy belowground. One she'll have to contend with.

Her mouth opens. Syrah disentangles herself from Ochai and plasters that stoic mask on her face. The one that she studied from Taron and now is replicating to perfection because Zehra lowers her eyes.

Ochai does nothing but comes to lean against the wall, allowing his glance to travel back and forth between the two women vying for his attention.

"I am leaving," Syrah says, dressing quickly. Love triangles are for cinema and romance novels. Real life is what she has to deal with.

She closes the door behind her without a word.

Chapter
Twenty-Seven

The threat from the topsiders' minion does not scare Romelo from the perspective of his home being discovered. But it does concern him for the Giants. He has heard the rootcast. The biologist and his team will be descending on the forest any day now. Humans who poke around do damage in their own way, mostly through callousness and ignorance. Some through malice. But this will be different. He has already developed a theory about the pheromones, the flow, which means that he might damage the trees while seeking confirmation. Vice will not allow it and wants them to accelerate its plans. First, Romelo must expand his test.

He leaves his quarters and strolls purposefully through the bends and curves of what they have affectionately renamed "Rhiza on High." As is his preference, everything has been cleaned and polished to a high shine. The bioluminescent mushroom sconces are a gift of theft, but they line the walls in bunches that provide the subtle but diligent glow. Stalactites and stalagmites uninhibited in their natural growth. Belowground, they live in harmony with the natural environment; they do not try to bend and break it to their will. Soon, though, after he is successful in righting these wrongs, the state of California will return to what is natural. Desert in the south, verdant green in the north, and whatever wins the battle between them in the middle.

Before he reaches the archway, the sounds of excited activity beckon him forward. His team is already preparing. He has given them this time alone on purpose. Time to gel as a group before he makes his entrance.

He does so with the style befitting someone who will be Keeper, despite Syrah's recent success: *Yes,* the lattice still whispers to him, *she was not granted the staff.* He thinks The Mother reserves that for him alone. First, though, securing their future. He stands just inside the entrance until a hush falls over the room.

He takes in the roots stretching from the pods to the ceiling in a great bunch. The refreshment center to his right, pitchers of waters, shiitake pies, and oyster chips at the ready. The excited, anticipatory expressions on his squad's faces. He meets each of their gazes, a tiny but necessary acknowledgment. A rallying and boosting of the troops.

Romelo straightens his back and thrusts his chest forward. He glides into the room as if floating and gestures for everyone to gather around. "I hope that you are all well rested, because today, as you know, is an important day. One that not if, but when, we are successful will change the course of human and Rhizan history forever."

Woots and claps wrap themselves around Romelo. The warmth of purpose and of support in their unified mission floods through him. Along with no small measure of gratitude. "You all know what we are here to do today, so I have prepared no long speeches. No words of encouragement are needed for those assembled. You have been hand-picked because you are the best at what you do. Let us get started."

A hand goes up. "The stories are all over the place about the top-sider scientist. What are we to do to stop him?"

Always a brave one, Romelo thinks. Someone willing to speak up and ask the difficult questions when others will not. Still, it grates that he is being questioned. "First, not once in a millennium has a human discovered Rhiza on their own. It will never happen. He will conduct his useless tests and be gone before we know it. As to the damage they may inflict while they are here, we will do what we do best and repair. But our test here today will ensure that nobody else will bother us. Now let us begin."

Romelo heads straight to the back and slips into his pod.

Once he is settled inside, feet itching to begin the connection, with a wave of his sure hand, the other rootspeakers take their places.

Romelo begins by working with Vice to erect his protections. What the topsiders used to call a firewall of sorts. Never before has a part of the lattice been masked from the rest. But Romelo reminds himself that he has managed what others, not even full-born Rhiza, could not. Whether by curiosity or acquiescence, The Mother is allowing it. There has been an unmistakable current of anger beneath Her silence.

When the time comes, she will be on the right side of the argument, his side.

Immediately he feels the presence of his crew. Ten of them in total. He tried to recruit Shansi to his cause, but he refused, choosing allegiance to Romelo's ailing adoptive mother instead. He has to admit a certain envy at how loyal the others have been to her. But he also understands. Taron was powerful, fair, and committed, though unwilling to make difficult decisions. For a moment, he allows himself to feel the full weight of her passing and his role in it.

But there is no time for regret or emotion. He must be single-minded in his next, most important task. *Begin.* It is a thought that traverses their portion of the lattice. And the rootspeakers respond. Each reaching out to one of the Giants that Romelo spent long hours into the night selecting. Trees that have, in one way or another, shown anger and resentment toward humans, in particular those trees that have suffered wounds or lost offspring at their clumsy, uncaring hands.

He also feels The Mother. Ever watchful.

Romelo has roots only for his nascent Giant, Vice. He feels his thoughts leap across the connections until he finds the tree. It answers his call with a childlike inquisitiveness that Romelo finds interesting. It communicates its needs: more sunlight and an annoyance with the nearby Giants for blocking so much of it with their full canopies. A question about why it is so warm already, concerns about the lack of snowpack and if it will be thirsty later in the summer. A wonder at why its lower branches are still so flimsy.

Romelo brushes it all aside. He observes the process of how the Giants and the other trees of the forest do their work. The sunlight is blocked by cloud cover, but the trees soak up what is there and begin the process of photosynthesis, taking in that light and transforming it into energy. Taking what nutrients they need and then sending them out through the lattice to share with the greedy fungi in a process of sharing that is as old as time. The mutual gratification communicated among them is that of the strongest brother- and sisterhood.

And then there is his goal. The air. Through Vice, he can almost feel the carbon dioxide enter through its bristling canopy. How it travels through the branches and trunk, down to the roots, where it is stored in the ground. How, in turn, Vice and the others pump cleaned oxygen back into the environment. The humans come and gawk in feigned awe, and they defile, but they do not have sense enough to appreciate it.

They will, though.

The lattice does not need words, and the communication is so much more visceral, so real. Thoughts are felt immediately in the mind and body. So when Romelo focuses on that intake of the poisonous carbon, gives the signal to his crew, Vice utters the command: *Stop.*

Ten trees participate in their test. The first three acquiesce before they hit a snag. Two of the trees are stuck in their cycles of pondering. Usually trees are not quick to actions that are different from those they have done by rote. In that way, they remind him of Taron. While the assigned rootspeakers attend to those two, Romelo counts off the next four acceptances. And then the last, General Sherman. The biggest and oldest of them all. They will need it more than the rest.

As Romelo is about to plug in to assist, something happens.

Vice. Romelo's tree leapfrogs them all and talks directly to the General.

It communicates its position as The President's offspring. The view, from a child's perspective, of all that is wrong in the forest. The baby Giant sounds surprisingly like Romelo, as if the words were coming from his own mouth. Vice's tone is just shy of whining, but it carries that childlike imperative.

Romelo can feel his and the others' tension growing near to bursting through their connection. Even Her focus is on them. The volley continues between oldest and youngest. Long enough that Romelo begins to feel the strain of maintaining the firewall protections and his connection to Vice.

Sweat plasters his clothes to his body. The tendons on both sides of his neck bulge with the strain. But Romelo resists the urge to interfere. He is fascinated by the exchange. They are all enrapt.

When Romelo is nearly ready to pass out from it all, She steps in. Shoulders just a sliver of the load. Emboldened, Romelo feeds Vice more nutrients, something to boost the baby Giant's voice.

It is as if they are all watching the two of them, Vice and the General. Even The Mother holds Her centuries-old breath. After a long time, longer than Romelo feels he can bear the strain, General Sherman does something unexpected. It says yes.

And the lattice erupts.

Chapter
Twenty-Eight

Rhiza
Syrah's quarters
April 2043

Syrah doesn't need her uncle's secret tree knock to tell her it's time to go back topside. Her manager made it clear, and the annoyingly self-assured Dr. Anthony reinforced it: she is to make herself available at his every whim during this farce of an investigation. Of course, already knowing what he does, maybe Syrah should stop thinking of it that way and take it for what it really is—a threat. Even if only a slight one.

For the five, maybe ten millionth time since her death, Syrah misses Taron. Her counsel was often delivered with a bite that stung, but she can't argue that that advice was more often than not on point.

The Mother? Syrah thought after she'd managed to connect with Her that the nature of their relationship would undergo some huge metamorphosis. But the joke is on Syrah. She still keeps her distance, is too silent. More cryptic than Taron ever was. She isn't fooling Syrah, though. The Mother watches and hears all.

She is changing back into her topside clothes when an insistent bang startles her. "Come in," she says, buttoning the last two buttons on her shirt.

Instead of Dhanil or Artahe, Shansi pokes his head in. "Something happened on the lattice. Something very peculiar."

"And you think I need to see it for myself?" Syrah says, finishing his thought. It is his way to lay out the facts and let you draw from them what you will.

He holds the door open for her, and they quickly make their way not to the largest root center, but to one of the smaller, lesser-used ones. Syrah's dread rises like a geyser. It is Yemaya behind them instead of Dhanil. Apparently, even the great sentry needs rest.

Inside, she posts Yemaya at the entrance and asks her not to let anyone enter. Shansi turns to her and says, "We do not have a retrofitted pod here."

"I am not a rootspeaker," Syrah says. "It does not matter for the one or two times I will need to do this." As she settles into the pod headfirst, unlike the rest of the rootspeakers, she turns to Shansi, who stands there wearing an expression that's a combination of dread and anticipation. "You want to give me a hint of what I am looking for?"

A curt shake of the head. "The best way to make sure I am not imagining things is for you to go in without any preconceived notions." He gestures with his hands after that; he wants her to hurry. But that will depend on the roots. She ignores the pinches and digs of a space that is meant for someone taller and oriented with their feet at the bottom, focusing instead on the task at hand.

It's easy now to call on her fungi. Almost as if in anticipation, before she hits the lever to open the panel, they stir, then spring from her skin. As has become her custom, Syrah inserts her hands into the earth, mostly because she likes the warm feel of it, but also because she's found that her touch helps coax the root filaments from their slumber.

Once she's settled into as comfortable a position as she can manage and has regulated her breathing to something lower than panic, the first filament strokes her fingertips. From the very first time to now, the awe is there. Amazed that something as grand as the lattice exists—an entire world that some scientists have theorized, been celebrated for, and, in a backstabbing reversal, been promptly ridiculed for by the same people who supported them. It's nothing short of amazing.

From the first contact, she feels history unveiled. And then more, what feels like hundreds of them, follow. All caressing her hands, wrists, and forearms. Her fungi begin to flutter. When they and the filaments converge, a quiver erupts along Syrah's body.

Instead of the skull-splitting pain she experienced the first time, she is now able to handle the deluge. Practice and perhaps The Mother, these things have taught her well. She sorts through the information about what's going on in the world, which flora and fauna are ailing or upset. She lets her mind and thoughts wander along the lattice, looking for anything out of place.

At first, it appears like a closed door that, with age, sags in its frame. Instead of kicking that door open, she forces herself through the crevices, around the edges, where something like light emits. She knows it's him. Until now, Romelo has successfully hidden himself from their view. Either he's getting sloppy or someone wants her to see, and see she does.

And what she observes horrifies her. For only a few minutes, certain trees simply stop taking in carbon and converting it to oxygen. Not enough for anyone to suffer any real harm, but she knows it is a test. A successful one.

The trees turn away from her gaze as if in shame. Back to doing their work now, of course. All project quivering leaves and communicate absolution to her. They waver, though. Wondering if she is the new Keeper or if . . . Romelo.

All the trees do this except one. She senses it's a newer tree, not one she's noticed before. She is inching closer, opening more gates, sliding through other gaps and fissures. The closer she gets, the more she is convinced that there is something odd, something even sinister, about this tree doing its absolute best to remain quiet.

Just as Syrah slips through another opening, about to find this Giant, a feeling like an old eighteen-wheeler slams into her, almost throwing her sideways off a trail. Syrah gasps in shock. The filaments retreat, and her fungi with them.

When Syrah drags herself from the pod, Shansi is standing there wearing a look on his face that matches the way she feels.

"It is true, is it not?" he asks, wringing his hands.

Syrah gulps around the splitting headache and the almost unspeakable truth of it. "My brother wants the trees to stop cleaning the air. He is going to try to poison every single oxygen-breathing creature topside."

Chapter Twenty-Nine

Rhiza
The library
April 2043

"You have to go," Artahe says.

She and Dhanil are with Syrah in the library. News of Romelo's plan has spread like the worst forest fire, with fear and disbelief acting as accelerants. Syrah tried to get ahead of it by sending out a rootcast that she's aware of the threat and is working right now to thwart it. Some were assuaged.

Too many were not.

Syrah has no time for this. She's supposed to be topside, checking in, but she's here dealing with her brother's latest, admittedly impressive, scheme, and the worried expressions of the people she's supposed to be leading.

Would a Keeper of the Canopy really be able to split time between two worlds? It's becoming increasingly clear that the answer is no. Taron's middle name should have been Right Again.

"And I also should stay," Syrah counters.

"When this biologist finishes his work, you must make a choice," Dhanil, ever pragmatic, states. She hates his tone. Condescension dripping from words that sound almost like a command.

The old anger for him stirs. "I guess you would handle things differently." Syrah turns on him. "Perhaps you want to toss yourself into the mix, huh? Feel like you should be the next Keeper? It's not like you didn't physically attack and try to usurp the last one. Somebody you served for a hundred years, no less."

Dhanil and Artahe exchange a glance. Syrah can see that Dhanil is struggling to keep his mouth shut for once. She shouldn't have lashed out at him, in her loose topsider style of speech at that. He's been nothing but loyal ever since his release. But he still has a long way to go to earn her complete trust. But Artahe? She's been her friend, her only real friend, since the beginning. And the way she's crossed her arms tells Syrah she's overstepped.

"I know you are trying to help," Syrah says to Dhanil. "I misspoke. I lashed out at you because I am scared and frustrated."

"There is something else," Dhanil says, and to his credit, he doesn't seem to linger on the slight. "We have spent an inordinate amount of time trying to find your brother. There is someone who knows exactly where he is. I request your permission to ask him and to keep doing so until he supplies an answer."

Artahe's eyes widen, and Syrah guesses she's feeling sorry for her. Syrah knows he's talking about Ochai. She should have asked him herself, a mistake she won't let her complicated feelings allow her to make again. "Permission granted," Syrah says, meeting and holding Dhanil's gaze.

The head of her honor guard positively sprints from the room. Artahe comes up and lays a hand on Syrah's shoulder. "I know that was even more difficult for you than that twitch in the corner of your mouth betrayed."

Syrah's chuckle contains not one ounce of joy. "He will hate me."

"Maybe," Artahe says, looking away. "Or perhaps he understands more about difficult decisions than you think."

"I will look like a coward for going topside while Dhanil comes for him. I had no idea how tough Taron's job was. I mean, Romelo was her son. And with everything he did, she still loved him until the end."

"Love no matter what," Artahe says.

Syrah sighs and gives her friend a quick hug before she leaves to deal with a biologist with a troublesome, inconvenient mission.

Chapter Thirty

At the veil
April 2043

Syrah emerges through the cavernous hole in the nameless Giant. Just before she steps into the tepid light of Sequoia National Park, she stops. She saw Taron do it the first time they met. When she and Dhanil, for all intents and purposes, kidnapped her. The old Keeper stood stock still, rolled her overlarge eyes back into that thick skull of hers, and disappeared somewhere inside herself, or . . . or was she in contact with The Mother, questioning Her decision to allow Syrah beneath the veil?

There was no long trek to the chamber. No waiting for root filaments to decide to facilitate that connection. It simply was. But how?

"Well," Syrah says aloud, "Taron didn't have fungi, now, did she?"

Africana fumosa. Syrah whispers their name, and they answer. She takes a moment to delight in the beauty of them, wondering how, in the beginning, she was frightened, even disgusted, by the enhancements to her body. Uncle Dane always says she makes things too complicated. Not this time. If you want different results, then you have to learn to try different methods.

As much as The Mother might disagree, fungi are the oldest organisms on the earth. There's a massive book in the library, *From Here to Eternity*, with half its pages dedicated to that debate. They not only have roots that connect to the earth, to the lattice, but their spores also travel on the air, taking their thoughts and essence far away from them.

Huh.

If the answer is sitting there, staring you in the face, then it is best to believe it. The key is a matter of thought and intent and air. She simply closes her eyes, releases a few spores coded with a message: *I need to talk to Her.*

You are learning.

Syrah nearly leaps out of her skin at the sound of The Mother's voice in her head. Tears of relief spring to her eyes. She swipes them away with the back of her hand. Talking to Her is like conversing with the most cryptic of riddlers on the planet. She has to choose her words carefully.

"We both have a choice to make," Syrah says. "I must choose between two worlds, and you must choose between your two human children."

A mother loves all her children equally, but she likes or dislikes them as individuals.

Romelo and Syrah didn't have a chance to develop any kind of rivalry as kids. The fire robbed them of a childhood full of angst. But the sibling competition has simply waited for them, now, hasn't it? "What do you wish for most?"

That my children not just live, but that they and all the native creatures of the forest thrive. None will outlive me, but my wish is that they have the long lives that are their birthright.

Native. Syrah catches the hidden meaning.

"We already have one team, likely combing the park as we speak. If my brother succeeds, if you help him or refuse to help me stop him, more will come. They may never discover Rhiza, but that does not mean they won't destroy everything else you hold dear in their search for answers. Humans need a culprit. If the air kills every single human being in this state, an army of them will come. They will get masks, they will get other equipment. They absolutely will burn down everything in their path, looking for a needle. It is their . . . our way."

With Syrah's eyes closed, she can almost see Her frown. An ostentatious one, just because she can. It lasts so long that Syrah wonders if she's severed their connection.

If this is what you truly believe, then you will stop him. The undoer, the breaker, and his misguided sapling. If you wish it, you will earn the staff and become Keeper. The choice and the route are yours to discover.

And then Syrah feels the break, something like the flick of a light switch that tells her The Mother has said all that she intends to. What else does she want? Syrah has connected in the chamber, and she now knows how to do so from the forest. What else does she need to do?

Something she'll worry about after she goes to check in with her family, and Dr. Anthony.

Chapter Thirty-One

Sequoia National Park
April 2043

As soon as Syrah emerges from beneath the veil, she senses something amiss. It's in the sound and feel of the forest. An announcement of sorts, a disturbance to the natural order. Or what little remains of it, anyway. She doesn't have to check anything else to know what, to know who, it is. They've come. Dr. Anthony and his investigative swarm.

She gauges the position of the sun, the coppery traces of morning giving way to clear blue. Small puddles of light litter the forest floor. Early, probably somewhere between eight and ten.

Where would they be? Syrah takes off at a trot as soon as the answer comes to her. He would start at the scene of the crime. The campground where everything started.

She encounters a few hikers along the way, ignoring their bright, untroubled waves and greetings. They have no idea. From behind her a voice shouts, "Screw you, too, lady! People are so rude."

Her footfalls catch the vibrations of too many feet concentrated in one area. Syrah increases her pace. The gurgle and whoosh of the Kaweah River guide her. Before long, she can hear the murmur of their voices, the clicks and clinks of equipment and monitors. She slows, preferring instead to appear to approach at her leisure.

Syrah pauses to straighten her clothes and wipe the sweat from her brow. Late April is a pendulum that wildly swings from spring to summer in the span of a week. She walks into a campground clearing that has been converted into a makeshift operations center. The tables have been pulled together and are covered with metal boxes and equipment. Luckily, the team members aren't dim enough to have food out. A tent has been set up in a corner. They've even managed to install an abomination, a porta potty. Syrah's blood boils. She counts eight team members. Dr. Anthony is giving his troops their assignments.

"Remember, we're working in small sections, no more than a half-mile radius for day one," he explains. "Collect your samples: bear scat, soil, and understory. We're partnering with NPS on the blood samples."

"You mentioned looking for anything out of the ordinary," a member of his team says, a woman of medium height and build. Young, with jet-black hair in a long ponytail down her back and a cap pulled low over her forehead. "I know you said you didn't want to give too much detail, but care to provide any specifics?"

Dr. Anthony is about to answer when he spots Syrah. He doesn't wave or say hello, nothing like that. But in his gaze is a bit of curiosity. "Between us, we have over a hundred years' experience in every national park in the country. Use that knowledge. That's all you need to tell you if something looks out of place."

Syrah can't argue with those instructions. The good thing is, they'll find absolutely nothing.

Dr. Anthony consults his watch. "Let's get started. We'll meet back here in two hours."

With that, the team fans out, and Syrah marches up to him. "I see you're on your way," she says, stating the obvious.

"Perceptive," the doctor shoots back. "What? No tours today? I could put you to work taking some tree ring measurements."

"I'll pass," Syrah says, knowing she walked right into that one. "I just came to see if you needed anything."

Dr. Anthony fiddles with a vial and tucks it into a loop at his belt. "No, you came because you have to. I can respect that."

He tugs on a fairly hefty backpack, then turns, and soon his long strides have him lost amid the trees and foliage. Syrah is determined to wait: not because she expects one of them to rush back with the discovery of the century but because she'd like to gloat when they return empty-handed. She's halfway into a seated position at one of the benches when her senses begin to prickle.

She abandons the bench and does a three-sixty, scanning the dense foliage surrounding the campsite. Vague noises, people, animals—nothing out of the ordinary at first. Syrah turns to her right, tilts her head, and listens. They move like wraiths, invisible to all but her. Canopy keepers, stealthy as the scarcely seen gray fox.

Syrah's blood goes cold. It's Romelo. She follows her senses and steps into the forest.

Dr. Anthony isn't as clumsy as your average park goer, but she can follow his trail nonetheless. She slinks between the trees, taking refuge behind overgrown chaparral shrubs. Despite the fact that she's no longer a firefighter, she can't help but wince at the state of the understory. Prescribed burns were put on indefinite hold after her catastrophe, but don't the brass understand that by doing nothing, they are all but guaranteeing a dangerous fire season?

Dr. Anthony's icy cry draws her forward at a run. Her fungi erupt along her arms and strain against the long-sleeved shirt covering them. Syrah gasps as he comes into view. She can hear footsteps converging. He is on the ground, and a contraption that has no place in the park is biting into the tender place above his ankle. An animal trap.

She scans the area, and though he's camouflaged, her brother is still human and isn't as good as the rest of the caretakers. He even drops it for a flash, just to shoot daggers at her with his eyes. "Idiot," Syrah mouths.

"Do you have a radio?" she asks.

Through gritted teeth, Dr. Anthony reaches for the radio at his right hip. Syrah snatches it. "Anybody there?" she screams into the radio. "We're going to need medical help out here. Dr. Anthony has stepped into an animal trap."

"A what?" Syrah recognizes Uncle Dane's voice. "Syrah, is that you?"

"Yeah," she says. Her eyes lock on the trap, the places where it pokes through the pants leg, the blood soaking and spreading. "Look, he's gonna need help."

"It's a scratch," Dr. Anthony says, pulling himself into a seated position, legs splayed out in front of him, hands on either side, supporting himself.

As Syrah explains where they are, her uncle tells them both that help is on the way.

"Every once in a while, this happens," Syrah says to Dr. Anthony after she ends the call. "Who knows the reason, but some people think this kind of thing is funny, or maybe they really want to hurt someone." While people leave trash, damage the trees and roots, the truth is, this kind of thing never happens.

"Coincidence that it happens now," Dr. Anthony mutters. He's gone white as a sheet of paper. And he's breathing hard, his lips thin. He falls backward, flat on his back, his eyes seeming to struggle to focus.

"You with me?" Syrah implores. "Stay awake now." And then she does something she'll later regret. She grabs the doctor's backpack and rummages around inside until she finds what she's looking for. A pair of sturdy work gloves. She slips them on and, without thinking, props Dr. Anthony's foot onto her lap, then takes the trap and rips it open.

Dr. Anthony is strong enough to pull his leg forward, away from the sharp teeth. Once his foot has cleared, Syrah drops the trap. It's then that she looks down at her own hands in mock surprise. The same surprise that's painted across the doctor's face. She knows she has more than enough strength to destroy the trap at will, but she has a part to play. "It was a piece of junk," she lies. Pokes and prods at his leg. "See, you're right, barely a few scratches."

A couple members of his team appear then, a man she'd barely taken notice of and the woman with the long ponytail. Their expressions are wide eyed and dripping with horror. "What happened?" Their words tumble out over each other as they drop to their knees, examining the wound.

"A bear trap," Syrah says, inserting herself. "A flimsy one."

Dr. Anthony is watching her with that look again. The same questioning stare. She paints a placid expression on her face, purposely letting her folded arms fall to her sides.

"We're going to need to call everyone in," Dr. Anthony says. "And tell them to watch their steps—who knows if there are more of these things out there?"

Syrah knows that her brother's act was intentional. He went after exactly who he wanted. There won't be any other traps. With the radio still beside her foot where she dropped it, she picks it up. "I'll call—"

"I'll call them back," the woman says.

Syrah raises an eyebrow at the hostility directed toward her. "Fine. I'll comb the area to make sure there aren't any more out there. Help's on the way."

Almost as soon as she says the words, the sound of sirens is pushing through the trees and landing at their feet.

Instead of the fire crew, it's an ambulance this time. They descend on Dr. Anthony like angels of mercy. As they try to explain where they'll take him, he interrupts: "Patch it up as best you can, and I'll stop by the hospital later. We've got work to finish."

With his crew's help, he's loaded onto a gurney and rushed off for whatever treatment one can administer to such puncture wounds. "Wait," she hears him call out. "Carthan . . . thank you."

She nods once before he's taken away. She'll do a sweep of the area, but more than any additional traps, she needs to find Romelo Thorn Williams.

Chapter
Thirty-Two

Rhiza
April 2043

"She has a small honor guard," Romelo explains. He and a hand-selected band of his followers are near the entrance to Rhiza proper. They have snaked through the Crystal Cave to the edge of what he thinks will be an easy takeover. "Aside from that, my sources tell me that without a true Keeper named, faith wavers. Now is the time to strike." What he does not add is that Vice suggested Romelo move now, preempting The Mother, lest she decide to pick Syrah instead of him. He also will not mention his apprehension, still so foreign to him.

"Her deference to the humans will keep her topside. She is probably helping the biologist lick his wounds as we speak. With luck, they will take her in for questioning. It will be enough."

"This is your time," Ezanna says, beaming. Murmurs of agreement follow.

With that, Romelo leads them through the first corridor. The caretakers who are there, some sitting in an alcove, others flittering through the pathway, all stop to stare. He holds up a fist for his team to come to a halt, and he separates himself from them. He doesn't say a word, just watches them, each of them, intently. The message, the challenge, is clear: *If one of you is willing to step forward, do so now, or stay out of my way until this is over.*

"No more Rhiza-on-Rhiza bloodshed." The speaker is someone whom Romelo has noticed a time or two, one of Artahe's mycologists. He moves to within inches of his opponent's chest.

"It brings me no pleasure to raise a hand against our own. But in service to our mission, I am willing to compromise myself. If you stand down, if everyone stands down, then . . ." Romelo stops, shrugs. "The outcome is not up to me."

When Romelo pushes past the challenger, intentionally bumping his arm, he remains silent. Like a band of travelers entering a station, he and his followers wade through the corridors. His intent is to get to Her. He knows the only way to truly become Keeper is by physically entering Her realm and undergoing whatever rites she imposes. That much he has read in the Keepers' logs he stole. The details of those rites, intentionally left out.

They pass more people. Hostility, fear, and is that hope he reads? It is there in the slump of a shoulder, the rise and fall of a chest, the narrowing of observant eyes.

Romelo's ego swells. Nobody dares challenge him. Not yet. With luck, he can—

"Turn right back around and slither beneath the rock from which you have emerged," Yemaya says.

She appears taller than Romelo remembers. And a layer of muscle has filled out her frame nicely. Sizing her up in a blink, he does not see outward evidence of the beating Ezanna gave her. He has heard that she has been elevated to an honor guard position. Perhaps now is the time to see if that promotion was well earned. "I give you just this one opportunity to step aside before we crush you. Do you really want to be a martyr?"

In response, Yemaya delivers a swift, torpedo of a kick to Romelo's gut. He stumbles backward into the arms of his crew. His middle feels like it has created a new space where her foot now lives, but he swallows the pain and waves everyone off.

His glance at Yemaya is a casual one. But in it, he has made a quick assessment. She kicked out with her left foot, her strongest. Her wide-legged stance is solid, even. Her hands, though, are balled up into impressive fists at her sides. She is taller than him by a foot. Decision made, Romelo sprints forward and feints to his right, her left, and her strength.

But he stops on a dime, waits for her fist to start arcing toward him before he ducks to the side, jumps up, and delivers a devastating elbow to the underside of Yemaya's chin. He lands and spins behind her, just as another caretaker stumbles upon them. He turns and runs off in the other direction, likely to rally the troops. Yemaya is left dazed on the ground.

"Go after him," Romelo shouts, and two of his team pursue the caretaker. Sounds of overtaking and beating follow.

Romelo leaves Yemaya to be finished off by a couple of others and gestures for the rest to follow him. Time is not on his side. All he has to do is make it to The Mother. Nobody will dare touch him once he has connected with Her. He does not want to appear hurried—such is not the look of a strong leader—but he picks up his pace nonetheless.

As Romelo passes the outcropping of stalagmites and stalactites, he senses his destination and his goal, firmly within reach. That is, until a sharp, pungent smell announces his next opponent: aside from Syrah, the one whom Romelo most hopes to avoid. All seven-plus feet of Dhanil block the entrance to Her chamber. Romelo's source was correct: he has been added to the honor guard.

Dhanil steps forward. "You will enter only in the unlikely event of my death."

Ezanna surprises Romelo when he shoulders his way forward. "For many years, I have dreamed of this moment. I will be happy to oblige."

Romelo loves Ezanna, as much as it is possible for him to love anyone. Perhaps as much as he once loved his sister. But he makes no mistake: he will sacrifice anyone in pursuit of his destiny. Ezanna was once a strong fighter, but age and time spent behind a desk plotting have sapped him of that former glory. Romelo knows what his mentor is doing, though, willing to sacrifice himself for Romelo, for the greater good.

Ezanna and the others begin to backtrack, and Romelo falls in with them. More, a few feet more. And then Ezanna, with surprising swiftness, strikes. Like an NFL tailback, Romelo spots an opening and maneuvers through it.

He turns to watch the fight unfold. Ezanna has shed his robes and produced a weapon from someplace. He is using it to fend Dhanil off, while the rest of his team easily handle the others. Romelo wishes his friend Ochai were with him at that moment.

He turns to make his way to the chamber, buoyed by his luck.

But when he gets there, the path is once again blocked.

"Sister," he says. "We meet again."

Chapter Thirty-Three

Rhiza
The Mother's chamber
April 2043

"You just won't give this up, will you?" Syrah keeps her eyes locked on Romelo's as she slowly ascends the steps. "A bear trap? What if one of the animals had stepped into that thing?"

"I would never allow that to happen, and you know as much," Romelo says. This time he maintains his distance. He will wait to see how committed this ostensible usurper is to stopping him.

"Even if I did let you pass, and that's not going to happen, you will never be Keeper, and you know it. She won't allow it. You aren't fit for the job, too emotional."

"This"—Romelo's chuckle is dry as a harmattan wind—"from a human? One who had Ochai Blaze freed like some lovesick teen? You should have freed the greatest Rhizan soldier you could find because that is what you will need."

"I know what you are planning to do with the air," Syrah says. "Not only will it not work, but you'll potentially kill every other living thing in the state. Have you thought about that?"

"You underestimate me," Romelo says. "You have from the first day you met me. It is that topsider arrogance. The flora and fauna may suffer, temporarily, but they will recover after the humans have gone."

"Died," Syrah corrects him. "After you have killed them all."

Romelo despises her. She has just arrived, and he has spent nearly his entire life here. Her hubris will be her undoing. He need only string her along. Still, a part of him hates Dane for finding her and not him. Why was she adopted and raised in a happy family?

And no matter what Ezanna says, her besting him has diminished him in their eyes. It is only with Vice that he has regained some level of status. "If you care for them, for the people who raised you, then you will tell them to leave the state now. I am willing to give you time to do that."

Her eyebrows climb nearly to her hairline. And for a few blessed moments, she keeps her mouth shut. Romelo relaxes his stance, gives her space and time. The war she fights is played out in a pattern of expressions ranging from hope to guilt to conflict.

"There's your answer?" Syrah moves toward him, then catches herself. "Send another one of your messages. Tell them all to leave. At least give them a chance."

Romelo scoffs. "To do what? Dismiss me like some zealot, as they did last time?"

Though she does not move an inch, Romelo can feel the distance between them spreading again. Syrah is a hypocrite. She does a good job of appearing as the topsider champion, but last year, when she was pushed, she had only begged to bring three people behind the veil.

"And just like last time, I won't let you do it."

Romelo realizes it then: when his sister flowers, the fungi emit a scent. Faint and sweet. Her arms are covered by shirtsleeves, but he can see their imprint bulging for release, and he smells them.

"Join me," Romelo says, reversing course. "Can you not see it? The Mother brought us together, to this very moment."

Syrah has been bracing herself for a physical attack. He's thrown her off.

"Why don't *you* join *me*?" She drops her arms and takes a few steps closer. "We find another way. A nonviolent way."

Romelo comes closer to her still. "How? Give me one good idea, and I will listen. Come." He reaches out for her. Syrah looks tentative. But it is time to end this. And it is his love that helps him.

"Romelo! They are tearing each other apart out there. You must stop this!" Artahe's voice holds them for a few taut breaths. The sound of her has always had that ability to calm him. He turns to see her running toward them, waving her hands like a madwoman.

It is enough to distract Syrah. He slides behind her and wraps his forearm around her throat. She twists and bends, throws all her weight into trying to fling him off, but his grip holds. He squeezes just a bit more, and it works. She sputters, her spittle on his arm, and when her fingers inevitably come up to try to wedge in a space in which to catch her breath, he has her.

Those fungi of hers are hidden beneath her topsider shirtsleeves, but he reaches his free hand over and gropes for them. They bulge and thrive beneath the fabric.

Romelo chances a look at Artahe and shrinks back at the pure hatred he sees.

He palms a handful of the fungi, crushes and wrenches their flesh, and with a ferocious tug, rips them from Syrah's arm.

All the struggle goes out of her, and she collapses at his feet, howling. A keening sound that slices straight through him. He looks up to find Artahe's eyes wide with horror.

He forces himself to tear his gaze away from her and glances down at his little sister. Her sleeve is soaked through with blood. With a combination of teeth and fingernails, she rips away the crimson-colored fabric.

Romelo gasps along with her.

Veronica G. Henry

Her arm is a ruin. Beautiful fungi tumble into her lap, the flesh beneath the wounds raw, angry. She cradles that arm like an appendage severed.

Romelo chances a look at the entrance to Her chamber, but Syrah's cries have drawn too many.

He whispers an apology, then turns to find himself the target of Artahe's deafening condemnation. As fast as he can, he flees, regret, like an unwelcome friend, mocking him all the way.

190

Chapter Thirty-Four

Rhiza
Syrah's quarters
April 2043

Syrah squeezes her eyes shut when she comes to. Unfathomable memories of what happened assault the darkness beneath her eyelids anyway. She knows she's in her room, in her bed, but that provides little comfort.

She mourns and she hates and she is angry at herself. A trifecta of simultaneously useless wars, and she's losing every one of them. A cry and a growl merge in the back of her throat and spill out of her mouth.

"You are awake," she hears Artahe say. Without opening her eyes, she can feel her friend hovering. And her nostrils inhale the scent of whatever concoction she's mixed up to try to do what Syrah feels can't be undone.

Her eyes fly open then. "Did you do it on purpose?"

Artahe backs away, as if Syrah's words are acid. She blinks. "What are you talking about?"

Syrah struggles to sit up and swings her legs over the side of the bed. "Pretty fucking convenient that you came up and distracted me just when I was getting to him."

Artahe narrows her eyes and blows out a breath. "You are hurt. You are angry. You must not, however, turn that anger on one of the few friends you have. And if you recall, I called out to the man I love and spoke for you. I told *him* to stand down."

Syrah's chest heaves with indignation. She forces herself to look down. Unbidden, her eyes close again. When she finally forces them open, it's like she can't focus, her eyes leaping around at anything and everything to avoid what she feels she'll be unable to handle. She musters a sneer for Artahe, not wholly convinced, and looks down.

Mercifully, her entire forearm has been wrapped loosely in a mossy green bandage. A spot, darker than the green here and there, suggests the remnants of fresh blood. "Will they—" Her voice croaks, and she can't speak another word.

Artahe is silent. When Syrah glances up at her, she's standing there glaring, with her arms folded. "I do not know if they will grow back. Do not disturb the wrapping. There is a poultice beneath that needs to go undisturbed for a time. Drink that." She jabs a forefinger in the direction of the small table beside Syrah's bed. "All of it."

With that, Artahe storms out of the room. And Syrah wants to throw something at her back. But she jumps down from her bed, a little unsteady on her feet. She looks at her arm and resists the urge to tear off the wrapping and face the reality of the damage. The pain, the shock, the fear. These things she recalls with the ease of a learned child reciting the alphabet.

All she's got is a dogged hope that the fungi there can grow back. She downs the dregs of her cup and the entire pitcher of the soup or drink or whatever it is. And, like always, it starts to work immediately. The lingering vestiges of pain are still there but have less bite. Like a fine crack through thin ice, a numbness spreads through her.

Why is it that you reserve your worst for the people closest to you? Syrah knows she was mean to Artahe. It was unfair to judge her. She'll apologize.

A rap of knuckles at the door, and Syrah rushes to open it. "Look, Artahe—"

But it is Ochai. She steps aside, and he moves inside as if propelled by an angel's wings and closes the door behind himself. "Romelo went too far."

"How kind of you to notice now." Syrah has a new target for her anger. "He went too far siccing bears and dogs and cats against people, but guess you didn't see it that way then."

Ochai shakes his head, and a few loose locs fall over his right shoulder. "You may not like the methods, but the mission is one I have not been able to bring myself to disagree with. But for what Romelo did to you, he must be brought before The Mother. I will not take the blame for this one."

He moves then to take Syrah into his arms, and too eagerly, she lets him. Resting her head against him is like the greatest comfort known to humankind. Tears? She has no time for them. But a dry, heaving sob . . . that she gives in to for precious, blissful minutes before she pulls back. "You must," she says. "You will take Dhanil and the honor guard to wherever Romelo is hiding."

Ochai thins his impressive lips, hesitates long enough to piss Syrah off again.

"What happened to having him pay?" she says. "For the love of God, both you and Artahe are enchanted by him."

"It is you that enchants me," he says. When he tries to kiss her, she pulls away and feels the loss deeply. She opens the door. "I will do as you ask," he adds.

With Dhanil off to find and capture her brother, Syrah makes a beeline for The Mother. If Syrah is to deal with him once and for all, she must claim her role as Keeper. She's determined not to leave the realm without the staff marking her new place as the head of the canopy keepers.

I wish I killed him the first time. She isn't proud of the thought. What would their birth parents think? What would her adoptive parents or uncle think of the kind of person who would contemplate such a thing?

For the first time since her early days here, wary looks trail her. The alcoves are empty, the halls absent of their normal buzz. She knows the source of the upset. Rhiza needs a leader and now, before their society collapses.

Unbidden, an image of Taron's disapproving face crowds Syrah's mind. She tells that image emphatically, *I will not let you down.* Taron didn't die and leave her—and, if she is truthful, Inkoza—prepared to take over for nothing.

"Why didn't you go with Dhanil?" Syrah asks Yemaya. The Rhizan woman is a fierce fighter, the only one who rivals Dhanil in skill. Someone who will prove useful if things get ugly.

"Dhanil was not comfortable leaving you vulnerable," she says.

Syrah is once again surprised at the turn of events. How he has become her fiercest defender, a leader even. She hopes inwardly that he is successful in subduing her brother and that he comes back in one piece. She wants to see Romelo conscripted for the rest of his life.

Once they are at the entrance to the chamber, Syrah turns to what in Rhiza amounts to a small army. "Forget the rules," she says. "Everything has changed, whether we like it or not. If something happens, if Dhanil . . ." She stops, clears her throat at the words that are near impossible to say. "If they are not successful and there is an attack here, you must enter the chamber and rouse me. If Dhanil returns with Romelo, have Shansi send out a rootcast to have everyone gather here for the ritual. I will waste no time sending him to his prison."

The group exchange nervous glances. She silences the protests with a sharp look. She clasps a hand on Yemaya's shoulder. "You have your orders."

Syrah leaves them and says a silent prayer that when she comes back from The Mother's realm, she will find her home in one piece. She descends the steep stairs. When she's finally at the base of the tree, she rolls up her pant legs, cradles her damaged arm across her middle, and lets the other fall freely to her side.

This time the root tendrils find her without haste. The Mother knows that something is amiss. Syrah floats through the in-between place more quickly and finds herself drifting down between the Giant's massive canopies until her feet touch down at the base of General Sherman, not Her.

And there, waiting for her, is her triple-great-grandmother, Cathay Williams.

Chapter Thirty-Five

Rhiza
The Mother's realm
April 2043

It is almost as if she has walked out of that photo that Uncle Dane showed Syrah. Like, as soon as Cathay Williams came to Rhiza, time stopped. But it is that way for all of them, isn't it? Syrah searches her face for clues to her past. Are those her birth father's closely set eyes? Did they have the same broad forehead? The nose? As hard as Syrah tries, she can't find anything they share.

Disappointment must show in her expression, because Cathay purses her lips and says, "You were expecting to find a carbon copy of yourself?"

Yes, that is what she's been searching, hoping for. Syrah wonders if other adopted children feel the same. It isn't that she doesn't love her parents—she does—but one never stops wondering at the history you don't have. The connection of a shared resemblance. She realizes it then: while her ancestor looks nothing like her, the bits of her brother are undeniable.

"Is it a bad thing to want to look like your grandmother?" Syrah says.

Cathay is wearing clothes similar to what men would have worn in the late nineteenth century. Loose wool slacks held up by a thick black belt. The long-sleeved shirt is clean but faded. And like all Rhiza, she is barefoot. "No, but it ain't necessary either. My blood runs through you and it runs through your brother, plain and simple. Hell, shared blood ain't all that makes you family either."

As Syrah thinks back to her parents, she knows those words to be truer than anything. She already likes her grandmother. Syrah isn't the affectionate type; she always squirmed out of her dad's persistent hugs, and that was never something she had to worry about with Mama. So why does she want, more than anything, to touch this woman whom she doesn't know?

Almost in response, Cathay says in her deep voice, "Come on over here, let me get a look at you."

Syrah comes forward and braces herself. Cathay grabs her by both shoulders, clasps them a couple times, then squeezes. "A good, strong woman," she says. Then she closes her eyes and traces her fingers across Syrah's face. Her touch is gentle but insistent. Syrah wonders what she's searching for.

Then she takes Syrah's bandaged arm between her hands. "He's sorry, you know."

"What?" Syrah shouldn't be surprised. If The Mother knows everything, it would stand to reason that Cathay does as well. That Romelo is sorry for what he did matters. But she's still angry. "Not sorrier than I am."

She goes to undo the wrapping. "No," Syrah says, but she's silenced with a look.

Cathay carefully undoes the bandage, and Syrah turns away. "Come on now," Cathay says. "You were a firefighter in this here same park where I worked. You seen worse."

No, Syrah thinks as she finally allows herself to look. *I haven't.* It's raw and patchy. Some of her fungi are there, but they appear limp and haggard. Patches of her skin are white-and-red swirls of unhealed flesh. "How can anything grow back?"

"We are made of tough stuff," Cathay says. "You would be surprised."

"Why didn't you come to me the first time?" Syrah asks.

"You didn't need me then; you needed Her."

"Why'd you come to Rhiza?"

"The question is, Why was I allowed to come to Rhiza?" Cathay begins walking, and Syrah falls in step beside her. "You'll have to ask Her about the why, but for me, I had no place else to go. I was kicked out of the army once they figured out I was born a woman. Didn't matter how well I served. I was sick, couldn't get nobody to care for me. So I came back to the place I love to die. Only, The Mother sent your Taron to get me."

That gives rise to another question. "Are you . . ." Syrah struggles with how to say this politely and then gives up. Hadn't Artahe told her that Rhiza speak their minds plainly? "Are you dead or alive?"

Cathay chuckles. "I'm as dead as it gets. Died March 3, 1893."

"And I started working here 150 years later."

Cathay inclines her head, swoops down, and picks up a piece of tall grass and works it through her fingers. "No coincidences."

"But how do you come here?" Syrah asks.

"Another question for Her. It's a beautiful place, but I don't make a habit of it. The dead exist somewhere else. Don't go asking me any questions about it neither; you'll know when you know."

Syrah takes that in. She has a million questions, but one stands out more than the others. "How are we related?"

"I had a daughter, one of her four sons had seven daughters, most of them sold off or dead. But one survived and had a daughter that became your grandmother. She gave birth to Ellis Williams."

"My birth father," Syrah says. She doesn't add that, as hard as she's tried, she doesn't remember him. That Trenton Carthan is her dad. He raised her and will forever in her eyes hold that title.

Is he with you? Are both my parents with you? Is Taron there? Do Rhiza and humans go to the same place after they die? A million other questions flood Syrah's mind. And she knows she won't be getting any of those answers.

"We're here," Cathay says.

Syrah hadn't even realized where they were going. This whole place is like a loop. The scenery: tall and low grasses, Giants, shrubs, wildflowers, all manner of flora, on repeat. There are no landmarks, at least that she's made out yet, that lead to The Mother. But when she glimpses the massive canopy, leaves and branches stretching outward and reaching up into that cloudless sky, she realizes they have indeed come to the crest of the hill she arrived at earlier.

"Don't worry. I'll be here when you get back," her grandmother says.

Syrah begins the descent, running. She isn't sure how much time slows here, even slower than in Rhiza, but she doesn't have much time to waste. "Everything in Rhiza will hold until you get back," she hears Cathay call after her. And she wonders if it's the truth. For all Syrah knows, her body is lying dead in the chamber already, Romelo having overtaken Dhanil and the guard and slain her while she was here.

But she knows that isn't right.

The Mother is the greatest of them all.

I do not condone what the undoer did.

That provides some level of comfort for Syrah, she has to admit. "I am ready to become the next Keeper. You know it is what Taron wanted, and I have done everything I need to. I have learned how to come here to your realm. I have learned how to contact you while topside. I have learned how to control my fungi. What other test do you have for me? I ask that you grant me the staff, so that I can defeat my brother and restore Rhiza to her glory. To your glory."

Do not presume to tell me what I must do.

"I . . ." Syrah stops, exasperated. "Please tell me how I am lacking in your eyes. I will fix it."

Want versus need. That is what you must decide.

Syrah frowns. "I do not understand."

Exactly.

That feeling of disconnection, like a ship unmoored, descends, and that means she is done speaking for now. If a tree could pout and turn her back, that is what Syrah envisions The Mother doing right now. Like a spoiled child. So much like Taron. Is this what will become of Syrah when she becomes Keeper? Maybe it's infectious.

Syrah is walking up the hill for a long time, and then she isn't.

I hear and see all. Obstinance is not a quality of a true leader.

Syrah finds herself hurtling away from the scene before being deposited somewhere farther away. A touch at her elbow. Her ancestor grinning down at her. "My own mother was so much like her. She spoke a language she called Mende to me when I was little. When they weren't watching and listening. Affection was an invitation for them to send you away, so she couldn't afford to show me any. But love was there in her eyes when she tucked me in at night. It was there when she slipped me an extra bit of rice too. What I'm trying to say is, love don't have to look the way you want it to for it to be there all the same."

Instantly, the frustration and annoyance drain away, leaving Syrah seeing that the only thing standing in her way is herself. She will try again.

"Why did you enlist?" Syrah leaves out the rest of the question.

Cathay lifts her chin, and her stance, and if pride were a picture, her grandmother would be it. "The same reason why you chose to work in national parks. It wasn't just a job; it was one with purpose. In a place that brought me more calm than anywhere. At the time, I didn't fit no place else."

Uncle Dane has told Syrah the story, but hearing it this way, let's just say she is grateful. "Why did you come all the way out west?"

A wash of sadness rearranges Cathay's features. "The only somebody that loved me, accepted me, besides my ma, was my friend Sally. Too sweet and innocent to have been born into what we were. I learned

Mama's lesson too late. We cared for each other, and they found out. So what did they do to hurt me? Sold her off, down Mississippi way. I searched for her after the war, but I never found her. Guess you could say I couldn't stand being there anymore."

Anger wells inside Syrah. Pain, no matter how old, never seems to leave you all the way. She's at a loss for words. But she's also anxious. She needs to get back and is worried about what she'll find.

"Ain't no need to go toting around guilt about everything. You got two things ahead of you. When the time comes, will you be able to face your brother? And will you be able to leave your family"—she stops and points—"in the topside world? That's what you need to settle in your heart before you earn that staff."

"But how am I supposed to stop Romelo without it?"

"Really think about that question, and you'll have your answer."

Seeing with Nascent Eyes
They will Write about me

Disgusting
That human dolt trampling all over my roots
    dares to lay his greasy palm against my trunk
    while he empties himself
of
His too-yellow crud all fouled
with chemicals
with poisonous drink
The stink of it puddles at my roots, splashes my
    trunk
I sift through the muck, extracting what little nu-
    trients I can
An elder nearby is in need of sugars and I slip a

little over, but the rest is mine

I must be strong for my caretaker, and despite
what She says, what they all say, he is mine

With his blood in my heartwood, I am invincible

Oh!

He is ready. It is, as the topsiders say, game time
(am I not clever?)

When I call to the elder Giants, many respond
immediately. They, too, are fed up.

It is those that need convincing that I focus on

I interrupt the flow of nutrients to them, for I
can do so

I am but a child, greediness tolerated

I pass along the message to them, imploring them
with one word

Stop

Do not clean the air for them, for now

Hoard what you need to endure until the worth-
less sacks of water and bluster have been
abolished

Hold the line

I stop taking in the noxious gas, refuse to be their
trash collector

They will know that we, the Giants, and their
caretakers, are wise and good

We are fewer, but still enough

Some of them balk, but now we reach out to the
firs and oaks and other species

They follow our lead, questions nonexistent

I swell with pride. And through the lattice, the
breaker congratulates me

I am growing

Getting stronger

She knows it and it scares Her
But a mother will not harm her children
Next time, though, she must join us and not
    stand idly by
This I decree
For I am Vice

Chapter Thirty-Six

Rhiza
The fungal farm
April 2043

Back in The Mother's chamber, Syrah is struck at how the image of Her here pales in comparison to what Her reality is in the realm. She listens for sounds of unrest as she sprints up toward the archway. Before she leaves, she thinks about the exchange with Cathay Williams. She's amazed that, through this world, she was able to come face-to-face with her. Rhiza is a place of what she believes to be still-untold wonders. Some of which are buried in those bulky texts that she's still only partway through.

Disappointment. That's what she feels when she see Dhanil standing there on guard. "You did not find him?"

He blows out a tired breath. "Yes and no. It was clear that where the undoer and his ilk were holed up was in recent use, but they had fled by the time we arrived."

Syrah curses under her breath. That brother of hers is a slippery one. Still, she's relieved that Ochai took them to him, her doubt about him, and whether he would remain loyal to his friend, silenced for now.

"Keep looking. I have to go topside to deal with the other threat," Syrah says.

On the way, she diverts to the fungal farm, hoping to find Artahe. There's the matter of an apology she owes her. A good leader doesn't own up to her mistakes just in her head.

The fungal farm, like the rest of their space belowground, is absent its usual thrum of activity. She spots Artahe in a corner, bent over a makeshift microscope.

"I lashed out at you because I am frustrated. It was wrong and I am sorry," Syrah says.

A startled Artahe turns from her work and fixes her with an admonishing glare.

"You have to help me out here. I thought Rhiza was different," Syrah says, running a hand over her head. "An apology is supposed to mean something. You are supposed to be so much more tolerant of each other. You put us humans down at every turn for being less evolved than you, but every day that I am here, I find we are much more alike than you probably want to see."

"I beg to differ," Artahe says. "Aside from some physiological similarities, we have little in common with topsiders. Just because we are imperfect at times does not make us them. And though you refuse to admit it, you are now more of us than you are of them. Recognize that."

This is not going the way Syrah wants. She rubs her hands over her face and tries again. "I should not have come at you like that. When you are ready, I hope that you can accept my apology. Until then, I need to go make an appearance topside, see the fallout from . . ." Now is not the time to mention Romelo's name.

"Dr. Anthony," Artahe says. "So far, he has been less of a problem than we thought."

"But the man stepped into a bear trap. Either that will make him turn tail and run or—"

"He will become even more determined. He will let anger drive him to his ruin."

Syrah raises an eyebrow at that "anger" comment, hoping her friend gets the message about her holding on to her own grudge. "They did not find him, you know."

"The Crystal Caves are larger than what your maps have shown you. Places that only we could navigate to. If he has abandoned that place, who knows where he could be. It would take years to track through it all."

"Time we do not have," Syrah says, then notices what's under Artahe's microscope. "What are you working on?"

Artahe's face finally brightens. "You," she says. "Come take a look."

Syrah is afraid, for she doesn't know if she'll like what she sees. What answers it will provide. But Artahe grabs her by the wrist and pulls her over. "This is a sample from your fungi. See what happens when I drop this mixture onto them?"

"Nothing." Syrah looks up.

"Now this." Artahe sprinkles a powdery substance on the slide.

This time when Syrah looks, the fungi begin to quiver. Tiny filaments that, even with her enhanced vision, she couldn't make out without the device. Just a few of them sprout.

There's hope in her gaze when she looks up. And gratitude.

"I do not have a full solution yet, but I will."

"Thank you." Syrah clasps a hand to her mouth. And, before emotion can get the best of her, she leaves.

Syrah pauses just inside the yawning hollow in a Giant, an entrance to purported paradise, an exit to purported turmoil. Neither place is everything that it believes. The light can't penetrate inside, but the air can. And immediately she senses something is wrong. The cloying earth smell of Rhiza still clings to her, and it permeates the hollow. She moves outside, camouflaged in case someone is nearby, and inhales.

It's as thin and light as a new leaf. Easy to miss; most people would. Her lungs have been on an evolutionary path that makes it impossible to not see. Northern California's air is different from that of the south, a little cleaner but always tinged with the hint of ash and smoke. When she visits her parents, it's smog that blots out huge swaths of the skyline.

That smog is the cost of human progress. Planes and fuels and too many cars left idling. The pollution in the park is thicker. Whether a small-scale test or a full-on attack, that means Romelo is dangerously close to trying once again to end everyone.

Does she run back beneath the veil, or does she run forward, warn everybody she can, and risk being taken for a madwoman?

Trust is not a strength of hers. But she has to learn to rely on the very capable people around her or risk losing them, losing herself. Shansi and the others will detect the disturbance. They're probably already investigating. If she's lucky, they'll have mitigation options ready for her to review when she returns.

Mother, she calls to the greatest of Giants.

Only idle mental chatter sounds in her head.

Mother. She tries again, adding as much urgency as one can when speaking into your own mind.

The chatter redoubles. Mama and Dad, Uncle Dane, the fungi that Romelo tore from her arm. Dr. Anthony.

Mother, I get it. This is a test for who succeeds and ascends to Keeper. I only ask that you hold him off. Give me time.

Syrah waits. That feeling you get when you think someone's watching you, but you look up and nobody is there? That's what she senses now. The Mother hears her; there's no need to respond because it's clear. This running back and forth, it's this struggle that she can't continue. There can be no coexistence.

As Syrah hurries off to her car, she realizes that at some point very soon, she's going to have to pick a side.

Chapter
Thirty-Seven

Sequoia National Park
Uncle Dane's cabin
April 2043

Syrah's dashboard, already dried and cracked by an unnatural sun, takes even more abuse as she bashes her comms device against its marred surface. Several times she's tried to call her uncle, and each time, the call hasn't gone through. Combined with everything else she's shouldering, she feels about as taut as a rubber band, its fraying ends threatening to snap with the slightest pressure.

It only serves to heighten her worry, even if she can't pinpoint the source. A gut feeling then. Something is wrong. Outwardly, everything looks like a typical weekend day at Sequoia. Serene, beautiful. A hush that signals all is as it should be in the forest. The lack of snow and the warmer temperatures have brought out a few more visitors than normal, but it's still a trickle compared to what they'll get in the summer. If there is a summer.

On a winding road to the cabin, Syrah spots one of the sleek new cars doled out like a winning hand to the park's security service. Money wasted that could have gone to so many other things. She immediately pumps her brakes, a telltale sign that she's going way too fast, tearing through the narrow, detritus-littered roads at a hair-raising pace.

She edges past the car and glances over her left shoulder, through the driver's side windshield. The park-issued hat, pulled down just above a stern face and disapproving gaze.

She picks up speed again once the trooper is out of sight. And doesn't slow until she's on the long gravel driveway and spots the little green pickup truck. She skids to a stop and gets out of the car, flinging the door open and leaving it that way as she heads up the stairs.

She fumbles for the key that he gave her when she got the post of chief of Fire Station Ninety-Three. She hasn't had to use it before now. She rushes inside and stops dead in her tracks.

Sitting in the spot at the table that she herself usually occupies but hasn't in far too long is Dr. Baron Anthony. They both take her in, Uncle Dane with a surprised expression, the biologist with casual nonchalance. She gives her uncle a questioning look that asks why the hell he has invited their enemy into his home.

"What's wrong?" Uncle Dane stands and comes over to her. He takes her bandaged arm. "What happened to your arm?"

Syrah pulls away, painfully aware of Dr. Anthony's assessing gaze on her. Uncle Dane's cough draws her attention back to him. It hits her then: the air is worse. "It's nothing."

Dane gives her a skeptical raised eyebrow. After another cough, he says, "Fine, come, sit down."

There isn't much space in the cabin, and with the unwelcome addition, it feels even smaller. Her uncle directs her to take his chair while he pulls over a round storage ottoman from the living room. She makes him take the chair instead. Dr. Anthony's leg is covered by long khaki pants. No crutch, no wheelchair. Nothing to indicate he's had anything more than an ant bite.

"How's your leg?" she asks.

"My boots took the brunt of the force," he says, lifting his left pant leg and pointing down to what looks like a new pair of black high-top work boots. "So thankfully nothing broken. A few stitches over at Three Rivers Hospital took care of the rest."

She wouldn't want to admit it to anyone, but part of Syrah was hoping for a broken bone, something to take Dr. Anthony and his team away from here. "That's so good to hear," she says. "I guess you'll be canceling the rest of the investigation, then?"

A smirk. Wishful thinking. "In fact I will, but the reason I'm here is because I trust my science, but I also trust your uncle's nose." He brings his hand up and points at Dane. Then Dr. Anthony wipes at eyes that Syrah realizes now are quite red.

"Something is in the air," Dane says. "And not in the proverbial sense."

"An unprecedented animal feeding frenzy, a bear trap found in the forest that I just so happen to step into. And now, according to our measurements, CO_2 in the area has increased. Fifteen hundred parts per million yesterday—already high, but such are our times. Guess what it is today?" Dr. Anthony's gaze swivels between them both. He isn't suspicious of them, and with a start, Syrah realizes he sees them as confidants. Rich. Allies in whatever is causing all this. *Little does he know,* Syrah thinks. "Just over twenty-one hundred parts per million. It sounds negligible, and to some degree it is, but why such a sudden shift? And in one day? It's unprecedented. And it might explain that cough you have there, Dane."

How to divert him? "Yeah, all of that sounds crazy when you put it together, but I'm not sure I'm following. What do you think is the connection?"

"That's why I'm here," Dr. Anthony says. "Nobody knows this forest more than Dane. And you practically grew up here with him. Together, you've got more insight into what is and isn't normal in this place than anybody. So I'll turn that question back on you both. You've got to have talked about the anomalies, to come up with some kind of explanation. Let's hear it—what do you make of all this?"

Syrah gulps, while her normally steady uncle fidgets with the salt-shaker. "Nothing," Syrah blurts out, and that earns her a foot nudge from Dane. "Actually, let me restate that." She tries to straighten herself on the ottoman, but no matter what, she feels like she's in kindergarten, in one of the kids' chairs. "Nothing about this state—rather, nothing about this country—is right. And it hasn't been since they put gasoline in the first car. You can't put poison in the system and then not expect some unexpected consequences. I mean, it's nearly sixty degrees outside. It's April."

Dane nods thoughtfully.

"So if I were to agree with you that climate can and likely has contributed to the anomalies, what about the bear trap?"

"Well, obviously somebody put it there," Syrah says.

"Someone who didn't want me digging into things."

"Or one of the many people who think that kind of stuff is funny."

"Or"—Dr. Anthony shifts, winces; the leg still hurts then—"wildlife biology kind of confirms what you say. We've seen changes in species to the degree that they look like something else altogether. Things that haven't even been released to the public."

Syrah stiffens and begins to sweat. "But—"

"Hear me out." Dr. Anthony puts up his hands, imploring. "You studied botany, so you know how scientists are. One person's slam dunk is another's 'Let's wait for more testing.' But I'm in the camp that says pheromones are real. What if one of the animal species has evolved to control the others? Control certain aspects of the flora and fauna here in the park? Or elsewhere, for that matter. Remember, this extended down to Three Rivers."

Syrah stands up, then sits back down. The man is close, though he doesn't even know how close or how much danger he's in. If her brother gets even a whiff of his theories, he'll make quick work of him. And maybe, Syrah thinks, she should herself. But she dashes the thought as quickly as she can. God help her, she's turning into Romelo.

"If I were an expert in these things, I'd call your theory a sound one," Dane says.

"I—"

"But there are approximately three hundred animal species, thirteen hundred plant, and another couple hundred insects out there." Dane gestures through the kitchen window. "And to your point, I'd add in another couple thousand insects alone that haven't been categorized. It would take a heck of a lot longer than a week to study each of them and test your theory."

Syrah does a mental fist pump. For a few moments, Dr. Anthony locks eyes with Dane and doesn't say anything. Then he looks down, his lips forming a stressed straight line, and he nods. He turns to Syrah. "Your uncle's reputation precedes him, and every bit of it was right. Wise man."

Syrah reaches out and squeezes her uncle's arm where it lies on the kitchenette table. It's a possessive gesture, and also a prideful one.

"It's only your second day in," Syrah points out. "I guess you'll finish up then, and head back east to reassess your approach?"

Dr. Anthony goes all pensive then. His gaze reaches out beyond the windowpane and takes in the towering green pines, the flock of band-tailed pigeons swooping by. Syrah's stomach clenches. She knows that look for what it is. Awe. Love. For the right kind of person, national parks have that effect on you, and it makes you want to stay.

"There's something special here, despite everything that's gone so wrong," he says, directing his thoughts to them both. "I've asked for an extension. An indefinite one. Maybe they want to get rid of me, but it's been granted. I'll be staying on here to complete my work. And if it's okay with you both, I'd like to take both your blood samples. See if there's something there that can point to any physiological stuff I can track down."

Chapter Thirty-Eight

Sequoia National Park
Uncle Dane's cabin
April 2043

Syrah and Dane stand on his porch, nearly shoulder to shoulder, watching as one of Dr. Anthony's assistants helps him limp into a government-issued truck and take off down the gravel path. They couldn't muster smiles but offered weak waves as he turned to go.

Then they hustle back inside. "I gotta say I'm impressed," Dane says. "He's looking in the wrong direction, but he couldn't be more on the right track." He closes the door and leans back against it.

"He'll never find Rhiza," Syrah says, pacing in front of the love seat. She's suddenly so tired, and she wants nothing more than to grab a blanket from the basket near the door and curl up. When was the last time she slept? "That isn't the problem. It'll never be allowed."

"'Never' is a strong word, don't you think?" Dane points to the sofa. "Sit. You're wearing a path in my rug." He goes over to set the kettle on the stove. Syrah's grateful that he didn't offer Dr. Anthony a cup.

Syrah plops down. "It's the possibility of collisions, though. That's the real threat. They've done a great job of avoiding humans, but it's easy because nobody looks that hard. The canopy keepers *can* camouflage, though."

"As can you," Dane points out, setting two cups and spoons on the table. "And that's exactly why you cannot give that man a blood sample."

"No way," Syrah agrees. "If you give one, I can make excuses until I figure something out."

Dane coughs again, and Syrah's heart leaps into her throat. "My brother is behind this. He's trying to get the Giants to stop cleaning the air."

"That would mean . . ." Dane looks up, wide eyed. Fear that nearly buckles Syrah's knees. "Hasn't he learned anything? Death is still the only way? What happened to him down there?"

"I pushed him from a tree and ran off and left him. Both his parents died in a fire. I had you, and then I got Mama and Daddy. He got taken in by another species and a woman—though, try as she might, she was not what you would call a 'model mother.' He latched on to the only thing he could: a cause. He may be wrong in his methods, but make no mistake, he cares for the Giants and this park just as much as we do." Syrah surprises herself. What she's just poured out sounds suspiciously like she's defending Romelo. And maybe she is. The Mother was right. She's still too conflicted.

"Wow," Dane says. "You told me he was charismatic."

"It's not like I'm on his side." Syrah crosses her arms.

"It's okay if you are," Dane says, dropping tea bags into their cups. "He's your brother. You can want desperately to have him back but also completely disagree with what he's doing. Sometimes you still love, even when you've got no stomach for it."

Syrah thinks about that. How many times has she done the exact opposite of what her parents wanted her to do? They may have argued, tried to change her mind on occasion. But eventually, they accepted all her crazy decisions, even coming here, and she never felt any less love from them because of it. "You are the smartest man I know," she says, getting up and folding herself into her uncle's welcoming, steady arms.

"Then you must not know a lot of people," Dane says before falling into a hacking cough.

Syrah pats him on the back, forces him to sit, and then fills the teacup with water from the kettle. "Drink."

He does, and Syrah chides herself. She's been wasting time she doesn't have. Hoping that Shansi or The Mother or someone other than herself will make this right. "You've got to leave," she says.

Dane is dipping honey into his cup, but he stops and gives her a side-eye. "This sounds so familiar. Unless you're getting in my little pickup out there and coming with me, I'm not going anyplace."

"And Mama and Daddy, hell, everybody—you're all going to have to leave. I . . . ." Syrah struggles to say the next part, afraid that putting it out into the universe will make it so. "I don't know how to stop him. In order to even do this, he has to have a sizable contingent of the Giants on his side. He may have The Mother as well." Syrah remembers how noncommittal she was. How bristly some of the Giants had been toward her as the orchestrator of taking the lattice down last time. She knew they would never allow it again. Nobody in Rhiza would.

"Say your folks and I did leave," Dane says as he stirs and sips. "How would you convince Anthony? Our bosses? The governor? You'd need that kind of support to stage a mass evacuation. That means a bunch of questions you can't answer. Am I right?"

Syrah snatches her own cup up and takes a sip, burning her tongue. "You could still go," she says weakly.

"Leave you here by yourself? And turn tail and run and potentially let the folks down at River View, your neighbors, everyone from north to south, die by the hands of a foe they can't even see? Does that sound anything like the people who raised you?"

A sad, curt jerk of her head. No. "Then what am I supposed to do?" Syrah's thoughts are a minefield. At every turn, every idea she's had on how to reverse this damage has unleashed yet more problems. Once again, she longs for Taron.

Dane massages his temples, a portent or an announcement of a headache. Another symptom. An omen. Her kindhearted uncle points to the chair, and Syrah slumps down, sulking. "You sit right there, and you come up with a way to stop him."

A bud of a plan. A delicate kind of thing that Syrah still isn't sure will take root and become something more substantial comes to her while she sits in her idling car, stewing and worrying. After a back-and-forth argument that had them both shooting daggers at each other, she had at least convinced Dane to go to the hospital, where he could be monitored and given oxygen.

Doubt, however, urged her to trail him from a distance, only turning away when he took the turn that leads to Kaweah Medical Center. She suspects that, by the end of the day, every medical center from here to San Diego will be full of people complaining of the same mysterious symptoms. Even Dr. Anthony. And when he gets there, waving his figures in the air, they'll know the depth of what is going on.

Unless she stops it.

Dropping an anonymous tip to a news outlet crosses her mind. A call that would unleash a panic, no doubt, and maybe get people smarter than her involved in finding a solution. But in this, the veritable witching hour of the information age, anonymity in anything you do is but a fool's mirage. A memory of yesteryear that's no longer guaranteed. Tracked, watched, analyzed. Reduced to a riot of qubits and quantum streams, more data point than flesh and blood. That is what it means to be a citizen of this broken world.

It's right there. So close. Generals Highway will take her straight to the fire station that she used to call home. She can warn them. Maybe *they* can help her.

Of course they can't.

Syrah is as alone as she was that night wandering the forest, when she set her brother on this treacherous path.

Her neighbors, the staff at her favorite cafés, the people she avoids saying hello to at the grocery store. They all matter, deserve a chance to save themselves. Selfish; she knows it is. Love is many things, selfish among them. She snuffs out the feeling because there are two people she must warn. Coded, cryptic, and cruelly blank.

"Hey, sugarplum," her dad says. The lightness in his tone makes Syrah's heart constrict.

"Hi, um . . ." Syrah's breathing is too fast. "Hey." She's decided to try to match his tone. "I was just thinking, I need to get away from here for a while. Clear my head, you know? Remember how you and Mama were always trying to get me to drive down to Mexico for a fun weekend? Let's go, like tomorrow. Just throw some stuff in a bag—don't let Mama try to overthink it and plan every second of the trip. Just start driving, and I'll meet you there."

She waits to see how her lie has landed.

The pause on the other end is long enough for Syrah to know that she can't quite pull off what she was aiming for.

"Is something wrong?"

Syrah lets out a breath that is neither relief nor anger. Resignation. That's what she feels. She wants to say *No, everything is just freaking peachy.* Except he'll see through her, like she's a flimsy piece of rice paper flapping in the wind. And her mother? The woman will hound her, wear her down until Syrah is nothing more than a battered nub. "Yes, something is wrong, and guess what? I can't tell you what. I just want you to get out of California for a while, okay? Can you just do it because I asked?"

"No." Mama barges in like an unleashed hurricane. "We can't do anything just because you asked. Now tell us what's going on, Syrah."

"Look, baby girl . . ." Daddy, forever smoothing things between them. "You got us all worried now."

The truth! It slams into Syrah's mind like a sledgehammer. "I've been working with a wildland biologist, and he's uncovered something unusual. Carbon dioxide levels in the air are increasing."

"The air around Los Angeles has been bad for the last fifty years," Mama says, and she's right. "Smog-free days are the exception."

"But this is different," Syrah says. "Have either of you been coughing? Any dizziness or headaches? What I want to know is, Do you feel off in any way?"

For once, Mama is silent, thinking before she speaks. "Trenton, you did say you were feeling extra tired this morning?" There's an edge of worry in Mama's voice that raises the small hairs on the back of Syrah's neck.

"Daddy, you're just getting over a stroke."

"Six months and a clean bill of health," he counters.

"This is serious," Syrah tries again. "If you don't want to leave, go someplace for a while—at least head to the emergency room and get yourself checked out. Both of you."

"We will." Mama is all business now. "And what about you? Are you heading to one of those medical centers? Maybe you should just head down to Kaweah Medical Center."

"As soon as I get off this call," Syrah says. "I just sent Uncle Dane there, and I'll be right behind him."

"Wait," Daddy says. "That biologist you mentioned, he works for the government, yeah?"

"Yeah," Syrah says, wariness a knot in her stomach.

"So they're going to do some kind of public announcement?" Mama, as usual, sniffs out the trail Daddy's lain and picks up the thread without a hitch.

"Any day now," Syrah says smoothly. "They may even have a solution: this whole thing may go away, dismissed as an anomaly before the day is out."

Syrah can sense the hesitation now, almost hears the words. *Well, maybe we should wait it out.* She's heard the same sentiment in communities across this country with fire practically licking at their doors.

"Call us as soon as you can." Syrah was counting on her mother's refusal to let her father so much as get a paper cut after the stroke, and she's gambled right.

"I will. Love you."

"We love you too."

Chapter Thirty-Nine

Rhiza
Another part of Crystal Cave
April 2043

It has begun. Romelo does not need fancy equipment or pronounce-ments from bloviating experts. The lattice tells him everything he needs to know. And the latest missive confirms the beginning of the end for the topsiders. Already they show signs of the impact. Echoes of their rough, hacking coughs ring out through the air. The staccato rhythm of heightened heartbeats thrums through the soles of their uselessly covered feet. Their stomachs empty in piles of chemical-laden stink.

But the forest, the earth, will heal herself after they have gone. Whether they die where they stand or they flee to the temporary safety of nearby states is of no consequence. The Giants will live. They will thrive. They will repair what is left of Sequoia. Perhaps they will revive the scorched-earth remains of Kings Canyon. The extra carbon dioxide they store along with the nitrogen and phosphorus will help them soar to their previous, stately heights.

Balance will be key, but Romelo, together with Vice, will manage it. His sapling has restored him to his previous self.

And the canopy keepers will experience the greatest renaissance they have ever known. They will take over the prescribed burns that will keep the forest and the Giants healthy, clearing the tinder that is both necessary and dangerous. It is how the Giants propagate, after all. Rhiza's numbers will increase; the population will rebound. They will spread throughout the state.

The country?

It is ambitious, but Romelo is the epitome of a visionary. He imagines himself standing topside, maybe at Moro Rock's peak. Looking out over the vastness of what will be his empire. The air will be clear. Giants will blanket the north, while other species thrive in the areas of the country best suited to their climate.

However necessary it was, Romelo feels a trace of regret over what he did to Syrah. She has no one to blame but herself for forcing his hand. If she is lucky and if he and Vice are forgiving, they may allow her a place behind him. If nothing else, she has earned a home in Rhiza. Romelo might have to detain her for a time. Keep her safe and close until she sees how right he is. How much better everything will become because of his efforts.

He will have a mate in Artahe, no matter what Keepers past thought about the practice. He finds it silly and unproductive. They will have children. The anticipatory sound of their feet padding through the corridors already warms his heart. He will have his own tree in Vice— again, a matter of dispute with Keepers, but that tree is his; there is no doubt. Of course, he will not let others have such attachments. They will not be as clearheaded as him when it comes time to make difficult decisions.

His children will have an aunt in Syrah. And, for however many years the old tyrant has left, Romelo will have a great mentor in Ezanna. He will have a real family again.

"Get your head out of the clouds," Ochai says. A full smile curls the corners of Romelo's lips. Yes, he will also have his best friend. The picture, the inevitability of it all, fills him up in a way he has not allowed for a very long time.

"You found us, old friend," he says. Romelo is so excited to see Ochai that before he can catch himself, he pulls him into an embrace. But he steps back coolly. Poking and prodding at Ochai's arms and chest. "You are well, then?"

Unease clouds his friend's expression. All the horrors he experienced while conscripted are spoken in that look. Romelo knows that Ochai will not be able to tell him about any of those things. This is their way, and another point that he agrees with. It is outlined in his favorite text, *Lives of Imminent Keepers*; mystery is far more detrimental. Imagination more powerful. Sometimes fear is necessary to rule, to keep order. The fact that only those who have experienced conscription know the depths of that horror serves as a powerful deterrent to disobedience—for most people.

"I am even better than before," Ochai says, slipping back into himself. That boyish grin lights up his playful eyes.

"And how is she?" Romelo need not say her name. There is only one "she" who binds them.

Ochai looks away. His chin dips ever so slightly before he lifts it again. "She is struggling. She tries to go topside to deal with matters there, and it divides her attention. She is losing more of the caretakers."

Romelo nods. "Ezanna brought back nearly a dozen more on his last mission alone."

"She and Artahe are fighting," Ochai adds. "I do not know what about."

About me, perhaps? Romelo envisions himself at the center of things. Is there any other way? "It does not bring me joy to see her like this. Especially when there is no point to it. The path has been laid. The Giants are already doing the work. We are succeeding, my friend."

Ochai looks away again.

"Do not worry, she will have a place in our new society," Romelo assures him. "Come."

Romelo leads Ochai through yet another undiscovered part of the Crystal Cave. A place that was once full of canopy keepers during the time when Rhiza was over a half million strong. They will return to their former glory and outpace it without humans to thwart them at every turn.

Sleeping quarters have been cleared out and made functional again. The fungi farm up and running, though not fully operational. He explains that it will be up to standard within one Rhizan month. Even an exercise and training center has been reestablished. He tells Ochai that as the canopy keepers' numbers swell, all these spaces will teem with life.

"This Lattice Affairs station is nearly as well equipped as the others," Romelo says, gesturing to the pods and the station like a proud parent.

"And The Mother has not intervened or tried to stop you in any way?" Ochai turns in a circle, taking it all in.

Romelo puffs up a bit. "She knows that my way is the righteous one. She has not so much backed me as not interfered with me. It is up to me to restore things to the way they should be. And then I will earn the staff."

"Not so fast." Ezanna's baritone is like a cloud, shading the room. "I have thoughts on that matter."

Ezanna's wizened frame is draped in his resplendent robes. Apparently he parried well with Dhanil but then, feeling that win he coveted slipping away, let the rest of Romelo's squad keep Dhanil occupied while he fled. He wears the severe expression and lined forehead of one whose thoughts weigh heavily on his mind. A tenseness to the shoulders, their hard edges softened with age. He is smiling, though. Except it carries the warmth of a winter's trek to the arctic.

"You led that oaf Dhanil right where we needed you to," Ezanna says. "It will take him and his meager group two decades to comb the caves. By then, his only task will be to clean them up and get them ready for other caretakers."

"Can you picture it?" Ochai says. "That colossal relic reduced to an underground scourge suppressor?" Ochai does that thing when he thinks he has said something particularly funny, throwing back his head and cackling.

"Fitting," Romelo says, almost joining in. It is only the second time the three of them have been together since Ochai's release. His mentor and his friend can sometimes be at odds, but this, the time they have when they are on the precipice of victory and can be jovial and light—Romelo looks forward to more of this.

"Not that it was necessary, but the caretakers I sent topside confirm what the lattice has already told us. The humans are already feeling the effects. It will not be long now," Ezanna says.

"What did they report?" Ochai asks.

"Every symptom that we discussed," Romelo says, answering for his mentor. "Soon they will be reminded how important the Giants are to their survival."

"Not that we want them to ever come back," Ezanna adds. "But they will come to understand that they are not the most important species on this earth. And it is a lesson that I am glad to teach them."

"But what will keep them out?" Ochai asks. "They are a dogged group. What if they invent another one of their machines to do the work of the Giants?"

A hush falls. All activity stops. Romelo's face contorts with outrage. "Do you think that I have no foresight? That I would not anticipate this?"

Ochai, to his credit, does not wither beneath Romelo's glare. He gestures to the onlookers, who have now recovered themselves and are back to their duties. "They can worship you. Nod stupidly at everything you say. Tell you all the things you want to hear." He stops and points at Ezanna. "He and I. That is not our job. We must ask the difficult questions. Your ego has nothing to do with it. Be glad of friends who are not afraid to make sure you have covered all the bases."

Romelo raises an admiring eyebrow. Ochai is right. Maybe that conscription did him some good. "You speak the truth," he is surprised to find himself saying. "They will try to fix things. That is their way. But by the time they do, the Giants and Rhiza will be stronger. We will repel their efforts."

"And what of the beasts?" Ezanna asks.

"They can endure for longer than the humans. They will suffer but survive. We may lose some, but in the end, the forest and the flora and fauna, if left alone, will recover and thrive."

Ochai fingers his chin. Ezanna shifts from one foot to the other.

"Come now," Romelo urges them. "What else do you believe I have missed?"

Shrugs.

"Then it is time for you to get back before you are missed," he tells Ochai.

Chapter Forty

She had expected, or rather hoped, that the park would be closed. But three cars are ahead of her, passing by the welcome sign. That means that either Dr. Anthony was unsuccessful in communicating the threat or that, as always, some people have chosen to ignore the warning. She can't worry about them now. If she is right, they will all be okay.

As Syrah steps beneath the veil, she stops to listen. It is a habit of late, borne out of the trouble they now face. She doesn't even bother trying to contact The Mother. The wizened tree has made it clear that she will watch things unfold from the sidelines.

Syrah walks through the passageways leading to Rhiza, nerves taut as a live wire. Dane, her parents? Who knows if they listened. All three of them can be stubborn. She can only hope. And as for Dr. Anthony . . . Syrah stops. She has one more call to make.

She doubles back and returns to her car, holding her device aloft, walking around until she gets a signal. She snatches his card from the car, where she tossed it that first day they met at the lodge. Uses voice commands to dial the number and holds her breath.

"Ms. Carthan," he says. "I'm glad you called."

Syrah isn't, not at all. "Did you have any luck with your leadership?"

"The fact that they allowed me to even lead this investigation was something of a surprise," he says. "Probably gave me the time just to keep me out of their hair for a bit. I told them. They'll do what bureaucrats do, assess. Then they'll meet. Perhaps five or six times. Someone will take minutes, and then, unless the world turns upside down, they'll forget all about it."

This level of honesty isn't something that Syrah was expecting. She isn't ready to call him a friend, but ever since the meeting at Uncle Dane's place, he's felt like less of a foe. "You should consider leaving." Syrah says this not only because she means it but also because it will be one less thing she has to worry about.

"I'm here for the duration," Dr. Anthony says, flatly. "As are you, or so it appears. I have to ask: Is there something you're not telling me?"

"After the conversation we had at my uncle's place, you still have doubts, huh?" Syrah is offended, but not for the reasons he might think.

"I'm a scientist. Hypotheses, theories, these are my marching orders. Inconsistencies, things in the margins, are the things I have to explore. You are at the center of this somehow. What I don't know is whether you know why and are choosing to keep silent, or if you really don't have any idea about your connection."

"You give me too much credit," Syrah says. "I'm a firefighter—well, I used to be. I work as a park guide because I love this place and want to see it survive. If that's all it takes for you to develop some conspiracy, then have at it."

A weighty silence falls into the gaps between their words, the accusations and denials. Syrah lets just a hint of admiration surface for Dr. Anthony. She doesn't know if either of them will survive what's to come, but if he does, he'll never know how close he was to the truth.

"I'm not your enemy; my only job is to find out what happened then, and what's happening now. My team and I aren't leaving. We'll be back at Sequoia today, this time not only taking animal samples but also from the trees. We need to see how much CO_2 they're storing."

"We want the same thing," Syrah says. "But your leg?"

"It's fine. Nothing would keep me from this. Will you be there today? I could use another pair of knowledgeable hands."

"I'll try to make it," Syrah says and then hangs up.

Dr. Anthony annoyed Syrah, but he also reminded her of something very important. She considers another call, but something invisible tugs her back in time. It's so close, minutes away. But Rhiza, Romelo.

The tug again. A little more insistent.

She hops in her car and soon pulls up in front of her old Three Rivers fire station. More confident that a call wouldn't do for the warning she has to deliver. She owes them that much. When was the last time she was here? It feels like two entire lifetimes ago but, in reality, has been less than a year.

And it hurts no less. To have everything you want and to watch it slip through your fingers.

She recalls the thrill of the run, the exercise. The sweet smell of adrenaline-induced sweat filling the cab. The sound of the siren blaring as the fire engine tears through the streets on the way to a call. The bright sear of the heat against her skin and watching the flames beaten back, the camaraderie of standing shoulder to shoulder with a crew on a single mission.

A life that is no longer hers.

And a position that now belongs to her rival turned friend, Lance.

One of the garage doors is up, letting in air more summer than spring. She checks the time and realizes everyone is probably at the morning briefing. So she waits, staring at the doorway to her old life. The intensity of the pull to walk through and resume her place surprises Syrah. It wouldn't be right to go in. She is not an employee of the fire service but a civilian observer. Except for when they called her back that one time.

Knock or wait? An inhale that tells her more of the poisonous greenhouse gas is in the air makes the decision for her. She strides up to the door and is about to knock when it opens. And the crew files out.

There are fewer of them than before. Too few. Alvaro and Lance are the only ones she recognizes. Didn't Alvaro tell her that some had resigned?

"Carthan," Lance says, his smile brighter than she expects.

"Chief," Alvaro says, earning a side-eye from Lance.

Syrah takes an awkward, jerky step forward, torn between wanting to run into their arms and maintaining the distance of a leader. Alvaro saves her. He gives her the one-fist-between-them man-hug. Lance shakes her hand.

"You got something from River View in there for us?" Lance juts his chin at the car behind her.

She wishes this were a social call. "Afraid not," Syrah says, and she takes in the inquisitive expressions on the crew's faces. "Can we talk? Just the three of us?"

Lance and Alvaro exchange a glance, but then they gesture for her to move to the front of the station, near what she realizes is a front door that's cracking and peeling. And the closer she looks, the more signs of disrepair she sees. A gutter dangling precipitously. The building number missing.

"What's going on?" Lance begins as soon as they're out of earshot.

"You're aware that a wildland biologist from the park service has been at Sequoia investigating the animal attack from last summer, right?"

They bob their heads, yes.

"Still don't understand what the man expects to find after all this time. They slash funding to help us repair the station and give it to these fat cats to waste," Alvaro says. He's wearing short sleeves, and Syrah notices that the scars on his arms, the ones that she put there with her carelessness, are smoothing out. She is glad for it.

"Couldn't agree more, but something good did come of it," Syrah says. "Any of the crew been sick?"

Lance perks up. "We have. Headaches, a little dizziness."

"And one of the crew didn't come in today, said she was feeling nauseous," Alvaro adds.

The confirmation doesn't make Syrah feel any better. She has to wrap this up and get back. "It's because carbon dioxide has increased, like nearly doubled in a day's time."

"What?" the men say in unison.

"I'm guessing the brass hasn't exactly told anyone."

"So how do you know?" Lance asks.

Syrah hesitates a moment before, "That scientist I mentioned? From the moment he wormed his way onto one of my tours and every day since, he's been a real pain in my ass. And my manager made it clear that when he says 'jump,' I need to get my track shoes ready. All that said, I guess we have him to thank—he's the one who told me and Dane about the readings."

"They haven't told anybody because people will be hysterical," Alvaro says.

"Exactly," Syrah agrees. "I had to warn you, though. I can't tell you what to do. I won't even suggest you take your families and get out of the state for a while, because I know you won't. But be ready is all I'm saying."

Lance clasps her shoulder. "Appreciate you, Carthan."

"That makes two of us," Alvaro adds.

"I gotta go."

Syrah can't stay to chat or ask after their families. She's already in her car, backing up and speeding down Generals Highway.

Chapter Forty-One

Sequoia National Park
April 2043

While Syrah drives, she does something she rarely does. One hand remains on the steering wheel while the other gropes toward the underused dials of her car's radio. Only a few stations reach them, mostly news, one that churns out a steady stream of eclectic hits from what they call music's heyday—the sixties through the midnineties. Her fingers swipe through a few staticky options before they land on KMJ talk radio out of Fresno.

It's the pitch and tone of the announcer's voice that still her fingers. Beneath that trained air of professionalism rides panic. He's freaked out of his mind.

"Reports from authorities are coming in.

"Residents from Three Rivers and down to Visalia are reporting symptoms from what we've learned are elevated carbon dioxide levels in the area."

Dead air while he pauses for a hacking cough.

"Please stay in your homes and tuned to this station for further developments.

"But now, we have a special guest, one Dr. Baron Anthony. Dr. Anthony, I understand you were the one who first discovered the irregularity. Can you tell our listeners more about that?"

What the hell is Dr. Anthony doing down in Fresno? Syrah beats a hand against the wheel, then catches herself. He's doing exactly what she needs. Getting the word out and giving people a chance in case . . . in case she fails. The man is risking his cushy government job, probably going against everything his bosses have told him. She'd bet her last cent that the bastards are holing up in some building with a state-of-the-art air-purification system, wringing their idle, useless hands.

Dr. Anthony clears his throat, then says, *"I'm here leading a team that was originally looking into the animal attacks that happened in the area last fall."*

"Strange business," the interviewer pipes in.

"Never seen anything like it," Dr. Anthony agrees. *"It was during this investigation that we discovered the elevated CO_2 levels."*

"I've got to ask: Why us? Why are you sitting here telling us this instead of the mayor? The governor? Some state authority?"

"You'd have to ask them," Dr. Anthony says. *There's venom in his voice, thick, deadly snake venom. The Dr. Anthony who first ambushed Syrah during her tour is back.*

"What—"

Syrah turns off the radio. If what is happening didn't seem real before, it does now. People will hear that, and some will panic; others will take refuge at home. Still others . . .

She blinks, gives her head a little shake. Is her mind playing tricks on her, or are the trees leaning closer together? Branches and canopies reaching out, one to another, like small children to a parent's outstretched arms. Coconspirators in Romelo's doomsday plan.

All along Quail Run and Sierra Drive, abandoned cars litter the streets like forgotten crumbs on a kitchen counter. Between the doors swung wide and the dented bumpers, the wounded loom. She hears the echoes of their cries and wet, rattling coughs. Some are running as if from an unseen but deadly assailant. The surge through the press of confused and terrified bodies, the muck of others, bent over at the knees, emptying their stomachs. Some are on the receiving end of forceful back slaps. All those things cause Syrah's breath to form an uncomfortable knot smack in the center of her chest. But what threatens to break her is what she spots next. A cluster of children huddled together, all tears and cries and scrubbing at their terrified eyes. Syrah wars between stopping. But to do what? To comfort them? To stuff as many as she can into the car and haul ass to Kaweah Medical Center?

A couple toting their own toddler makes the decision for her. They run out of the house the kids are in front of, gather them up, and hustle them inside.

Syrah turns away. She carefully maneuvers around the obstacle course made of human and plastic vehicles, small frenzied animals darting into the roadway. Cursing that she's losing precious time by having to slow down. Behind her, she hears the roar of a fire engine siren and knows that her old friends have been called into service.

She wishes she were with them.

A clearing, finally. With a frustrated growl, she gets moving. All the madness around her becomes a disembodied blur as she whizzes by. Romelo cannot be allowed to get away with this.

Mentally, she is imploring people to stay indoors, to not panic. At the same time, her comms device blares with a Three Rivers emergency alert notification. Too late. All of them.

Use air-conditioning or home filtration, the electronic voice warns. These are things that were about as rare as buffalo nickels in the state as recently as a couple decades ago, but soaring temperatures are making them relative fixtures now. She was about twelve years old when her parents gave in and had a mini split installed. How much life has changed for them all.

At least Dr. Anthony has gotten the word out.

Thankfully, nobody is there to stop her as she streaks past the **Welcome to Sequoia National Park** sign. But it doesn't take long for her to come upon a slow-moving line of cars blocking her way. She rides her car horn like a jockey riding a prize horse inches away from the finish line.

A hand from the car window in front of her reaches out and gives her the finger. She rolls down her window and screams something foul.

Then she takes a gamble on the two-way street. She swerves into the left lane and floors it. One, two, three cars and a small RV later, she swerves back and goes way too fast around those dangerous Highway 198 curves.

Finally.

There are too many people at Wuksachi. Cars wedged into every makeshift space like hundreds of blocks of carbon fiber litter, obnoxious and ugly. Would it make sense to go to one of the other campgrounds? No, she'd probably find the same thing there. Syrah screeches to a stop behind a truck parked dangerously close to the trees and just about leaps out of her car.

It makes sense. If there isn't a fire at play, the air here is always cleaner than anywhere else. While others mill around, she moves with purpose and speed. The sight of her raises a few eyebrows. She doesn't care. Whoever sees her in the parking lot catches only a glimpse; she is but an indistinct smudge that blasts past them all, into the forest and beneath the veil.

Mother.

No answer from the ancient, obtuse, thickheaded mother of Giants. Syrah also feels her fungi; they're oddly weak, and when she tries to call on them on her free arm, they don't bloom as fully. It has to be the carbon dioxide.

Syrah tears through the grid of pathways that lead to Rhiza. The air in the caves is blessedly clearer.

Dhanil's pungent aroma hits her, and a moment later, there he is, standing sentinel stiff, waiting for her. "Any change?" she asks him, not bothering to slow down.

"Since I met you, everything has changed," he mutters from beside her. Usually, he's either ahead or behind. A strange thing for Syrah to notice, but she does. In the dim light from the mushroom sconces, she shoots him a look.

He glances down at her, a mask of contrition or maybe exasperation etched into the lines of his face. "If you are asking if Ochai led us to your brother, I am unsurprised that he did not. He took us to the place in the caves where he and his followers were living, but they were no longer there. My patrols continue the search."

And you left them, to come and wait for me. Syrah keeps the thought to herself.

"Have Artahe and Shansi meet us in the library," Syrah instructs him as she turns off to make a quick stop at her room and change. "And Inkoza, bring him too."

As she bounds through Rhiza's normally bustling corridors, Syrah feels as if she's wading through a sludge made of nervous tension. Thick and impassable as a thousand-year-old root. There's an uneasy buzz in the air. They won't be affected physically, not like the topsiders, but it is the Giants that are the source of the concern. If Romelo has convinced them to stop cleaning the air, similar to what she did in taking down the lattice, it is something that has never happened before. So they have no idea what the impact will be.

Word of her return has spread, though. Dozens of pairs of eyes follow her as she walks, a few whispers of their traditional greeting, *Peace be with us.* There is hope in those gazes. And expectation. If she is to lead them, she will have to navigate them through this, the latest crisis. It isn't lost on her that she and her brother are the source of all their problems. She tells Dhanil as much when they get to her library.

"You know what The Keeper would say, do you not?"

Syrah thinks for a moment. "Taron would set her shoulders and say, 'Do not waste another second with your pathetic guilt,'" she replies in a near-perfect imitation of the former Keeper's voice.

"She was right then, and it still holds. I have thoughts on how to stop it without hurting the Giants."

"You still don't like the humans, do you?"

Artahe and Shansi enter then, and Dhanil waits for them to sit before he answers. "I had time to think about this. About my mistake in challenging The Keeper. It was because of hate. And it solved nothing. Liking humans is also irrelevant. I do not think they are aware of how much their actions hurt others, hurt each other. I find that more sad than anything."

Syrah is dumbstruck. Once again, Dhanil has surprised her with his wisdom. "I have an idea. What is older than the Giants? Maybe older than The Mother?" At this she senses what feels like a burr in her mind. This—who was first—is a matter of contention with Her.

Artahe, the mycologist, lifts her chin. "The fungi. It is a matter of debate, of course. They assume somewhere around five hundred million years, but we Rhiza know the reality. The first mushroom varieties date back one billion years."

Even Syrah is awed by that answer. She wonders if she'll eventually develop a relationship with all fungi, similar to what The Mother has with the Giants. One that will tell her the history of how they came to be. "As far as I know, I'm the only human-fungus hybrid that has ever existed." She taps her arms, sans bandages. "They live within me. This is how I will stop my brother once and for all."

"I found something," Shansi says. "You masked it from us, but it seems that the Giant wanted to make itself known."

"It did? Which Giant?" Syrah asks.

"The lattice suggests that it is the offspring of the one the topsiders call The President," Shansi replies.

"Killed by a human," Artahe adds, her voice bristling.

Shansi shifts, exchanging a glance between Syrah and Artahe. "That one. This Giant cannot be more than six months old, but it is much larger than it should be. And it . . . well, I can only say this plainly. It hoards. It is taking in too much of the carbon dioxide. The balance is off. The fungi and the other Giants have tried to warn the sapling . . . ," Shansi says, trailing off.

"It has to be tied to Romelo," Syrah says, earning gasps and downward-cast eyes. "Yes, the scrolls say we cannot have allegiance to one tree, but we know that Romelo did. The President saved him, and he never forgot it."

"So he has naturally gravitated to the Giant's offspring," Dhanil says.

"And it to him," Syrah adds.

"There is something else. The lattice has told us," Shansi says. "The undoer has control of the trees."

"The Giants, you mean," Dhanil says.

Shansi shakes his head. "No, all of them, not just the Giants. Stretching beyond the forest. How are we to stop him?"

"The relationship between the trees and the fungi is symbiotic. It is through that relationship that each thrived and have managed to exist longer than anything else," Syrah explains.

"And you think you can control the fungi?" Artahe fills in.

It is why she was brought to Rhiza, Syrah believes, but she does not say this, not to them. It is as if all this time, The Mother has foreseen what is coming and has allowed them both in anyway. She'll have to puzzle out why later. If there is a later.

Syrah stands. "I know that I can."

Seeing with Nascent Eyes
Manifestation

They called my father The President
They call my caretaker the breaker
They will call me the aftermath

I flex my roots and the forest trembles
My leaves shimmy to the rat-a-tat of my bass
thrum and deer run off in search of more ap-
pealing food options
I stretch my canopy to the sky and it bows down
to meet me
Because I am Vice

My brothers and sisters
Foremothers and Forefathers
My tree kin

I am them and more
They grow jealous of me but they listen and obey
Us

When my caretaker was not up to the task, it was
I who made them stop and
Let them choke on their own tech, the toxic fruits
of their tirelessly damaging labor

We have the carbon and we will keep it

I store more than all of them, drunk on the gas
They try to tell me to stop, to slow my roll
But I do not

When the humans are gone and they no longer produce their poison, how then will we
survive?
By storing
So I take it in and I hold it tight in my roots

The fungi will have to wait, I will stomp their
   greedy little filaments

Sharing is for the weak
When they have expended all their resources, I
   will have more

I will share
If I must
But I will not sacrifice myself, nor my caretaker
Beneath the forest floor, I can feel The Mother
   watching
More than that, it feels like hero worship

The breaker and I, we are the new order of things
Together, we are Rhiza

Chapter Forty-Two

Rhiza
April 2043

Her friends are watching her. Dhanil is standing, of course, near the archway, managing to angle himself so that he can watch her and the corridor equally. Artahe sits in the chair in front of the desk, across from Syrah, her fingers knitted in her lap. Shansi paces near the bookshelves that house The Keepers' volumes. Syrah feels oddly protective of these but stops just short of telling him to get away from them.

Even before she became a canopy keeper, Syrah didn't have much use for television. The paid variety of the earlier part of the century had returned to the free, ad-supported version after most of the streamers went belly-up. Even then, there was little of interest to her aside from old British mysteries.

In Rhiza, she'd found it a good thing that, had she been tempted to mindlessly stare at a screen, the option would not have been available. Right now, though, she'd give a week's pay for just one hour. The voyeuristic need to watch how this fiasco is unfolding has her bouncing off the walls. How are people faring? Has California declared a state of emergency? What about the rest of the country? The world?

They will either watch, clucking useless tongues and shaking their heads, or they will throw everything they can into the fight to figure out what has gone wrong and how to fix it, fast.

Syrah is what Mama likes to call a seat-of-her-pants kind of person. She has yet to prove that overthinking has ever done anybody any good. And at this moment, thinking too much will only muddy her mind. She needs a clear head to do what she has to do next.

There is an uncomfortable truth, blindfolded and gagged, right there in the library with them. Like an unwritten book. Romelo will not go quietly. He cannot be reasoned with. He will not change his mind. His path, his destiny, is likely something that The Mother herself has set in motion.

Twice he's plotted humanity's demise. Last time, he set every creature, walking or crawling, against them. For his encore performance? Poison. Pollute the whole damn environment. And if he survives this one, what will it be the next time? A full-on physical assault?

There is only one way to stop him . . . permanently.

Kill him.

The Keeper Grail: Artahe's high voice springs into the silence as if on righteous wings, reciting the missive:

1. You cannot willingly harm another member of the society;
2. You cannot through action or inaction harm a tree;
3. You cannot divulge the location of the community to outsiders.

Gooseflesh erupts along Syrah's limbs as voices from outside the library join in. As do Shansi and Dhanil. Syrah even adds her voice to the mix.

"One of the first things you told me was that Rhiza speak plainly." Syrah gathers herself and leans forward, forearms rubbing against the desk's smooth grain.

Artahe fixes her gaze on Syrah. There's some bite to it, but then it fades. "You are becoming more Rhizan with every moment that passes," she says. "We are all thinking the same thing."

"This cannot continue," Dhanil cuts in.

Artahe flicks an annoyed glance over her shoulder. Dhanil throws up his palms in mock surrender. "Are you prepared to break rule one of the Keeper Grail?"

And kill the person whom, even from this distance that we cannot cross, I still love. And regardless of whether you want to acknowledge it or not, you love him too. "Rules are all well and good," Syrah says, keeping her thoughts private, "but even Keepers past knew that sometimes, life requires us to take a bit of license. When the safety of the collective is at risk, all bets are off."

They raise their eyebrows. "You know what I mean," Syrah says. Now isn't the time for nitpicking her diction. There's a straightness to her back. A certainty in her eyes as she takes in each of her friends. An evenness to her breathing. Her body believes what she's just said, but that blinking light behind her eyelids isn't going to be convinced as easily. "Are you all right with that?"

"I am not," Artahe says, surprising Syrah. And, from the looks of it, surprising them all. "However, my duty is to Rhiza, and I will not stray from that path."

Not for a human, at least. Syrah tastes the bitter flavor of blood as she clamps down on her tongue.

"The lattice is alive with chatter," Shansi tells them. "Humans are piling into the forest, bringing their sickness and mania."

"What is so unnatural about that?" Artahe says sarcastically.

"The breaker has opened the lattice to us, almost as if he wants us to see what he is doing. He has total control of the Giants, it seems."

"And most of Rhiza," Syrah fills in. "Plus, make no mistake, it is Vice in control. Romelo's a tool."

The trio falls silent again. It's a heavy, weighty silence that makes the room feel smaller.

"Dammit," Syrah says, finally. "I wish they would close the park. All those people are just going to complicate things."

"You have a plan, then?" Dhanil says.

"One that I know will stop him," Syrah says aloud. Then silently adds, *And cement me as the new Keeper of the Canopy.*

With her honor guard protectively ensconced outside, Syrah bounds down the steps toward The Mother, praying that her parents and uncle have gotten themselves somewhere safe.

This time when she connects, she whizzes past the in-between place and lands on the other side of the river circle from Her.

Syrah feels the difference a split second before her eyes confirm it. The Mother is . . . "nervous" is the word that comes to mind. Maybe excited. Her leaves are peacock flashy. Her branches are slightly trembling. Her canopy is positively standing on end.

They know not what they do. Her voice is that of a being that has held the world on Her Giant shoulders for too long.

Just as Syrah is about to answer, the world shakes.

Chapter
Forty-Three

Sequoia National Park
April 2043

He doesn't like most of the park, but the Giant Grove, that's a different story. Which is why, after he got so sick of his parents and their constant fighting, he slipped away from them and from the rest of the people piled on top of one another.

Something about the air. He knew it before the panicked exodus. This morning, he'd woken up before everybody and grabbed for the inhaler tucked in his nightstand. Breathless, he looked out through his window at an innocent-enough-looking sky.

A couple of inhales still hadn't cleared his lungs, and then Dad burst into his room, without knocking, and flung three words at him: *Get dressed, now.*

They piled into the truck. No time to shower; forget brushing his teeth or using the bathroom. His parents were already at each other about what they had packed and what they'd had to leave behind.

His stomach growls now, and he's glad that Dad tossed a couple of packs of meat into the cooler, along with some charcoal. They can use the grills in one of the campgrounds if worse comes to worse. Steak for breakfast, yeah, cool. Luckily, he picked up the lighter before they left and stuffed it in his jacket pocket, or they'd all be shit out of luck.

But there will be no school today. Or, if things are bad enough, the rest of the week. The thought twists his stomach. School's the only place where he doesn't feel the weight of his parents' dysfunction. Then, and when he goes to visit his grandma in Georgia in the summer.

On the drive, he turned his headphones up a notch too high and tuned them out with eighties rap music. Until the battery died just after they'd eased past the entrance, along with a long line of other cars.

Sequoia National Park.

There's almost nowhere to park, so they pull up onto some dirt and dried grass. They mill around with all the other families; he recognizes a couple from school, but he doesn't rush over to say hi, as his mother suggests. Like he hasn't told her a million times that he doesn't like any of them. They don't bother him, keep pretty clear of him, but nobody wants to hang out with a kid who has to whip out an inhaler if he laughs too hard.

And he kind of prefers his own company anyway. A few graphic novels and he can while away an entire Saturday afternoon in his room.

His stomach churns again, and with a sinking feeling, he realizes it isn't hunger. He hasn't had a chance to go to the bathroom. His eyes dart all around, but he doesn't see any buildings, let alone a bathroom. Signs point to campgrounds, one mile to the left. Another is three miles back the way they came. His gut protests, and he doesn't think he can make either.

He's seen it done in movies, old Westerns, where bathroom conveniences weren't a thing. Leaves to wipe with. The whole thing makes him sick, but what choice does he have? And won't nature take care of it? He slips away, into the Giant Grove.

At once he feels so small, and he sees his parents and their petty fighting the same way. There's such a hush to the place that he decides he'll come back to visit sometime. When he gets his driver's license next year, he will come by himself.

He winds his way deeper into the forest until he's reasonably sure nobody but the trees will witness what he has to do. He grabs a couple of too-dry leaves, wondering at the same time how he will wash his hands. No time to think about that now.

Sweatpants and boxers down, squat, strain it out. Wipe.

When he stands up and takes in the stinking pile of mess he's made and looks up at the Giants, he somehow feels judged and gets an idea. He wipes his hands the best he can on a few more leaves and spots a thick branch.

He carves out a small hole in the dirt, then uses the branch and another one he's grabbed to push his shit into the hole. He tosses the branches and a couple of leaves on top. He's turning to head back when he feels the weight of the lighter in his pocket.

Incinerating toilets. They use them in the homeless shelters' tiny homes down in Visalia. He's seen it on the news. He can burn away the shit and be done with it.

He grabs the smaller branch from the pile, lights it on fire, and tosses it back onto his shame. He scoops up a few more leaves and drops them into the fire, since it's having a hard time getting started.

The whole thing goes up, and he steps back with a smile, admiring his ingenuity. When an ember leaps up and lands on a dry-looking branch nearby, he rushes over to stomp it out. But then, as he's turning back, he notices that the fire he's started has grown larger. He stomps his feet in that, too, shit and flames now on his shoes. He jumps around, trying to shake off the mess.

And then his eyes grow wide. A trail of fire, following dead leaves and branches, is snaking off into the depths of the forest.

He turns and runs.

Chapter
Forty-Four

Sequoia National Park
April 2043

Syrah has been tended to enough times to know the feel of Artahe's hands, shaking her shoulder. She opens her eyes to see the Mother Tree's root filaments slinking away. Reclaimed by the soil and earth. Her own fungi in full bloom, fruiting like a spring maple tree, before abruptly retreating to slumber once again beneath her skin. She is healed.

She tries to stand, but dizziness drives her back down to the soft earth. "What's going on?" Syrah mutters.

And then she hears the alarm, a piercing, shrill thing that seems to go straight to her throbbing temples. Dhanil hovers over her, coming into view, and he doesn't have to speak the words. One or more of those idiots have done it again. Someone has started a fire.

This time, Syrah comes to her feet and is steady as a surgeon's hand.

"Ochai is rousing the Blaze Brigade," Dhanil says as they run up the steps. There's no sneer in his voice, only admiration. All business. For all his faults, Ochai is the best at what he does, and Dhanil has no issue with that.

All the same, Syrah's heart constricts at the mention of his name. The same way it did for every fire crew member she'd ever faced the flames with. But that's a lie. This is different because she feels something more for him. Something she's afraid to give name or voice to.

Artahe hands Syrah her socks and boots. "Return to us," she says before she spins on her heels and leaves.

In the hallways, members of the Blaze Brigade stream past like rafts on an agitated river. A voice, at the end of the corridor, rich and deep and in control. She searches through the bodies encircling him and catches a glimpse of his topknot. A shift of a shoulder, then a head, and she sees him. And him, her. Before the bodies crowd around again, blocking. In that glance, a kind of limbo.

The Giant Grove.

Syrah doesn't have to wonder where the thought has come from. She takes off in the other direction, heading topside, with Dhanil right beside her. A feeling that she can't explain overcomes her, and she stops him. "You need to stay here," she says.

His eyebrows knit in anger. "You would take away my most important duty? If there is a fight, then I should be there with you."

"And if I do not return, I need you to be here," Syrah says, unable to finish the thought: if she doesn't survive, Rhiza will need a leader. She thinks back to all the ways in which Dhanil has proven himself to be just that since his release. How he's accepted responsibility for his actions without question. Accepted her without question. Provided key bits of advice. Led his team.

"But will you—"

"Look at me," Syrah commands. She thinks of how callous Romelo is. How he would so easily kill what remains of her family, even the man he also once called uncle. How dangerous it is to leave a foe like him lying in wait, just to strike again. "I meant what I said. I will kill that bastard where he stands this time, and I will not lose a moment's sleep because of it." Syrah doesn't wait for a response. She falls in line with a few straggling members of the Blaze Brigade. The sight of the small animals skittering through the warren of caves tells them that things are already bad. Soon she steps outside.

And into a free-falling madness.

The smoke is already so thick that it blots out the early-evening sky. Syrah and the others have slipped into their camouflage like protective cloaks. To all but each other, they are invisible. Wraiths made of earth and fungi and ancient things. All except Syrah and Romelo. They, the breaker and the deliverer, are something else altogether. More or less, she isn't so sure anymore.

Syrah's vision adjusts, and she homes in on the area emitting the thickest plumes of smoke. The Giant Grove. The Mother wants her there. She takes off at a run, heading south and east. Skirting the trails that may be overrun with people and slicing her way between the oaks and pines and firs.

Dead and dying things litter the path, from animals large and small to smoldering branches and blackened leaves.

Already the Blaze Brigade is a half dozen paces ahead of her. Their long strides have them streaking away, blotted out by encroaching, deadly darkness and smoke.

It thickens as they move closer.

A cluster of piercing screams cuts through the thicket of trees and grit, each one overlapping the other. How many of them? How many caught and confused, stumbling only minutes away from potential salvation. The forest can be confusing during the day, but at times like this, it's impossible to see your very hand in front of you.

Syrah hesitates only a second before she veers off course, darts away from the Brigade, and sets off in the direction of the worst of the cries. Her shoulder catches the edge of something. A tree? Another Rhiza? Whatever it is spins Syrah away with a force that makes it hard for her to stay on her feet. She stumbles forward, hands outstretched, finding nothing but the feel of air and ash.

She rights herself and stands stock still. There, behind her. The cries are faint and dying, drifting away. Syrah's feet are moving, taking her deeper into the thick darkness and farther away from the grove. Torturous moments later, she spots them. Three figures huddled, frozen with uncertainty. Two men, a child. She knows what they feel. How their minds are at war, focused on one unanswerable question. Which way is out? And another. Gnawing, agonizing. *Is this how I'll die?*

Irrational as it is, they are the first topsiders she's seen, and she wonders if one of them started the fire. Syrah maintains her distance and camouflage but shouts, "Follow me, follow my voice!"

Each head, one by one, swivels around, bewildered. "Where . . . where are you?"

"Here," Syrah calls again and again until one of them swivels his head in her direction. He looks right through her. He picks up the child and takes the other man by the arm. Together they take their first tentative steps forward.

"Come on," Syrah implores. "This way." She turns then, tuning in to the sounds of the river and charting the path toward it. She can hear their staggering footsteps behind her. Their coughs and sputters. She glances back and urges them on: "That's right, keep moving."

As she turns, a force slams into her. Her fungi bristle. Ever since Cathay touched her, they've felt better, but she hasn't dared to remove the bandage. The person, she's sure it was a human being and not an animal, streaks off, even after she calls for them to wait. She turns back to the three and guides them through the forest to the edge of the trail.

The comforting, familiar sound of a fire engine both revives and frightens her. How many crews? Certainly her old one. "That's good," Syrah calls over her shoulder, the words trickling out like clues pointing to an unfound treasure. "Just a little ways now."

When they get to the Tokopah Falls Trail, the sound of many footsteps on the path stops her. "Come forward about ten steps and you'll be on the path. Just keep going. The firefighters are here."

Syrah watches as they stumble past her. "Where are you?" The voice is indistinct, wary. Syrah slinks back into the smoke-filled shadows and watches as they make their way down the path. She doesn't peel her eyes away from them until they're in the ready arms of a firefighter. No, not just any firefighter. She barely makes out the smooth angles of her friend Alvaro's determined face.

Syrah is off again, tearing through the forest. She leaps over a group of squirrels, sidesteps a stag, and gives wide berth to a snake slithering down from what was previously the safety of a tree but is now on fire. No more people appear, but she can hear them. Hear their wails and cries and sobs and smells, an incense of burning flesh.

Three miles south from the veil. Three miles of increasingly difficult terrain.

The Giant forest isn't some neighborhood park. Though the home of the last stand of Giants is massive, it is but a fraction of what it used to be. Contracted by one devastating fire after another, this montane area of the forest spans just under one thousand acres. Down from close to double that at its peak.

As she comes upon the edge of the towering grove, the heat goes from tepid to torrid. She narrows her gaze, searches through the dark. Syrah advances until she can make it out. A few hundred feet inside the barrier, near the center, so many Giants already engulfed in flames. The fire crew hasn't made it here yet, but there are Ochai and the Brigade. It's the first time she's seen them in action, and the sight of them takes her breath away.

Chapter Forty-Five

The giant sequoia. This veritable last stand of groves is home to some of the most ancient trees in the world. The most venerable, the most wise. Those that have worked the hardest to keep the air clean enough for humans to enjoy in their unaffected ignorance.

So, so many of their canopies writhe in agony. Orange-tinged flames reach up toward the darkened sky like deadly, many-fingered tendrils.

A snarl ensconced in a sob pours from Syrah's throat in a grief-stricken torrent.

Like pinpricks of stars blinking in and out of sight in the night sky, Syrah perceives Rhiza's illustrious firefighting squad. Rigid as oaks, each of them. To the untrained eye, their arrangement would appear haphazard. But Syrah spies out the pattern, the chessboard precision. All of them equidistant from one another. Their shoulders and heads thrown back. Arms stretched out from their torsos, palms open. Their clouded eyes seeing but not, only trained on the task at hand. The flow cascading from their bodies.

Some are arrayed in circles around an almost totally consumed Giant. Others angled between, deterrents, try to keep the other Giants safe. Dangerously, sickeningly close to the heart of the flames.

Syrah's stomach curdles around a hard-edged nest of despair. Already, she realizes that so many of the trees may be beyond saving. A too-warm spring has stoked a fire that burns too hot, its flames singeing tender bark.

But the canopy keepers are making headway. The flow sends off undulating ripples that collide with the flames and snuff them out. Rhizan pheromones turned extinguishers. They weaken the fire by manipulating oxygen. Transpiration of the flow is the key. Fire can't live without tinder and oxygen. Unfortunately, the Giants are the tinder.

Syrah has the flow, but she cannot use it as they do, or she would join in. But then she spots it: a branch the size of two thick Rhizan thighs snaps. It falls away from the trunk, crashing toward the ground. Syrah takes off and launches herself into the unsuspecting brigadier. The branch lands with a crash, and a flame leaps onto her pants leg. Her fungi spring out but writhe helplessly.

She bats at the flames with her hands, burning them before the brigadier she saved swats her hands away and puts out the fire himself. A look of gratitude crosses his face before he's back on his feet and fighting the flames again. Vaguely, Syrah feels the beginnings of the burn on her leg, the wail of her fungi there.

Syrah resolves to do what she has just done. When the Rhiza are fighting a fire, they're nearly transfixed, in a state of focus so intense that something as simple as a fallen branch can take them out. This is why they always keep a lookout among them: another Rhiza who can alert them to impending trouble. Like branches, like people. This deep into the grove, she doesn't know when or if the human fire crew will make it, so this is what Syrah resolves to do. The burn on her leg is beginning to make itself known, but she pushes the sensation away and throws herself back into the task at hand.

Then she notices something odd. The grove is massive, yet there is one curious absence. Of all the fighters here, Ochai is not among them. Their leader. "Where is Ochai?" Syrah asks another of the lookouts.

No answer, of course.

Syrah feels herself drawn away. A tug. Like a string attached to a balloon, she's pulled away from this battle and into another.

Chapter Forty-Six

Sequoia National Park
The Giant Grove
April 2043

Once again, the humans threaten to ruin all Romelo's plans. Everything he has worked for. It was working. The Giants had stopped transpiration. The air had begun to be clogged with the excess gas and slowly, painfully, but surely driving them away or sickening them.

But Romelo's plan had unforeseen consequences. Do not all good plans suffer the same? He did not anticipate that some of them—wise, now that he thinks of it—would choose to take refuge here in the forest. The place where breathing would be less encumbered.

Where the humans go, trouble follows. It should not surprise him as much as it does. That someone, in their ignorant carelessness, would start another fire.

The lattice alerted them a moment after Romelo had heard Vice's alarm, the one meant for Romelo's ears only. Despite his differences with Taron, with his sister, they are all Rhiza, and their mission never wavers. They are the canopy keepers, protectors and caretakers of the Giants. He did not hesitate to send his own members of the Blaze Brigade to fight alongside Syrah's.

But he and a couple of the crew made a beeline for his tree. Exactly what his adoptive mother and all The Keepers before her had warned about. He had diverted resources to help aid a tree with which he had a personal connection. An attachment.

Camouflage does nothing to deflect the intensity of the heat. His body feels near to burning; it seems as if all the small hairs on his body are withering and blowing away in the smoke-filled air. He lifts a hand to shield his eyes as they run through the forest, heading for Vice.

The sounds of people reach his ears like the tolling of a bell. There is no siren, but the clanging of equipment tells him that the topsider fire-fighters are near. Something like gratitude fills Romelo. There are some humans who have the same mission as theirs. His sister was once one of them, which is the only reason he holds a sliver of respect for them.

For years, Rhiza fought alongside them, unseen. In every great fire, they have been responsible for stopping the worst of it. That has not stopped the humans from blindly taking credit.

But this will only complicate things.

When they finally make it to Vice, Romelo's heart sinks. Several of the trees near his sapling have been caught in their own infernos. Vice is perilously close to a tree whose canopy is a mass of orange flames.

"That one," Romelo shouts at Ochai. "You two do what you can to contain that one."

While they set to work extinguishing that tree, Romelo runs over to Vice and lays a hand on its nascent bark. Warm. Too warm. "Do not worry, my friend," he says. "I will protect you." And he will, if he has to call over every member of the Blaze Brigade to make it so. He would willingly sacrifice every other tree in this forest for his.

No. The thought surfaces, and Romelo removes his hand. That does not fit the rules and ways of a Keeper. He refuses to let Taron be right. The Giants, all of them, are too important.

But. Already he has spotted the Giants' cones littering the earth. Some of them will take seed. Many of them, perhaps. They will grow. They *could* grow like Vice, could they not? With his help, his blood. He could repopulate the entire forest. Assuming his other plan succeeds and the humans flee.

Romelo grabs a hefty fallen branch and drags it through the understory, trying to surround Vice with a makeshift fire line. It is rudimentary, but maybe it will be enough to stop any flames from traveling along the ground. Ochai and the others just have to stop any embers falling from overhead or carried on one of the charring gusts of wind.

Footsteps. Fast Rhizan footsteps. Romelo turns in their direction. He squints, takes a few steps forward.

He should have known.

Chapter Forty-Seven

Sequoia National Park
The Giant Grove
April 2043

Syrah should have known.

Romelo would be right here, selfish enough to try to protect one tree over all the others. The worst of the fire is back at the other part of the grove, and he's pulled away two of the Blaze Brigade—

Syrah's gaze slowly slides away from her brother and skips over to the two forms she makes out. They are doing an admirable job of subduing the flames attacking one of the Giants, lost in the semitrance of the flow. One's silhouette reveals the strong curve of his shoulders. Sculpted thighs in a wide stance. Arms and head thrown back, strands thrown free of his topknot.

Ochai.

How . . . when? Has he been in touch with Romelo all along? Syrah nearly doubles over with the certainty of it.

Movement between the trees. The effort it takes for Syrah to turn away from Ochai is considerable, but she does it. Through the speckled light and dark, her brother is advancing, stalking.

She does the same.

"You would save one tree and sacrifice the others?" Syrah says, feeling her fungi struggling to break free. *Not yet,* she implores them. *Not just yet.*

"I expect that you already know that I have sent all members of the Blaze Brigade who follow me over to the worst of the fire. They are there alongside your crew. Those are not the actions of a selfish person," Romelo says. He's taken a stance, a fighting stance, but his face is placid, searching. "All except a couple essentials," he adds, with a hint of a smirk as he gestures over at Ochai.

Syrah wants to smack that grin off his face. She refuses to let him see that he has, that they have, hurt her. "What now?" she says, swinging her arms wide. "Your plan has backfired, and because of you, another fire may claim more of the Giants."

"Because of me!" Romelo bellows. "Are you as blind as you are sentimental? It is the topsiders, always them."

Syrah won't waste time arguing the small details. "After we stop this fire, and we will stop it, stand down. For good. Come back to Rhiza proper and accept your punishment."

Romelo makes an incredulous sound. Syrah flicks her gaze over to Ochai. His camouflage flickers, then resets. He's noticed them. Good.

"When is the last time you have checked your numbers? Have you any idea how many caretakers have joined me? You have already lost and are too blind to see it. What will happen when we finish this is that I will come back to Rhiza proper. *You* will stand down. *You* will work with me, as you should, or you will not. The choice, a final one, is yours."

Around them, it's hard not to notice the heat of the fire intensifying. Even the Blaze Brigade's ardent leader may not be enough to stop what is building. The crackle and hiss of burning, the roar of the wind and flame. It's in Romelo's face; he senses it as well. He chances a glance back at his tree. It's only then that Syrah notices he's made an amateur attempt at establishing a fire line around the young Giant. She knows that it won't be enough. Romelo probably does too.

She advances. Her fungi stir and flare. Syrah remembers the last time they fought. How her very own big brother had latched on to her arms and ripped the tender buds from her flesh.

Blots of light poke through the murky smoke, illuminating a small clearing. The expression on Romelo's face spurs Syrah on. He isn't quite so sure of himself.

"You are not strong enough," he says with what Syrah perceives to be genuine pity or resignation.

"And you are not smart enough." Syrah raises her arms, and her mushrooms' hyphae ease away from the stems. She has her own flow. Different from that of Ochai and the others, but more deadly. It was Cathay who helped her see it. The Mother too. Her spores meet with those rising up from the earth and coil together in one rapturous unit. Judging by Romelo's disbelieving expression, he sees them too.

He lets loose a string of curses and backpedals. Syrah pursues. But she doesn't have to run, and this time, there won't be some epic battle. Her spores have hitched a ride on a gust of hot air, and now her beautiful horde surrounds Romelo. Like a sculptor molding a mound of clay, Syrah cajoles the spores into her weapon and gives them permission to proceed.

Instinctively, he covers his nose and mouth with his forearm, whacking at the air with the other. But it is too late. The morphogenetic proteins are on his skin, sinking in, tiny enough that they've already slipped past his arm and into his nose and mouth.

The two humans, the breaker and the deliverer, have evolved along disparate paths. Romelo has become Rhiza's greatest rootspeaker, able to communicate with trees on the other side of the country. Syrah has become a welcome host to the fungi.

Recognition blooms in his face as he takes one last look at his Giant, almost but not quite raising a hand toward it before sinking to his knees. The whole scene is surreal. Syrah sees him there, against the backdrop of an apocalyptic sky. The fungal infection is eating up his lungs and blistering his skin.

Syrah doesn't rush to his side. She stands there, numb. Holding back her emotions. Her fungi have retreated, their mission complete.

Romelo writhes on the ground, likely wondering how the fight he was hoping for had ended before he could land a weighty punch or swift kick. When their eyes meet, the iced-over part of Syrah's heart splinters. All around them, the flames intensify, with Ochai and the other brigadier still holding off the worst.

Syrah reaches her brother just as he cries out in pain and coughs. He reaches out a hand for her, and she eyes it like it's a viper. But then she takes his hand in hers. Sores are forming on his skin, and she imagines his lungs are a ruin.

And the floodgates open. Syrah is bawling. Hiccuping, racking cries.

"I would not have killed you," Romelo says around a wince of pain.

She doesn't know if he's telling the truth, if he's capable. But that sliver of doubt forces more tears from her eyes because she knows that she has, in fact, killed him. "Why couldn't you see reason?"

"The same reason that you could not," Romelo sputters. "Reason rests wholly in the eyes of the beholder."

Syrah thinks oddly that Romelo would have made a gifted poet. "What am I supposed to do?" Syrah says, wiping her eyes. Her tears have finally abated. "How am I supposed to go on knowing what I did to my own brother?"

"That is for you to figure out," Romelo says, and then his gaze goes someplace else. Someplace in the past. "Fitting, is it not? That I would die here this way? The way it should have been when our parents died."

When I pushed you. Syrah doesn't speak the words, but they both know the truth of them anyway.

"Take me over to Vice," Romelo mutters, pointing at the young Giant.

So he has given it a name. Fitting, as The President's offspring. Syrah lifts her brother with an ease that no longer surprises her. He rests his head against her shoulder, the way she used to rest hers in the crook of his arm when they were children. She crosses his fire line and lays her brother down and props him against the bark.

"This is your life," he says. "Do with it what you want. *You.*"

"Rhiza is going to need a leader," Syrah says.

He tilts his head, regarding her. "You are not convinced, then." He chuckles. "All this time, I thought it was what you wanted. You know I was right, though: the humans will not stop until they destroy this place and us with it."

"That won't happen," Syrah says without much conviction. "I'll do my best to make sure it doesn't."

Syrah can feel the heat. It's becoming unbearable.

"Go," Romelo says. "I am exactly where I should be."

"No—"

"Ochai does love you, but he loves me as well. He is Rhizan through and through and will defend it until the end."

Almost as if on cue, Syrah feels a hand on her shoulder. "The area is going to be overrun soon. You should go beneath the veil."

Syrah sees the conflict in Ochai's eyes and hears the urgency in his voice. She stands, pulling away from him. To the other brigadier, she gestures at Romelo and says, "Take him belowground."

She doesn't look back as her brother weakly protests to be able to stay by his tree to die. She is marching back to the worst of the fire; she will not run and hide. She will do what she can to defend the Giants, not quiver beneath it all, waiting for whatever outcome befalls them.

Syrah is grateful that Ochai walks alongside her, silent but steady and sure as the fire chief she once was.

Chapter
Forty-Eight

Sequoia National Park
The Giant Grove
April 2043

Syrah and Ochai don't speak; they run. They don't glance over at each other, their gazes fixed straight ahead. To be fair, she's felt him chance a look at her a time or two. She has no desire to return the favor.

All around them, smoke and ash and murk. Bits of fire flare sporadically. Ochai stops to try to put those flames out himself, but Syrah pulls him away. She knows, they both do, that the bigger fire, the one that needs them most, is still ahead of them.

Cutting through a dense thicket of brush and trees, Syrah glances up and sees plumes of smoke that remind her of images she's seen of the atomic bomb. A cloud so massive and thick it will likely drift as far south as Mexico in the aftermath. Whatever that will be.

Voices, snatches of anxious raised shouts and cries. They're close. The flames have gone white, burning the hottest, and Syrah is momentarily blinded, but she blinks it away. Her knees nearly give out. Canopies engulfed, flames climbing up massive trunks as if on a ladder.

And her crew is here. Both crews. Camouflaged Rhiza and human. Fighting side by side as they have for centuries. In fact, it looks like every fire crew the state has ever known is here. It's getting harder to maintain her camouflage, but Syrah slides into it again. Ochai touches her, a gentle brush of fingertips on her arms. She doesn't want to, but she looks up at him. He doesn't have to say the words; sorrow and regret craft the visage of his expression. This is no movie. She does not fall into his arms. There is no time for a kiss or an embrace.

He simply moves off to join his team in this, the latest of battles. There are words Syrah wants to say to him, some biting, some loving. But there's no time.

She fumbles around for something to do. All around her, others are taking action. Her heart sinks at the sight of the fallen. Long-limbed branches, blackened leaves and cones. But it is the Rhizan blaze brigadiers who get to her the most. Whether from exhaustion or having come too close to the flames, they litter the forest floor like shorn blades of grass. Scourge suppressors are there, dodging human and animal alike, carting away some of their fallen friends. Syrah can only hope that Artahe is able to save them.

No ambulance has arrived to deal with the handful of fallen firefighters.

Everything Syrah is witnessing threatens to overtake her. Her heart thunders in her chest, her breathing coming in short bursts.

Then she snaps herself out of it. It's too hard to maintain the camouflage, so she runs to the edge of the grove, near the trail. And she comes up behind the crew. No hat, no equipment, nothing but bare hands and a stone-edged will.

Lance is at the front of the line, holding the hose and laying down water at the base of a Giant. The firefighter behind him falls, and Syrah rushes up and jumps into the line, taking hold of the hose when it almost slips out of Lance's hands. One thing people don't realize is the strength required to be a firefighter. Almost two thousand kilopascals of pressure coursing through this tube, and she's seen how, so many times, a hose can jerk right out of your hands, and it takes a major feat to regain control.

But she is infinitely stronger than she used to be. She could hold the hose by herself.

Lance has no idea who has taken up the slack behind him. A good leader doesn't stop to check, but keeps their eyes and intention set to the task at hand. She can feel the questions coming from the others at the back of the line, but there they will wait until later. Maybe she can slip away before she has to answer them.

For what feels like hours, they crouch and fight this most resistant of flames. Around them, other crews are sent to other areas to fight. Syrah doesn't look, but she catches a glimpse of Ochai and a few others running to another hotspot.

After the flames on this Giant have been subdued, Lance has stood and is turning, ready to point the firefighters to the next crisis, when his gaze lands on her. Shock, disbelief, confusion. They're all there, but then Lance is chief again. Something like relief and determination draw him back. She knows what he's thinking. There she is, come out of nowhere, with no gear, not even a mask. But he doesn't waste time. He gestures to the next area he wants to target. And Syrah and the crew hoist the hose and follow.

In this way, they and the Rhiza take on this, the latest in a series of devastating forest fires. More losses on both sides. Even a few collisions that, in the dark, nobody notices. Here and there, Syrah seeks out Ochai, despite herself. And she is both angry and comforted when she sees him still in the midst of the battle.

Alvaro is now right behind her. Lance, Syrah, Alvaro. It has always been the three of them, at odds and on the same side. She is amazed at how much comfort this whole scene gives her, even though she wishes they weren't here. That the Giants were not screaming and dying.

Vaguely, Syrah feels another presence. It's Her. The Mother. She doesn't interrupt Syrah, but she knows. The oldest tree in the world can see all. Syrah knows that in Her own way, she is doing whatever she can to help them. She and the rootspeakers are directing the Giants to share resources. To redirect water to thirsty roots. But will it be enough?

They are all focused on one Giant. Her old crew and the new one. Ochai and the others are arrayed, the flow wafting off them. She and Fire Station Ninety-Three, using water and retardant. And then two things happen at once.

A thundering snap startles them all. Syrah looks up in time to see a large branch break off and fall from near the top of a Giant. Her gaze follows the trail. She drops the hose and runs and shouts at the same time.

Ochai is lost in the flow trance, his glorious head thrown back. He is still standing there when the branch topples him in a whooshing roar, crowned off by a hiss of sparks.

Syrah hears another cry go up and turns. Lance has lost his mask somewhere in the middle of the fight, and he is down. His eyes are closed. Alvaro is bent over him.

Syrah is halfway between them both. Ochai and Lance. She sinks to her knees and screams.

Chapter Forty-Nine

Rhiza
May 2043

History and the Keepers' logs will record May 3, 2043, as the day an assault from pure thin air precipitated a fire that left another one thousand irreplaceable acres of Sequoia National Park a scorched wreck.

A week that began with what to the Western world will remain a baffling spike in CO_2 levels in the state of California ended with an elemental and human massacre that claimed eight human lives and five Rhiza. Twenty-four Giants that Syrah could not protect.

Among those lives, two men: one whom she can only now admit she loved and another whom she had come to respect. Love is funny that way. It is relentless in its pursuit once its sights are set on you. You can try to turn away from it, deny its very existence. Refuse to acknowledge that flutter in the heart, that unabashed perking up when the object of your love is near. The anticipation of them.

Love is a mean and sneaky opponent, undefeated in smashing hearts as soon as it's won them.

What a complicated relationship Syrah and her brother had. She had almost killed him once by childishly shoving him off a tree branch. In self-defense (she is convinced of this), she had taken another shot at it on Moro Rock. And when that didn't work, she used her fungi to polish him off.

Yet she calls *him* the madman.

You did the right thing. It is not your fault. You had no choice. This from her friends, Dhanil and Artahe. They mean well; it's just that those words are all platitudes you say to somebody who's done something so wrong you've got nothing else to give them. Maybe pity. Because right or wrong, it hurts like the seventh level of hell when she thinks of her brother's baby-smooth cheek covered in festering pus and sores, all his idealistic rants annihilated by her.

She runs the tips of her nails along her arms, caressing her fungi. She calls to them more often now for comfort than for defense. They've got a sound to them, quite like a contented cat's purr.

Nature can give life as easily as it can take it. People like to think they're in control, but that couldn't be further from the truth.

Syrah is in her room, wearing clothes that smell of smoke. When she shakes her head, ash drifts to the ground like thin snowflakes. Her body is at that space well beyond her physical and mental limits, but she can't even think of sleeping.

Open on her desk is *The Keeper Book of Rituals*. She's read the section she needs three times over. There will be two burials. She turns her gaze to her bookshelves, overflowing with the thousands of words that Taron demanded she read. She's only gotten through half of them. And more await in the library. It would take two human lifetimes, reading ten books a day, to make a dent in the stack. No matter how much time slows for her here, it doesn't stop. She'll never get through it all.

Before she slunk back beneath the veil to deal with the aftermath, she'd stolen time to check on her uncle and her parents.

Mama didn't play when it came to Syrah's father, not after watching him suffer the stroke. She had hustled him into the car and, to Syrah's surprise, driven past Compton's only hospital and right across the border to Mexico without stopping. They were on the way back home now, safe and sound. Uncle Dane had also surprised her by going to get himself checked out before returning to his cabin.

In the midst of the fire, the Giants all but forgot Romelo's directive, their collective minds and canopies focused on survival. Whether because of his death, because The Mother interceded, or because they saw how tirelessly the humans they had sought to end were fighting for them, even giving their lives for them . . . Syrah doesn't know. But they have gone back to doing the work of cleaning the atmosphere, both of the lingering smoke and the carbon dioxide that has built up and made everything infinitely worse.

Dhanil's gruff order turns away yet another person who has crowded near her door. The person waits while she cowers at her desk, trying to decide where to take them, these people who are looking for her to lead them. Somewhere.

Syrah hears Artahe's voice and rushes to open the door. She pulls her friend in and closes the door behind her, comforted by the fact that Dhanil is there. And she knows that, despite their rocky beginning, he will always be there for her and for his people. He has a single-mindedness to him that Syrah admires . . . and covets.

"You cannot stay here forever, you know," Artahe says.

"I do indeed know," Syrah says. "That does not mean I will not stretch out my time here for as long as I can."

That earns her a sound of exasperation, too much like what she'd expect from Taron when she thought Syrah was acting childish, like she is now. That's the old Syrah. The new her knows better.

"Everything is in place. You must complete the ritual. It is what is required of a leader."

Syrah makes a show of looking around her room. Lifting the thin blanket on her bed, peering in corners, lifting and dropping Artahe's arm. "Hmm, do you see a staff around here anyplace? Because I do not. And you know what that means? That means I am not yet The Keeper."

Artahe plants a hand on her hip. "For the love of Rhiza, please grow up!"

"What are you talking about? I have done everything you all have asked of me. Even accepted everything you did without my consent. It does not get any more grown than that." Syrah's eyes are boring into her friend's by the time she's finished rattling off her list of accomplishments. They sound tiny, though, even to her own ears.

"Taron is gone—"

"Don't you think I know that—"

"The Mother will not just hand you the staff because you want it; you have to earn it—no, do not interrupt me. I believe you have done that. Especially after . . ."

This is when Artahe's voice breaks, and Syrah's angry resolve disintegrates right along with it. This time, they both know that Romelo is dead. Grief and regret unify them now. She wonders if the very same thing will rip their friendship to shreds later. Syrah, like her mother, is not one for physical displays, but she gives Artahe an awkward half hug anyway.

"He is gone," Artahe sobs. "I saw him, you know. I tried to sway him, but he, he would not listen to reason."

Syrah pulls back then. Have both Ochai and Artahe been secretly visiting Romelo behind her back all this time? Anger is about to flare, but Syrah does something that makes her immensely proud. She watches it, sees that ball of bad emotion just waiting to manifest in a litany of expletives and accusations . . . and lets it go. Watches as it slips away, losing ugly, hateful steam as she releases it. "You had every right to try, and I am glad you did."

Artahe composes herself and gestures toward the door. "You go out first; I will follow at a distance."

Chapter Fifty

Rhiza
May 2043

An impatient swarm of bodies packs the narrow passage outside Syrah's door. Among the multitude of their gazes, she reads a desperate, hungry need. Like a ship with no mast, they have been drifting along these past seven months, especially since Taron's recent death.

For more years than Syrah is able to fathom—thousands or more—Rhiza has never been without someone at the helm for more than a couple of days. That this small community, one that she and her brother have split nearly in two, has held it together for this long is a testament to the Rhiza, not to Syrah. The fungi, the Giants, the canopy keepers (in that order, she thinks), the most resilient and hardy organisms that have ever lived and ever will.

They have waited long enough. Each and every one has stood by, probably gnawing their tongues raw, waiting while Syrah and Romelo, even Inkoza, have vied for the title.

Keeper of the Canopy.

Dhanil. Talk about irony. Aside from the kid who wanted to give her a beating on her first visit belowground, he was the person who was most willing to openly display hostility toward her. She appreciated it in a way, since it gave her someone to focus her own anger on. Now the person who once beat her nearly senseless, then attacked both her and Taron and locked them away, has now become her most trusted companion and adviser.

Time is a stand-up comedian.

Seeing him there with a sliver less than his customary scowl gives her the strength to come out of hiding in her room. He gives her a curt, expectant nod. Bruises to the chin and left eye. A nasty cut on the left side of his neck. Well earned.

Dhanil's entire visage is one of such pride and determination that it straightens Syrah's back. She swallows whatever the thing is that has kept her holed up in her room and takes the first leaden step. With him a half step behind and Artahe bringing up the rear, each step becomes surer and easier.

As she leaves her personal oasis and marches toward The Mother's chamber, Syrah meets dozens of gazes. She doesn't shy away, nor does she flinch. Syrah wills herself to embody all the traits of a leader. Her pace should be strong but not hurried. And the eyes are the window to the soul, aren't they? Her eyes, her entire expression, should show the stern look of someone who's always thinking, always ahead. Strong as the oldest Giant, languid as a hibernating bear.

She can't help but think of Taron. The old Keeper was, in a word, at ease. Two words, then. Despite whatever madness was jumping off at any point, there was never any doubt that she was in control. Even when she wasn't. Was she always that way, or is that something that Keepers develop over time?

Time is a thing that Syrah will never have as much of as they do. It hits her then that if she has even a slightly extended life in Rhiza, say, fifty human years, she will outlive everyone she knows topside by spans and spans more. Time without Dane, her parents. Time without her brother and Ochai.

Syrah trashes all those useless thoughts and concentrates on where and who she is now. All she wants to convey is her determination. Purpose as strong as that of the string of her predecessors. Smiles and nods, and the occasional *Peace be with us*, follow her like an escort along the route to the chamber. Murmurs in the crowd both gathering behind her and the one that is mere steps away, already gathered for the ritual.

She finds it more difficult than it should be to enter. Where, after all she's done, is this lingering doubt coming from? It's fear; she calls it for what it really is. Maybe a tinge of regret, along with a healthy dose of pain.

While she was topside fighting the fire, Dhanil was here below-ground, grudgingly, fighting his own battle. He had taken the advantage. With Romelo trying to save his tree, Dhanil had wrangled a bit of information from Ochai before he, too, joined the fight. It lessened her pain, some. Ochai had given Dhanil the location of Romelo's sect, and he had rooted them out like creatures burrowed into a foxhole.

Dhanil had suffered some injuries, but not enough to harm him. Syrah didn't think anything would. He was the thickest and most solid of the honor guard. He had served Taron and Her for longer than any of humanity's toughest generals. But he had successfully tracked down those who hadn't already defected by the time news of Romelo's death hit the lattice.

Ezanna and a few others were the last holdouts. Syrah meets his steely gaze now as she descends the stairs to join him and the other captive deserters at the base of The Mother.

Well done.

The words come to Syrah's mind, and she warms at Her touch and kindness. She's come to accept the nature of their relationship. Like any mother, she will let Her children grow as they need to. She knows when to interfere and when not to, so that Her children will learn the lessons necessary to be successful for the next in a long series of life's challenges.

Syrah doesn't have to say anything back. To Her, she is an open, plot-twisty, unfinished book. Syrah does not always understand, but she is no less grateful to be here in this place, with this most incredible species. For the opportunity to lead them.

Off to the side are several bodies, wrapped in the traditional burial cloths, plain, colorless, utilitarian. One, noticeably smaller than the others.

Romelo Thorn Williams.

The breaker.

The Mother whispers, a hint of sadness like a heavy sigh against Syrah's skull.

Syrah tears her gaze away before emotion can get the best of her. She focuses her ire on Ezanna and marches up to him. She stops a few feet short. She hates having to look up at his already raised chin. Stripped of his precious robes, he stands there in standard-issue Rhizan clothing, just like Syrah and everyone else. Without Romelo to back him up, all the bite has gone out of him. The other traitors cower behind him.

Syrah turns to the crowd, still making their way to the benches and alcoves. Her heart breaks that the numbers are fewer than they were the first time she was here.

Dhanil and Yemaya are on opposite sides of the dais. The raised birchwood platform has a podium at the center where the recovered text, *Lives of Imminent Keepers*, rests. The Mother is at her back. Ezanna and his crew are to her right. Syrah faces her people. "Recite the Keeper Grail."

In unison:

1. You cannot willingly harm another member of the society;
2. You cannot through action or inaction harm a tree;
3. You cannot divulge the location of the community to outsiders.

When the last echoes of their raised voices die down, Syrah, by herself, recites the Keeper Code:

If one shall fail, we raise the veil.

Her voice is nearly not her own. It is loud and strong and it belongs. Belonging is a thing Syrah has coveted and denied she even had any interest in for her entire life. All eyes are plastered on her. Even Ezanna's attempt at a murderous scowl. Beginning with Ezanna, she calls them each out by name, then asks, "For the crime of treason, how do you plead?"

Ezanna steps forward. Without his robes, he seems lesser somehow. "Crime? You dare call what we did a crime?" He stops to gesture at his comrades. "The crime is up there. Our job is to protect the Giants, and ever since Taron's reign, we have done nothing but lose. And now more. Those who should be punished, current company aside, are up there as well. The crime is that they will live to do it again and again until all of us are no more. And I anticipate that if you proceed with this farce, we will see the end of Rhiza and the Giants during her reign. I—"

The entire massive chamber vibrates. The Mother, previously watching as if unconcerned, has lit up like the greatest of Christmas trees. Syrah feels that thrum deep in her belly, like she used to as a kid. But this time, it sets her teeth on edge. Everyone sways on their feet, frightened, for the full minute that it lasts. Even Ezanna cowers. He has called out something that she has made clear she will not stand idly by and watch happen to Her children.

That scares Syrah more than Romelo ever did. She gathers herself and continues: "Is there anyone who would debate? Anyone willing to speak up for the accused?"

Her heart swells. Not one hand, or voice, is raised. They are united—behind her. Syrah pauses, her eyes rolling back, to listen to The Mother. Instructions. "For the crime of treason, you will be sentenced to conscription for a period of twenty-five suns."

Unlike humans, Rhiza don't argue. There are no tears or pleas of innocence. Once their fate is handed down, they inexplicably, docilely, accept it. All except this time.

Ezanna stupidly launches himself from the dais and tries to dash up the side of the chamber. Syrah is about to take off after him, or to at least call for one of the Rhiza to trip him up, but one glance at Dhanil tells her she doesn't have to. Her guard does not run after him either; he merely raises a hand, and several members of Rhiza stand from the seats. One, closest to Ezanna, makes her way over, then is joined by two more. Ezanna is soon surrounded. And the other members of the expanded honor guard are eyeing the rest of the room and those on the dais who haven't moved.

Without touching him, they escort Ezanna back down to Syrah. They are all positioned near one of Her massive roots. Syrah lays a hand on the trunk, feeling the warmth spread through her. Roots spring from the ground and grab each of the convicted.

One by one, they are held until they go rigid and stiff; then the earth opens up, and The Mother swallows them whole. Soon nothing remains of them except their pain-stricken faces, carved into her bark. Where, if Syrah has any sway at all, they will remain forever.

Chapter Fifty-One

Rhiza
May 2043

For this next thing, only Syrah and Artahe remain. The two friends stand shoulder to shoulder. The tears have been shed. The regrets shared. The losses feel like an eternity of cessations.

Syrah wishes that her uncle could be here for this. She has often been angry at him for never finding Romelo when she was a kid. Irrational, but isn't that what people are most of the time? She had felt like an idiot when he'd explained how he never stopped looking for her brother. It was only then that Syrah saw, really acknowledged, his guilt. The sadness that seemed to surround her uncle despite his ready smile and good nature.

Well into her thirties, she is finally growing up. It is long past time to turn away from herself and start seeing the adults in her life as people and not window dressing there to support her and tend to her every need.

She supposes The Mother is like that. Syrah wants to know Her story, but wonders if she'll ever share it with her. A matter for after.

Fingers grope for hers. Artahe wipes away what Syrah knows is a tear with the other hand. That shard of hope that they both held on to last fall is no longer. Romelo's dead body is wrapped lovingly in front of them. His and Ochai's.

They mount the stairs together. Syrah doesn't care if she's supposed to let Artahe do so or not. It's time to write some new rules into the Keepers' logs.

Syrah speaks to The Mother in her head, and soon, they see the ground swirling. The moist earth gives way. They watch as their loved ones sink and are covered over with earth. Where they once lay, a small flower has sprung.

Seeing with Ancient Eyes
An Ending and a Beginning

We, the trees, speak in a subtle, cultivated
    language
Though they see us and take us for granted, only
    a chosen few humans will ever hear the wise
    words and warnings we convey
We make the world a place they can and want to
    live in
My children and I, we make life possible

But they know this not
We are social beings all the same
We share food, stories, nourish our young and
    infirm
We relish in the few gains and suffer together the
    many losses we have been dealt by human
    hands and nature herself
We and the fungi, we created the lattice and our
    connections grew

Our canopies soared
Every one of us a valued member of a forest
    community

The humans are shortsighted, perhaps because
    their time is so very brief; for this there is no
    blame
They can only be what little they were born to be

My love is for all trees, but my greatest affection
    is for the Giants, for it is upon our shoulders
    that survival rests most heavily
And for my canopy keepers, who exist alongside
    us, careful ardent caretakers
We live in the slow lanes of existence while the
    humans are forever in the fast

The undoer's pain has subsided
He is with me now, he and his friend of the
    Blaze Brigade wander my forest in their easy
    companionship
Already, he has passed time with his ancestor, the
    buffalo woman, and this, to gaze upon his face
    and relish in the sound of his voice, genera-
    tions removed, brings her the greatest of joys

He visits me often, sits and says nothing
But I know he is content now

Giant sequoia
More of us lost over this past century than in all
    others combined
Our numbers are perilously thin

There was a time when I believed that new suns
were plentiful
I, The Mother, contemplate an emotion that I
have never before allowed entry into my con-
sciousness . . .

Fear

Chapter
Fifty-Two

Rhiza
The Mother's chamber
May 2043

After Artahe leaves and Syrah is once again alone with The Mother, she waits.

She is no less awed now than she was the first time she saw Her. When Taron marched Syrah into this space and changed her life forever. The words she has to describe the being before her have not increased. "Majestic" sounds silly. "Wondrous," something out of a badly worded novel. "Exalted," another century or two.

The Mother, Syrah decides, is not a being who needs human definition.

Syrah listens to the sounds drifting down to her from the corridors outside the archway where she knows Dhanil waits for her. Life, as well as it can, is trying to reassemble itself into whatever their new normal will be. Death has visited them again. Rhiza have raised hands against one another. As much as Taron tried to sell them on being a peaceful, benevolent species, even she knew that was maybe not as much of a pipe dream as it is for humans, but a pipe dream all the same.

Violence cloaked with purpose is no less violent. Just ask the families of the people lost to this world's many wars for a cause.

This time when Syrah opens her eyes, she's already here. Past the tall grasses, through the thicket of Giants. The circle of water gurgles softly at her back. Like the Kaweah River behind her home in Three Rivers. Her old home.

You have become who you were meant to be; you have slain what for some would have been insurmountable obstacles, and you have transcended.

Syrah brightens at what she perceives as the highest praise. She wants to ask about her brother. About Ochai. About Cathay, her great-great-great-grandmother.

You have already asked, and they are well.

Relief is swift and sweet, like a first breath after an eternity submerged underwater. After all he has done, Syrah still does not want her brother to be angry at her, to feel she is at fault for what has happened over this past year.

And an aching buds within her, one that Syrah knows is the manifestation of Ochai's absence. It will become her companion now.

"I am ready to lead," Syrah says. "I am ready to be the next Keeper."

Are you?

Syrah blinks. "Yes. I have studied the texts . . . well, mostly. I have learned how to use my fungi; I have carried them through the worst and come out on the other end. The caretakers accept me . . . well, again, mostly."

You fought the fire well.

A smile curves at Syrah's mouth. "I only did what I had to do. I don't have the flow, but I know very well how to wield a fire hose."

And it made you happy, did it not?

"It did," Syrah says without hesitation. "Tell me, how do I get a staff?"

You will walk back through my forest. Linger among the Giants and the flora and the fauna. Come to know my land as you know yourself. Greet and accept the wisdom of whomever you meet on your journey. When you come to the end, the staff will await the next Keeper.

Syrah thanks The Mother, and anxious to take up her newest and most important role, she turns and leaves. The Mother doesn't say anything else. Syrah is overwhelmed by being in this realm. Like Her, it is beyond description. She wonders if this place is like human heaven. She's past questioning what can't be explained anymore. Her time in Rhiza has convinced her that all things are possible.

Soon, she sees a figure heading toward her, and she's thrilled to recognize the form.

Taron is whole. She wears traditional Rhizan gear. Gone are the outward scars and bruises from her fall. Not really a fall: a push, by her adoptive son. One who is here, somewhere, in the same place she is. Syrah thinks about the fairness of that scenario and once again is confronted with how much she still has to learn about the canopy keepers. Taron walks with her staff, not because she needs it to assist her but because she's earned it.

"I must say that I was unsure that you would make it this far," Taron says by way of hello, after all this time. Syrah expects nothing less than a biting quip.

"Have to admit, I shared your lack of confidence," Syrah says, shifting uncomfortably on her feet. She wants more than anything to reach out and grab that staff.

"Do you nurse any guilt for what had to be done? For killing your kin?" Taron is watching her with that unflinching gaze.

Syrah wonders if this is a test, a part of the process that she must also pass. She opens her mouth, too fast, a response on her tongue, but she waits. She is Rhizan, and they speak plainly. "Guilt . . ." She pauses, searching the swirl of dark and light sky above her, then finds the words. "What I feel is more like regret. I had to take a life, and that it was my own brother's . . . no, I can never forget that. But what I wish is that I had whatever skill I lack that would have enabled me to convince him to not hurt you, to not tear Rhiza apart."

Taron raises her eyebrow and nods. "You were so obstinate."

"And you so self-assured." Syrah shows great restraint in not calling her an arrogant prick.

Taron's laugh is not something Syrah has heard before, and it takes her completely off guard. It is a stilted, croaking sound that makes Syrah join in with her. She can't remember the last time she laughed. And within her, there is a melting. The feel of something heavy and terrible loosening its grip on her.

Syrah's gaze flitters over to the staff; her chin juts out. "Is this the part where I take that and begin the next era as Rhiza's Keeper?"

"It is here." Taron takes the staff in her hands and holds it in front of Syrah. "Before I relinquish this to you, ask yourself two questions and answer in the Rhizan way. To yourself, no one else."

Syrah had reached out, but now, she pulls back. "Okay . . ."

"Anissa Carthan, Trenton Carthan, Dane Young. Are you prepared to forsake them forever for the caretakers and for Her?"

Syrah is about to speak, but Taron gives a short, curt shake of her head.

"Second, are you prepared to make all the duties of The Keeper your life's work? Will you stay belowground and man the library while the next fire erupts in the forest? Are you prepared to watch your friends at the fire station from the sidelines?"

Syrah has developed the patience of the people she has lived among for the last year. She knows what it means to wait and to think. She doesn't jump to an answer, like she would have before. These aren't questions she hasn't considered.

The staff is held there between Syrah and Taron like a challenge. From the corner of her eye, she catches movement. She turns in time to see two forms she knows well. One taller, the other slightly shorter. One with locs flowing freely down his back, the other with his customary topknot. They walk together, through the trees, laughing at something Syrah wishes she could hear. She is drawn to them but stays rooted where she is. She isn't ready; none of them are.

Syrah turns back to an expressionless Taron and makes a decision.

Chapter
Fifty-Three

Rhiza
The Mother's chamber
May 2043

When Syrah comes out of it, Dhanil is pacing back and forth in a corner and Artahe is perched on the edge of the bench closest to her, gnawing at her fingernails. Comically, they both freeze when she stands. Their eyes are searching, as if trying to discern whether she has changed physically. That or—

"What happened?" Artahe is on her feet.

Syrah gestures for them both to join her, near The Mother. "Dhanil . . . ," she starts, then stops, at the untimely cracking in her voice. Some kind of leader she is. She swallows the lump in her throat and inhales. What she has to say will be the most difficult thing she's ever done. "Who has surreptitiously read every book in Taron's library?" She still hasn't worked up the nerve to start calling it hers.

He does the shrug-hitch thing before looking over at Artahe, who also shrugs. "I did not think it was wrong to read from The Keeper's library, I—"

"Who was willing to sacrifice his own life, going against The Keeper he served, in order to do what he thought was the greater good?"

"I accepted my punishment—"

"Without denying or justifying," Syrah says. "And who crushed Ezanna and restored order while I was up there?" She gestures at the ceiling with her finger. "Fighting a fire, not protecting the caretakers? You know more about Rhiza than I would, even if I were able to live three human lifetimes. You have proven yourself a leader time and again." Syrah nearly breaks before she says this next thing. Meeting his gaze is like lifting hundred-pound barbells with her eyelids. "You have to do it now." Her voice is a blade of grass over a whisper. "Connect to The Mother, make your peace with Taron, and claim the staff."

First gasps. Then mutters of indignation. Some denials. Artahe's fists are planted on her hips, her words coming out in a tangle that Syrah only snatches bits and pieces of. "Coward," "abandoning," something about fairness.

Dhanil takes a few step backward, as if putting distance between himself and what Syrah is asking of him.

"But . . ." He stops, glancing around and behind Syrah then. In that gesture, Syrah knows that both he and Artahe are just now realizing she hasn't emerged with the staff in hand.

When the leader of her honor guard, her . . . friend, doesn't move, Syrah trudges over, gets behind him, and gives him a gentle push forward. The last time she touched him was during their slugfest in Taron's chamber, but oddly enough, that memory doesn't have the steam it once did. She can't for the life of her muster any anger about the betrayal, and that makes her immensely happy.

Dhanil walks like a person stilted, like he is moving toward a guillotine instead of the most important job in the world. When he finally makes it to the spot near the large root Syrah favors, she sees him take in The Mother. His jaw drops open slightly, his neck bent to try to take in the canopy that brushes the sky. When he looks back down at Syrah, his expression is one of someone who has seen greatness and will never be the same.

Syrah shows him how to sit in order for the tendrils to feel comfortable enough to seek him out. Artahe respectfully turns her head, but Syrah asks her not to leave.

"Just stay here. Wait as long as it takes," she instructs Dhanil. "I can tell you no more."

Dhanil's back is straight, his long legs stretched before him. For a minute, Syrah thinks he is about to regale her with some long speech, but that's not him at all. He only says, "I was prepared to serve you for the remainder of your days, but this . . . this feels like the right thing." And then Syrah no longer matters. Dhanil focuses, intent and deliberate on his task.

Haughty and single-minded, sometimes to a fault. But always thinking. He will make a fine Keeper.

Syrah turns and strides up the stairs, stopping only to take Artahe's hand in hers. Together they take what to Syrah feels like a funeral march up the steps and out of the chamber. She stops just outside the archway and glances back over her shoulder. She can't still the pang of loss in her chest, can only hope that, over time, it will subside.

The friends meander through Rhiza's unusually quiet corridors. There's a twitchy hush as the caretakers await their next leader. Syrah takes in the alcove where she and Romelo sat having one of their tense tennis match conversations. Artahe's mushroom farm, the smell of earth and growth wafting out and stirring her fungi. Lattice Affairs, the station where Syrah connected to the mycorrhizal network and brought it to its knees. The exact corridor where she first saw Ochai. And Syrah's cozy room. She doesn't stop. Some part of her prefers to leave everything just as it is. *Just in case,* she thinks.

A thousand words come to Syrah's mind, likely the same for Artahe, but they stroll on in silence. Only the occasional shudder when their arms touch, as Artahe tries to suppress her sobs.

At last, they come to the end of their journey together. They stand in the hollow of the Giant that opens and closes the door to Rhiza.

A slant of bright sunlight cuts a sharp angle into the space. Outside, smoke and ash remain.

"I did not say so before, but Shansi says your uncle left the signal," Artahe says, almost as if she's afraid to say the words.

Syrah's gaze is fixed at a distant spot outside the hollow. She takes in what her friend has said without reaction. She has no space for anything else. Worry flares, but if something has happened to her parents, or him, for that matter, she will find out soon enough.

"He is happy," Syrah says, turning to face Artahe. "They both are."

Artahe opens her eyes, which had been closed. Syrah can just make out the relief on her friend's face. "You must return to us," she says.

Syrah gives her a long, shattering hug, then turns and hurries from the tree hollow. The sounds of the forest accompany her like the sweetest of repetitive melodies.

With a whimper of regret, the veil heaves and lowers behind her.

Chapter
Fifty-Four

Sequoia National Park
May 2043

The Giants have gone into overdrive, trying to clean not only the built-up carbon dioxide but also the smoke from the latest fire. Because of them, the earth will once again repair itself. The fire started and was largely concentrated in the worst place possible, the Giant Grove.

The result is a dystopian sea of char and ash. Blackened husks of dead or dying trees, canopies muted by erasure. An arboreal graveyard.

Syrah has a different set of eyes than those she had when she first came to this place. Because of this, she is selfless, unselved, through the blight, a gift unbidden, the ecology of regeneration. Some trees inexplicably remain untouched. The cones littering the ground will soon shed their spores; the wind will carry them to fertile spaces in the ground, where they will nest and sprout. New Giants, with the knowledge and wisdom of the old. A spotted skunk wobbles by; a whiptail lizard slowly scales a tree trunk. Somewhere in the distance, a black bear clicks its tongue and grunts.

To be a living creature on this planet is to be imperfect and painfully immortal. But rebirth and evolution, they keep us going.

Syrah and her fungi are two things that have merged in a mutual exchange that has made them one. She supposes all relationships are that way, all identity, when the kinship becomes so close with another that it fuses into something fresh and new.

Syrah emerges from the Twin Lakes Trail at Lodgepole Campground, and a grin breaks out at the sight of her uncle Dane, leaning against her car. She isn't the slightest bit ashamed to rush into his arms like she is a little girl again and lay her head on his very capable shoulder.

Dane holds her and, thankfully, aside from assuring her that her parents are fine, allows her to be quiet.

She knows he's got questions, and she will answer them, but for now, she just needs to be a vulnerable, sad, nerves-in-tatters mess.

When Syrah finally pulls away, she tells her uncle everything that has happened. About the battles, about Romelo's death, about walking away from Rhiza and her responsibilities there. She does not, cannot, tell him about Ochai. Her feelings, the loss, will be hers to bear alone.

Syrah wonders if her fungi will remain without Artahe's constant tinkering and the special diet they consume and realizes she doesn't want to lose them. Not them or any of the enhancements she's had from living and working alongside her subterranean family.

"He's gone," Uncle Dane says then, his expression a wash of caution and pain. "You can't be okay with that. Let yourself feel it, or you'll never see the back side of it. Just don't build a house out back for that grief—let it go, all right?"

Syrah nods, thinking back to the burial ceremony and how the earth swallowed Romelo. How at peace he seemed in his final resting place with The Mother. "You have a deal—no new construction."

"And what about your decision? Any second thoughts? Thirds or fourths?" He chuckles, but that sadness hasn't left his eyes.

Syrah thinks. Of course she does. Not about Dhanil's ability to lead, but about her decision to leave. "Truth is, after what I've been through, I think I'll always question myself, but I've made the right call. The tough part will be living with it."

"I still wish I could have had a chance to see the place."

"Maybe you'll still get your shot."

They hop in their separate cars then, agreeing to meet after she swings by her Three Rivers home. She feels like it's been years since she was there.

As she's driving out of the park, a pang tugs at her heart. After a quick call home, she motors through Sequoia's exit and doesn't dare look back.

Chapter
Fifty-Five

Syrah pilots her car down the long half-moon curve of her uncle's drive-way. Her escorts, the towering evergreen pines, their pointed peaks flirt-ing with a full yellow afternoon sun. That feeling she gets whenever she's in this precious little nook of a place—a kinship, a belonging—relaxes her shoulders and evens her breathing.

Syrah didn't always believe in miracles. They were reserved for mov-ies with happy endings and people with much better luck than she'd had. Then she discovered a world that shouldn't exist and a brother who had lived his life without her. And now she sees her own mini miracles more clearly. Survival, for one. Being adopted by those nosy old people down in Compton. Uncle Dane, more family than the brother who is no more.

The most impressive miracle? That nature, God (Syrah actually thinks they are one and the same), the universe, or whoever watches over this place has saved his little cabin in the woods each of the far too many times fire has threatened it.

Returning to this place after yet another fire? Syrah has to shake her head. It's where everything began, and coming back lets her see how every pin in her lifetime map connects. It was almost a foregone conclusion that she would end up here. Each decision she's made since she left Compton has kind of laid the breadcrumbs. Picking one job over another, choosing this state instead of that one, each choice littered with potholes, one-way streets, and detours, eventually guided her right where she needed to be.

When she thinks about her future, the picture gets a little fuzzy. The people are there, even her home, a handful of her favorite things. But she isn't sure which path to set her foot on; she just knows it isn't back the way she came. She inhales and knows the spores are there, will always be there. They are single-minded on survival and don't really have much to say otherwise. Syrah is left to ponder the thought: *What now?*

One figure sitting on the porch is her uncle, his pickup parked at an angle on the far side of the drive. Another car has pulled in, arrow straight. Another person is with him. Sitting in *her* chair.

Syrah parks closest to Dane's car, and when she gets out, she recognizes the other vehicle. One of those boxy white, standard-issue government vehicles from the visitors' fleet down in Fresno. Her fungi twitch, then settle. She and Dr. Baron Anthony started off on the worst possible footing, with him ambushing her during a park tour. Trampling all over the forest and not-too-subtly threatening her, insisting that she knew more than she was letting on. Yes, he was right, but he was not going to jeopardize Rhiza.

But he *did* help her, didn't he? She can't imagine what he had to do to get himself that radio spot. His spreading the word about the carbon dioxide probably saved a lot of lives. It also caused the panic that sent everyone to the park. One of those people caused the fire.

So where does he stand now? Is this investigation still underway? Enemy or foe, that remains to be seen.

Syrah plasters her most good-natured expression on her face as she mounts the stairs. She shoots her uncle a look, to see if she can read anything there. He's as blank as she is. Both men stand as she reaches the top step.

"Thank you for what you did," Syrah says, speaking first. She has to see where his head is. She may have walked away from Rhiza, but she is no less protective of them.

"I'd do it again," Dr. Anthony says. He's in street clothes: dark-wash jeans, a flannel shirt, steel-toed boots. That air about him that initially unsettled Syrah hasn't gone anyplace. That predator's gaze. Those green, soulless eyes that don't blink nearly enough. "I warned them first, you know. I tried to follow the chain of command. Those bureaucrats sat around writing reports and scheduling meetings, so I had to do something."

"That warning saved a lot of people," Dane says then. He's inched closer to Syrah, though, and she smiles inwardly; it's such a fatherly, protective gesture.

"And drove them straight to the park, where one of those idiots started a fire. Do they even know how many Giants were lost?" Syrah doesn't try to mask the bite in her voice. The lattice has already told her how many Giants were lost. A number she tries to forget.

Grim nods all around.

"An unexpected consequence," the doctor adds, and she sees genuine regret in his eyes before he lowers them.

Syrah can't wait any longer. "So what does this mean for your investigation?" She wonders if that annoying little notebook of his is tucked away in his back pocket. He'll probably try to convince her he's now on her side, then whip it out and assail her with one of its dangerous questions.

Dr. Anthony blows out a breath. "It was already too late; I'm well aware of that. You know how long it takes to get approval to do anything. With the fire"—he pauses for a defeatist shrug—"any semblance of evidence I thought to gather is gone. I'm still convinced there's a reason for what happened. In a surprise to nobody, my funding has been pulled, right along with my team. Everybody is back home."

"Except you," Syrah says.

"Except me. I quite like it here."

Ugh! Syrah does not like where this is going.

Dr. Anthony continues: "I thought I'd stay on awhile to see if I could help the local NPS in any way."

No, you can't, Syrah thinks. Her fingers brush Uncle Dane's, and she gives his pinkie finger a good squeeze, one that says *Help me out here.*

He tries. "I doubt there will be much you can do. The cleanup alone will take months."

"I suppose you're right. I'm at the Buckeye Tree Lodge. I'll stay on awhile longer. Eventually, they'll yank me back east, but I'll likely never turn away from this place completely. There's something out there, an explanation for what happened with the animals. And this thing with the Giants and the air?" He gestures outward. "It only convinces me more. I'll wait and then ask again, assemble another team. We'll be back to this wonderful place."

And I'll be waiting here to stop you if I need to. Syrah's promise is as sure as the sunrise.

With that, Dr. Anthony gives Dane a fist bump, and when he offers to shake Syrah's hand, she shakes her head. "One too many virus variants—like my uncle, I stopped shaking hands years ago."

"Yes," he says, "I can respect that. Well, best of luck to you both. Stop in at the hotel if you want to go to River View again. Love that place."

Syrah and Dane stand on the porch and give him final waves and fake smiles as the biologist drives away. "Why did you take him to our favorite restaurant?" she says, playfully punching Dane's shoulder.

"Don't blame me." He mock targets her stomach for a return shot. "He'd heard of the place long before he got here."

"Give me a minute, and then we'll go grab some food. Just us," Syrah says, and they take their rightful places in the rocking chairs.

Her old boss, Khatir, answers immediately when she calls. "Carthan," he says. "Good to hear from you." There's something in his voice, something not quite right. Syrah guesses it was the fire.

"Khatir," she says, "I have something I wanted to talk to you about."

"If it's about Lance's services, there won't be any. Apparently, he was quite clear—you know how he was when he had his mind set on something. He didn't want a funeral."

"A what?" Syrah is on her feet.

"Oh no," Khatir says. "I thought you knew. They said you were there."

And I had to run off to deal with my brother, Syrah recalls. "Lance died in the fire." Dane looks stricken. Syrah turns away.

"It was the smoke," Khatir says. And Syrah remembers when he lost his mask and how he kept fighting on without it. If she hadn't been sure about this decision budding in her mind, she is 100 percent convinced it's the right one now.

"I want to join the fire service again." Syrah is so relieved to hear the words come out of her mouth and to see the boyish grin break out across Dane's face.

"Alvaro will be chief," Khatir says.

"As he should be," Syrah says.

"Fill out your paperwork online, and stop by the office tomorrow," Khatir says.

Syrah hangs up, turns to her uncle, and thinks about her short but illustrious career as a park guide, her face splitting into a devilish grin. "I quit."

Epilogue

Seeing with Nascent Eyes
He Has Become Death

They called my father The President
We called my caretaker the breaker
And his sister the deliverer

When the fire threatened, he came for me
And did the work of a caretaker dedicated to his
    Giant

And now, because of them, he is no more
I am lonely but not alone

Without him, though, my growth is slowed
Stunted

My tree family
They never forget a slight
Because they think me a child, they chastise me for

What they call hoarding, I call survival

The Mother mourns
I rage
I tried to give them an end they could not see
A death strike
A merciless last breath full of poison

But the topsiders persist, oblivious

I will grow tall, my roots will stretch wide and
    deep, I belong to no being but the earth and
    the mercurial sky

Drop one cone and a decade has passed
Listen to a bit of birdsong and another follows suit

The cycle will continue
The battle between the two-legs and Giants is
    not over

But *she* lives
And perhaps one day, she will see things for what
    they are
One day, she *will* accept her new nature and re-
    turn to us

The deliverer and I, we are family
Together, we can become the new world order
Together, we can usher in a new Rhiza

Acknowledgments

I can't remember when I first heard Neil Gaiman's now-famous commencement speech in which he so eloquently bade the class to, no matter what, "Make Good Art." The message was that life, in its infinitely mercurial wisdom, will toss all manner of potholes and poison darts your way and that, through it all, art would and should still be there for you.

Those words were never truer for me than they were last year. Let's just say it was a real shitkicker. But Neil was right: the words, though fewer, and at times awful, carried me through it.

There was also an entire village of people who helped me make it to the finish line, and I ask that you grant me the grace to shout out a few of them here.

My agent, Mary C. Moore, without whom my words would still be fodder for my hard drive.

Adrienne Procaccini, the editor who granted me the gift of a treasured new career.

My brilliant new editor, Selena James, who asks all the right questions.

My developmental editor, Clarence Haynes. It was with the utmost affection that I called him cruel and ruthless.

Robin Miles, for being the epitome of excellence and for the photos that gave me just the right description for the sky.

A huge thank-you to the entire rock-solid crew at 47North and Amazon Publishing. Copyeditors, proofreaders, cover design, and everyone else I'm missing. You are publishing's unsung superheroes.

My mom for enduring.

My sisters (Carol, Tammy, Kim, and Ursula) for allowing me to be myself and not treating me like a bird with a broken wing.

My LS's, who showed up and showed out. Ours is a lifetime bond.

My family, for the love and support. And for overlooking my absences and distance.

My nephews and nieces. My joy and our family's future.

My friends Eden, Nicky, DaVaun, and Marcia for regular check-ins.

Cadwell for saying yes and for a most welcome invite.

Readers for keeping my dream alive.

Last, but certainly not least, Eric, who never wavered.

About the Author

Veronica G. Henry is the author of *The Canopy Keepers*, the first book in The Scorched Earth series; *Bacchanal*; and, in the Mambo Reina series, *The Quarter Storm* and *The Foreign Exchange*. Her work has debuted at #1 on multiple Amazon bestseller charts and was chosen as an editors' pick for Best African American Fantasy. She is a Viable Paradise alum and a member of SFWA and CWoC (Crime Writers of Color). Her stories have appeared in the *Magazine of Fantasy & Science Fiction*, *Many Worlds*, and *FIYAH* literary magazine. For more information, visit www.veronicahenry.net.